D0094911

ADVANCE PRAISE FOR *MOTHEREST*

"MOTHEREST is a moving story of loss and loneliness and parenthood and love, in all their vast human multitudes. It's an intensely perceptive and honest novel about the sometimes unbridgeable gap between parents and children. Kristen Iskandrian's narrator is an extraordinary character: a woman searching desperately for connection, an island trying to become a peninsula. You will want to yell at her, as I did, and you will want to cry with her, as I did, and you will be transfixed until the very last page."

  —Nathan Hill, *New York Times* bestselling author of *The Nix*

"One of the most unforgettable protagonists I've read in recent years—as if a Dickens heroine was reimagined by a literary girl gang made up of Deb Olin Unferth, Katherine Dunn and Lydia Davis."

  —Porochista Khakpour, author of *The Last Illusion*

"Kristen Iskandrian has done more than write a book: she's created a world. So particular and familiar is its setting (the '90s; college), so nuanced is its narrator (broken, whip-smart, wildly perceptive and yet frozen in her own fate), and so poignant is its writing (there are poems in these paragraphs!), you'll find yourself lingering in this world long after you've turned the last page. MOTHEREST is a fresh and devastating deep dive into womanhood, motherhood, teenagehood, and grief, and is an important reminder of the aches and wonders of being alive."

  —Molly Prentiss, author of *Tuesday Nights in 1980*

"Kristen Iskandrian is an utterly thrilling voice, and MOTHEREST will slay you with its inventive, spiky, and heartrending investigation into the dark mysteries of family life—and the quest for a private identity within it. A smart, gorgeous, and singular debut."

  —Laura van den Berg, author of *Find Me*

"This is a book of wombs, physical and metaphorical, an exploration into the ways we make spaces to become ourselves—both divine and misguided—and what it means to be a daughter. Kristen Iskandrian's prose is both compulsively readable and structurally unique, investigating the mysteries of human feeling through a beautiful epistolary form."

—Melissa Broder, author of *So Sad Today*

"I highly enjoyed MOTHEREST—a powerful, moving, complex, wry, sensitive novel about crying, laughing, waiting, leaving, pain, loss, endurance, secrets, surprises, ambivalence, possession, parents, pregnancy, childbirth, college, home, and love."

—Tao Lin, author of *Taipei*

"Taut and tender, MOTHEREST one-ups the messy teenage page-turner, finding real human truths in its story of a vanished mother and a struggling daughter, a source for the sourceless longing of growing up."

—Amelia Gray, author of *Isadora*

Motherest

A Novel

Kristen Iskandrian

TWELVE

New York Boston

Twelve
Hachette Book Group
1290 Avenue of the Americas, New York, NY 10104
twelvebooks.com
twitter.com/twelvebooks

First Edition: August 2017

Twelve is an imprint of Grand Central Publishing. The Twelve name and logo are trademarks of Hachette Book Group, Inc.

The publisher is not responsible for websites (or their content) that are not owned by the publisher.

The Hachette Speakers Bureau provides a wide range of authors for speaking events. To find out more, go to www.hachettespeakersbureau.com or call (866) 376-6591.

Library of Congress Cataloging-in-Publication Data has been applied for.

ISBNs: 978-1-4555-9444-3 (hardcover), 978-1-4555-9445-0 (ebook)

Printed in the United States of America

LSC-C

10   9   8   7   6   5   4   3   2   1

To Brian—
for seeing me.

O children, O my children, you have a city,
You have a home, and you can leave me behind you,
And without your mother you may live there forever.

—Euripides, *The Medea*

I broke a mirror, in which I figured you.

—John Berryman, *The Dream Songs*

Book One

The Mother Hole

Chapter 1

When my mother caught me rummaging in her nightstand, she said, *You must never look in there again.* She said, *Certain things are private. Do you know what private means?* I did, but I told her I didn't, which was maybe my version of what private meant. *When something is private,* she said, *it belongs only to you.* From then on, I understood my mother to be private, in how she kept herself to herself, and in how, in my mind, she belonged only to me. I really thought I was entitled to her, to the most intimate parts of her, which seemed to be in that drawer: photos, a Bible, stacks of letters held together with rubber bands, a diary. None of it helped me. Most of it probably wrecked me. But sometimes, that's how you know something is working. The world may have been destroyed by a flood—but that doesn't mean we don't still need the rain.

Dear Mom,

The thing about college is the bodies. They are everywhere. I feel like we were all sent to one place to figure out how to be in one, what to do with the fact of them, and how close and how far to move them in relation to one another. I try to imagine what we might look like from space, clustered and worrying, how we would probably only be discernible in clumps, the solitary ones not registering on the infrared screen or whatever the technology is. I've been in some rooms that reek of desperation, that rapey cologne smell of boys sitting around marinating their impulses, their collective ideas about girls like some weird psychic orgy. Those are the rooms, the parties, you run away from. Or to, depending, I guess.

I want to tell you about how many boys I've laid under (2) and how both of them felt the same. I want you to come here and wash my sheets and tell me the truth about my clothes, about the people I've met. I want you to see me working in the dining hall. I want you to come with me to my classes, comment on my professors, on what they're making me read. None of this will happen, I know. It wouldn't happen even if you were another mother. But being the mother you are, it's not just impractical. It's impossible. You are not available. You don't want to be summoned.

Lately I've been thinking about my whole life in terms of having grown up at the end of a cul-de-sac. I'm beginning to wonder if there's a certain "not a thru street" psychology to my time here. Everyone seems busy planning their futures, whereas I honestly can't even imagine tomorrow. I think I like the sense of safety that only a dead end can offer.

There is that picture Dad took on my first day—the last day I saw you—where I'm standing outside the student center, the place they told us would be "command central" or whatever, where we'd be spending all of our time outside of class, checking our mailboxes and praying for packages, or playing fucking PINBALL, or getting quarters for the laundry, or watching movies, or just generally loitering around with our backpacks, being coeds. I never go in there. My roommate, Surprise, whom you guys didn't get to meet because you left too early—that's actually her name, by the way, because she was supposed to be a boy but came out a girl—checks my mail for me. In the picture I am squinting and doing that ugly thing with my jaw. I seem to be saying, "1993, what else you got?" Dad took that picture and must have developed the roll because the next week I got it in the mail with a note that said "First day memento, Love Dad." It's funny how a picture of me reminds me only of you.

I thought it was odd that he sent it to me, tried to imagine him putting it in an envelope and addressing it—looking up my address, carefully copying it down—and I couldn't, at least not without feeling sad and sorry for him, the same way I've felt watching baggers at the supermarket handling eggs with great care. I guess it was that feeling that prompted me to call him to say thanks. Thanks, too, for the book of stamps he included with the photo. And it was when I asked to speak to you that I knew you were gone.

Anyway, I've never had a pen pal, but this seems as good a time as any to try it out. I'm good at remembering details and I have a lot of time to record them. Though "pen pal" suggests a back-and-forth that's impossible here. Lucky me, then. Now I have unlimited space to talk about my favorite subject besides you: me!!!

Love
ME
(Agnes)

Chapter 2

Surprise asked me, "Is it okay if we don't talk in the morning? Like not even 'hey' or 'have a good day'?" Then she told me a story about how her dad used to drive her to school, and he'd have on talk radio, and he'd ask her little questions, and one day she sort of blew up, snapped off the radio, and told him that she wasn't awake yet, and she just wanted it to be quiet. They drove in silence for the next two years, but she said she felt so guilt-ridden that they might as well have been talking. "It was so loud inside my head, you know?"

I know, I tell her, and leave it at that. I don't say how silence seems to be a member of my family. I like Surprise too much to burden her. Or maybe even more than I like her, I want her to like me. In either case, I wish we slept in the same bed sometimes.

It's late afternoon and I'm on my way to English, wondering if I should skip it, trying to remember how many I've skipped. I see the boy from my philosophy class coming toward me. I have an unbridled desire for him that wearies me and takes up a lot of my time. My face feels out of control. I concentrate on my shoes, the six-eye Doc Martens I bought with the money I'd saved babysitting the horrible Nolans, and remember my mother's arched eyebrows when she saw them ("Those?"). I study the ground right before each shoe hits it.

"Hey."

"Hey."

I keep walking. He slows down a little as if to chat, and I move faster. I want to turn around so badly that walking feels like pushing through the heaviest revolving door in the world, but I keep going. I don't trust myself around him. When I get to the humanities building, I stop.

This boy, this thing of beauty—I call him Tea Rose.

Dear Mom,

I go through Surprise's stuff all the time but it's so disappointing. Almost lurid in its boringness. She has one sexy pair of underwear that still has its tags on. There are cards and letters from her parents and aunts and stuff. In one drawer is just sheets of tissue paper, which she uses when she packs to go home. She wraps her nice sweaters and skirts in tissue. It smells faintly like her perfume, Love's Baby Soft.

I think I found your diary too young. I wasn't ready for it. I don't remember much of what was inside but I mean I wasn't ready for the fact that you had one. Knowing you had a secret life still haunts me. As a result, everyone's secret life—all the things I can't see, not because they are innately invisible but because they are deliberately hidden—consumes me.

Last time I flipped through your diary, scanning it like I was a metal detector, was a while ago. I remember, in particular, the way you never ended a sentence. That you seemed exclusively to use dashes and ellipses. I guess I have a natural aversion to endings too.

. . . Agnes

Chapter 3

It's Friday night. I have to write a paper on one of the following topics: the theory of forms, Cartesian dualism, the Zeitgeist, or Kant's categorical imperative. What I want to write about instead is physicalized loneliness, my dead brother Simon, waiting as a form of punishment and/or prayer. Or some combination thereof.

Everyone is at the bars or off-campus parties and I want to be somewhere too. I get a Coke from the vending machine in my dorm. I was hoping to find boys with whiskey hanging around but there's not even a trace of them, no beer can tabs or baseball caps in the kitchenette. I put the Coke in my coat pocket and leave the building. Outside is chilly and has the hormonal whiff of the weekend to come.

At the start of our first philosophy class, our professor asked us for some examples of philosophical ideas in everyday life. Fortune cookies, someone said. "To be or not to be," another person offered (but couldn't name the play it came from). Tea Rose raised his hand. "If a tree falls in the forest," he said. I'd been thinking the exact same thing.

Overhead, the spindly tree branches look as though they are trying and failing to hold hands in the stiff breeze. I can't decide if my mother is the tree or the forest or if I am one or the other. And she's just the person who's not there.

Dear Mom,

Last night I wandered around campus in your long coat with a half-empty Coke, looking for booze. I knew where a couple off-campus parties were, so I went to one. Surprise was there, excited. She just really likes college. Her eyes were a little drunk and she put her arm around my waist to "introduce me to people" but she was still mostly her tidy self. I broke away after a few minutes and found a bottle of whiskey in the kitchen. Most people were hovering around the keg. I poured whiskey into my half-empty Coke can and put the bottle back. What did Dad used to say? If you see the glass as half empty, just fill it? I was always puzzled by that whole scenario. Whether it's half empty or half full, it's still only half of whatever you might want it to be.

I wanted Tea Rose. I wanted his whereabouts. I thought for a second that he was at the party but it was some other tall boy. The disappointment of this was enough to make me want to leave, so I headed back toward campus, keeping my head down.

I always hear Simon when I'm alone at night. "What the fuck are you walking around by yourself for? Do you have the mace I gave you? How are you going to defend yourself, Agnes?" When did he first give me mace? Do you remember? I think it was the Christmas that I was eight. Ten years ago now. And he's been gone for less than three—the three longest, shortest years.

I'm a slow sipper and the whiskey was doing its thing to warm me up. It's midterm time and the library stays open until midnight or later. I always think about staying in the library after it closes, spending the night there, like those kids did at the Met in that book I loved. I want to do this with Tea Rose. I want to do so many things, inarticulable things. Not like "go hot air ballooning in the Alps" type of stuff but like "sleep in a library next to a boy."

I have to write a philosophy paper. If you wrote me back, I'd just turn in your letter.

Agnes

Chapter 4

I get a B+ on my philosophy paper. There are red checkmarks and plus signs in the margins, a couple "!"s. The note at the end says, *A fascinating essay, though gravely lacking in source material and proper citations. I'm eager to see what you could do with more research.* There's fifteen minutes left of class and I'm upset that Tea Rose isn't here today. His paper is sitting on the corner of the professor's desk along with the other absentees'. I'm thinking about how I can get it for him, deliver it later, when a tall blond girl raises her hand and says she lives in his dorm.

"I think he's sick today," she says, smiling sweetly. "I'll bring it to him." She looks like one of those women in commercials for feminine products. I picture her itchy and rash-ridden and try to calm down. I leave class to go to the bathroom and stare at my face for a while. I have no idea what I look like, even looking at myself. Sometimes I wished for the blankness the girls in magazines had, the nothing gaze, the empty eyes, as though they'd unlocked the meaning of life, and the meaning of life was meaningless, and there was nothing left to do. But my face always seemed vaguely worried, searching, my dark eyes somehow darker than they needed to be, my thick eyebrows an additional source of shadow, my longish hair tangled by nature and heavier than they made brushes for. It just doesn't seem like a face, I think to myself, that could ever set anyone at ease. I decide against going back to class and head to work early instead.

Mr. Figgs, the dining hall director, has asked me several times whether I want to work "front of house," serving food or replenishing the salad bar, which I hear are the more coveted positions. I'm happy washing dishes in the back. The time goes fast, and it's rare that anyone tells me what to do or asks to give them a hand. I wear industrial-grade latex gloves up to my elbows and keep the water scorching. Today Terrence is mopping a pool of salad dressing off the floor. There is the overwhelming smell of Caesar. Surprise, who has no scholarship or work study, often asks me about the smells. "How gross is it back there? How bad is it on taco night?"

The thing I like about this work is how uneventful it is. It's a spill here or a shortage there, but mostly it's predictable in ways that other things can't be. Like if a heavily manned large-scale kitchen could just be the context for every situation, we'd all know exactly what to do with ourselves. When I get back to my room after work, Surprise is there, folding laundry.

"Your dad called. You should call him back."

"Did he leave a specific message?"

"Well, he said that he got something about Parents' Weekend in the mail, some hotel rates or something, and wanted to talk to you about coming."

"Oh." I take a piece of Juicy Fruit from the pile of packs on my dresser.

Surprise is holding a very small sock. I can't understand why it's so small. "That sock is tiny," I say.

"It stretches. It's for working out. So did you not tell your parents or dad or whatever about Parents' Weekend?"

Even knowing that the sock can stretch out does not help me come to terms with its size. "Can you put that on right now? I can't believe that it fits a human foot."

"Okay, Miss Change-the-Subject. Hope you don't mind but I told your dad that they should definitely come up. We could do a lunch on Saturday or something, if you don't have to work. By the way, you smell like . . . mayonnaise?"

"Sorry."

Surprise steps out of her fluffy slipper and pulls the sock on. Incredibly, it fit.

"Why can't they make all clothes like that? We'd have so much more room to work with."

She shrugs, taking off the sock and finding its mate. "It'd probably be really expensive."

I put a few books in my bag.

"Where are you going? Call your dad."

Dear Mom,

So what I want to know is, is "leaving" a verb or a personality trait? Like, do you do it because you are it, or are you it because you do it?

I've had two Simon dreams this week. How about you? Do you even dream?

The other thing on my mind regarding word usage pertains to vanity. You call your dresser your "vanity." And it has those big mirrors, one on your side and one on Dad's, and then you have that big mirrored tray with all your perfume bottles on it. So I could sit on the bed and watch you get ready in three planes: real life, vertical mirror, horizontal mirror. Usually I just used the mirrors. I felt I could be more invisible if I looked at your reflection, rather than directly at you. I never wanted you to catch me looking, but you never seemed to mind or notice if I was there. Of course my favorite combination was the yellow dress with the red belt and red shoes, and then the cloud of Chanel.

We have the same crooked mouth,

Agnes

Chapter 5

There are these strawberry-flavored muffins, bright pink, at the coffee shop on campus. They taste like the marshmallows in cereal. There's also something called coffee milk, which people here are obsessed with. It's like chocolate milk but it's flavored with coffee instead of chocolate. I pick one of those up along with a muffin, and I'm in line when I feel a change in the air and hear the tinny clatter of music issuing from somewhere very close to me.

"Hey. Nice dinner." His voice is loud and deliberate, his headphones neon yellow, their cord rising out of the pocket of his olive-green barn jacket. I take him in entirely, his cheeks flushed with cold, his slightly rumpled hair, the torn canvas of his sneakers. To hide my panic and excitement, I try to concentrate on paying and probably look like I don't know how to add up money.

"Do you want a bag for this?"

I shake my head and put the stuff in the pockets of my big coat. I stand there while Tea Rose pays for his small coffee.

"Don't you work at the dining hall?"

"Yes."

"So can't you get better food? Like, secret food?" He is still too loud. We move to the side.

"It doesn't really work like that. Usually we eat before whatever

14

meal we're working, so I'm not very hungry, and afterward I don't always like eating what I've been around for three hours."

"Ah." He puts his headphones around his neck. There is suddenly no sound between us. "Hey, do you know Nirvana?" He says it like we are at a party and he is our—mine and Nirvana's—mutual friend.

"Um, yeah. Doesn't everyone?"

He rolls his eyes. "I don't mean like, 'Smells Like Teen Spirit.' I mean their early stuff."

How could he know I had an older brother once who knew everything there was to know about music? "You mean like 'Bleach'?"

Tea Rose lights up. "Yeah, yes. Totally. That's exactly what I was just listening to. It's fucking brilliant. Do you want to sit somewhere?" He looks around for a table.

"I have to go, actually. I need to get some reading done. And call my dad. And do some laundry." I don't know why I'm doing this. What I want is to stay with him more than anything in the world.

"Wow. One excuse and two alternates. Impressive."

I think if I kissed Tea Rose, I would definitely keep my eyes open. I'm convinced that if I loiter too long in his presence, I will reach out and start rubbing his face. It reminds me of the polished minerals I used to covet from the gift shop of the museum of natural history. Agate. Calcite.

"I'll see you in class."

He raises his cup a little, as if to toast. "Okay. That's a big coat you've got there."

"Thanks," I say, before realizing he isn't necessarily complimenting me. "I mean, it's my mother's." Now I'm practically mumbling. "I like to be prepared. You have no idea the stuff I can keep in here."

Tea Rose laughs, an easy sound. "Maybe we can get together and listen to Nirvana sometime. Or, you know, talk about coats."

I don't tell him that I don't really care about music anymore. But I would listen to whatever he wanted. And then I am extra grateful for my coat, which feels like it's actually keeping my heart, now spinning as wildly as a piñata after the first hit, inside my body.

. . .

At the start of Parents' Weekend, I meet my dad at the student center and we hug each other, and I have to try very hard not to let loose the ball of unexpected tears in my throat. His beard tickles my neck and he smells like Pour Homme, the drugstore cologne he's been wearing for a thousand years.

There is a breakfast set up for students with their parents, and I don't have to work. We go to it, the stench of powdered eggs rubbing against our faces as we walk through the door. My dad puts a lot of food on his plate, and when he runs out of room, he puts it on my plate. Eggs, French toast, sausage links, bacon, a muffin, hash browns, fruit, and a few packages of saltines from near the silverware. The saltines are part of some final, desperate act. The last grabbable, edible thing.

We sit down at the end of a long table. At the other end, a group of girls sits with their parents. All of the girls seem to be wearing some combination of pink, green, and white, with scarves tied through their belt loops or in their hair. Their mothers are aged holograms of them, incandescent in their crisp white shirts, with their crisp white skin and frosted hair. Their fathers sit in pleated and plaid button-down shirts, silent and embarrassed. We listen along with them as their wives and daughters decide on the places they want to hit and do.

"So, okay, we'll do the museum, then," one of them is saying.

"Yes!" says another. "The museum!"

"We'll do the museum, and then we'll hit the mall, and then we can squeeze in a quick run—"

"Or tennis!"

"Ooh! Tennis! Yes. Let's totally do tennis. And then…maybe Cactus Fred's for margaritas?"

"Yes! Totally! We should definitely hit Cactus Fred's!"

My father and I watch the same way we watch television at home. I turn to him after a while.

"Dad."

"Hmm?" He is hovering over his food, as if newly reminded of it.

"Should we do the museum? Or would you rather do Cactus Fred's? Or we could, you know, do both, with a little fro-yo in between . . ."

My dad smiles, a bit of ground pepper between his front teeth. "What's the museum like?"

I tear the tops off three packets of sugar at once and empty them into my coffee. "There's a Mary Sargent collection, I think. And a few suits of armor."

"Sounds pretty good."

The coffee won't get sweet. I stir it some more. "I'm kidding about wanting to go."

"Oh. Well, whatever you want. Whatever you want to do." He is staring at one of the mothers. He is thinking about my mother, because we are always thinking about my mother.

The girls and their parents disperse after some prolonged good-byes and a few more rounds of schedule recitation, dumping their trays of egg-white omelets and fruit at the trash station and exiting through separate doors, linking arms with their mothers while their fathers trail behind.

We wind up at the outlet mall and walk around and around, not saying much. We buy caramel apples, each the size of a baby's head, and eat them down to their cores. My father keeps eating past the core, seeds and all, until he's left with only stick, which he holds in his mouth like a giant toothpick. We are in front of a sneaker store when he finally removes it.

"So you'll be home for Thanksgiving, right?" he says.

I look at my dad, taking in the rough, sad terrain of his face and the garish mall carpet and the dozens of sneakers in the display window next to him. *Home* seems like the most taboo word, subject.

"I don't know."

He's looking at me now. It's not really in our contract to be looked at this way. I am unaccustomed to the openness in his eyes, the want, the sadness, his very here-ness. I want to disappear into the carpet, the sneakers.

"I'm just . . . not sure I can handle it right now. "

How to tell him without hurting his feelings that without Simon and without Mom, there's no home to speak of? He who is, after all, there, home, alone.

"Where does that leave me?" He is pinning me here. He is not being rhetorical. The possibility for more sorrow is thick between us. My mouth is gluey from the caramel. I don't want to answer his question, and I can't answer his question.

My dad returns the apple stick to his mouth, tries a different angle.

"She might come home if you do."

"Dad. That's a lot of pressure."

His whole body is a frown, head and shoulders tilted forward as if bracing against a stiff wind, knees buckling slightly against all the feelings and objects of the world, namely, hope and the mall. I have been looking at and not seeing his face for my entire life. I close my eyes briefly and try a composite sketch in darkness, the stiff beard and mustache that conceals his small mouth; the tired, deep-set eyes; the bald head now reflecting the sickly overhead light, the hair at the back of his head surprisingly dark and silken, the hair of a much younger man. I look nothing like either of my parents. When I open my eyes again, he's attempting to smile.

"Sorry," he says. "I'm not trying to put pressure on you. The situation with Mom is . . . complicated. I myself don't . . ." He trails off, rubs his face. "I just would like to spend more time together. With you."

I used to be his helper. Yard work, grocery shopping. He always put an extra pack of Juicy Fruit gum on the conveyer belt at the very last second, for me. The predictable thing that was somehow still a surprise every time. When did I stop being his helper?

. . .

Later we're in my dad's hotel room, each on a bed, eating Vietnamese takeout. We are two people who generally connect via eating. The food is our euphemism, everything we can't say. The news is on mute.

"When's the last time you saw her?"

My dad jabs his noodles with a plastic fork. "What else is in here? Tofu?"

"Yesterday, a month ago...?"

He chews for a minute. "Hmm, something like that. Things haven't been easy for her. She's very sensitive." He looks at a piece of shrimp on his fork for a long time, as if searching for answers.

"Don't you think this is abnormal?" It's unprecedented for me to be this direct.

Dad puts the shrimp in his mouth just as a commotion breaks out in the hallway. A crash and someone saying, "Sir, sir." The sound of squeaky wheels and a slow rubbing against the wall, as if someone is dragging someone else against it.

"This is a strange hotel." My dad puts the paper container on the nightstand, unmutes the TV.

We watch the second half of a *Law & Order* and then another *Law & Order*. Eventually, we put the food containers back into the takeout bag and try to squeeze the whole mess into the tiny wastebasket. My dad puts it out in the hall. "Wish we could open a window," he says.

"Fresh air gives people too many crazy ideas," I say, purposely not making the joke about suicide. Not that it'd even work, I think, here on the aspirationally named "garden level" of the hotel.

We take turns using the bathroom and getting ready for bed.

Then, lying in the dark, each in our own double bed, we take turns making settling-down sounds—I sniff; Dad clears his throat; Dad sighs; I yawn—as though to dissuade one another from talking.

"Dad."

He waits a few seconds before answering, as though debating whether he should pretend to be asleep. "Mmm-hmm?"

"Remember when it was my seventh birthday and you drove me to school because Mom wasn't home, and we had to stop at the deli to get stuff for my lunch and you felt bad so you bought, like, a huge paper bag worth of stuff? Like a family-sized bag of chips—I shared them with the whole lunch table. And you did my hair that day; you tried to braid it."

"I think I remember, yes."

"Where was Mom? Why wasn't she home? I mean, it was a weekday. And my birthday! But the craziest thing is how it didn't seem strange to me then, the way it does now."

My father adjusts his pillow, slaps it lightly, clears his throat. "I guess she was visiting her sister? Or wait. Actually, I think she'd gone to find you those what's-it-called, those dolls you liked? One of those cabbage dolls? Cabbage head dolls?"

"But couldn't she have done that before my actual birthday? Remember we were all sitting around after dinner? And Simon really wanted to go out, and you kept saying we had to eat cake first."

"Well, your mom went all the way to the city for the cake. She wanted it to be really special."

I start to respond but think better of it. There can be no definitive family history. We will always have our own versions. In mine, Mom walked into the kitchen, where we were all sitting—waiting—with nothing in her hands and gave me a distracted hug and kiss. And then told us she'd forgotten something and left again, the car peeling out of the driveway. My dad scooped ice cream into bowls for the three of us and lit a candle in mine, and sang Happy Birthday, and then gave me some cash and a set of marbles. Simon gave me a kiss and a beat-up

Meat Is Murder cassette, which I listened to almost every day for the next year. Later that night, when I was trying to fall asleep, my mom came into my room and gently touched my face. I woke up and there was a slice of cake on my nightstand and a Cabbage Patch doll in a brown shopping bag, and we shared the cake and freed the doll from her plastic trusses. I realize now that it's still one of the happiest memories I have of any birthday, despite the fact that she missed it almost entirely.

"Dad?"

He doesn't answer, not even when I try again. He has fallen asleep, or committed to pretending.

Dear Mom,

Dad wants everything to be fine so badly. "Fine so badly" seems like a good description for how we relate to one another, how we pass the time not being fine but not wanting to hurt one another with our own pain. You have made us so polite.

Good work (sarcasm).

Agnes

Chapter 6

My dad and I say goodbye on the walkway outside my dorm. He brings me two bags from the store filled with instant oatmeal, saltines, Juicy Fruit, cans of grapefruit and pineapple juice, mixed nuts, detergent, legal pads, and toothpaste.

"Thanks for coming, Dad."

He hugs me briefly and hard. "Let's see you at Thanksgiving."

"I'll let you know."

We look at each other through a veil of something. Campus is quiet. Everyone is at the final luncheon. There had been a moment earlier when Surprise's parents had asked if we wanted to sit with them. Both of us had reacted strongly, deferentially, citing the long drive ahead. Surprise's mom, Poppy, gave us a big smile, but her eyebrows were having another conversation.

I look up for a moment and the sky is like paper, the branches overhead a sloppy crosshatch.

"Bye, Dad."

"I love you, Agnes." He turns in the direction of the parking lot, his beige pants and beige jacket some kind of official uniform of leaving.

"You too."

. . .

On certain days I just want to play the piano and wish I'd gone to a school where that was all I had to do. I don't know anything about those schools because I've never been good enough to consider them. I imagine them like the ones from television: passionate kids who are passionate in a general way about everything, writhing and crying on piano benches, bony hands whittled from practicing. My own hands seem lazy and lumbering in comparison.

At the music library, I borrow a Chopin waltz. Early October has become unexpectedly warm, and there is a feeling like an awakening across campus, a broad desire to *do things*, a low-level excitement not directed at any goal.

Earlier today I took note of people on benches outside. Classic bench behavior—chitchat, sunglasses, books in a heap on one end and bodies leaning lazily on the other. One of the bodies on one of the benches was Tea Rose. He was facing forward but angled sideways toward a girl's ear, saying something, and she was laughing quietly, the laughter of an intimate moment. I'd walked quickly past, blood suddenly echoing in my ears. I was strangely embarrassed, as though their mild affection was a public announcement of my hunger, my loneliness.

The music library is empty. I take the sheet music and walk through the breezeway to the practice building. The girl at the desk has fuzzy blond dreadlocks and paint-chipped nails but otherwise looks like a young Joan Baez, like the photo of her on the cover of *Diamonds & Rust* in my parents' collection: dark eyes, full high cheeks and forehead, lips that seem preternaturally parted.

"You're in my Energy and the Environment class, right?"

I look at her face. All I can think of is Joan Baez, about my father saying her voice was celestial, and my mother arguing that her voice was reedy, and me saying, over the chords of "Sweet Sir Galahad," that they could both be right.

"I usually sit behind you."

"Oh. Hi."

"Hey. That class is not going smoothly for me! I thought it'd be all easy. Did you do the homework for Tuesday yet?"

"No, I haven't started it."

"Me neither!"

There is something that she wants me to do. She looks at me openly, expecting something. After a moment, she looks down at the notebook on the desk.

"Looks like all the rooms but one are empty right now. Do you have a preference?" She wrinkled her forehead and kind of shuddered at herself. "Not that it would matter since there's just the one room."

"I don't think so, no."

"Here's 4A. Do you have your ID?"

I hand it to her. Her nails are the color of a nail polish I had as a kid that came with a set of other makeup specifically made for kids. Tinkerbell? I remember biting the lipstick, one of the times I locked myself in the Pink Bathroom to be alone and do weird things. It was so smooth, waxy, impossibly shiny, and it rolled up like a whisper from its plastic case. I'd rarely put it on. I'd take it out, roll it up, and dare myself to bite it. And then one day I just did it, bit the whole stick off. It tasted like candy you're not supposed to eat. I held it in my mouth for a moment, without letting it touch the sides and then spit it into the trash. Mostly I'd just wanted to sink my teeth in, to leave a mark.

We are still looking at each other, the girl and I.

The Tinkerbell nail polish, on the other hand, I used frequently, in its correct application. I'd splay out my fingers on the side of the tub and do my best. Afterward there would be half-moon smudges that I would forget to clean off. My right hand would look badly wounded when I was finished. My mother didn't approve but she never disapproved. By which I mean she probably didn't notice. Before long, the shame of a job poorly done would have its effect on me and I'd lock myself in the Pink Bathroom again with nail polish remover and cotton balls, trying not to breathe in the acetone but also allowing myself to breathe it in a little. My time in there always seemed busy with secret putting on and taking off, furtive denials and indulgences.

The girl notices me staring at her hands and folds her nails under. She thinks I am judging her but I am just using her as the portal of a memory, which maybe is a compliment. I take the key and put my ID away, try to lift my voice. "Thanks so much. I'll see you in class. Good luck with the homework."

She smiles a little, an uncannily Joan Baez smile. "You too."

I trip through the piece for as long as I can. At a certain point it's less hesitant and starts to sound like something, and I play it a few more times, adding some pedal and experimenting with loudness. It's getting dark when I return my key to a different girl and head toward my room.

Dear Mom,

It's funny how much you insisted on. Choir, piano lessons, an abiding sense of decorum and frugality, discipline in all things, and God. How did you enforce those things so rigorously when you were always disappearing? Even as you entered a room, you were already halfway out of it.

How I watched you, how I paid attention. I listened to everything you said and find myself waiting now, like a jilted girlfriend, for the phone to ring. And it's like all of the things you stood for were concentrated—like, maybe you didn't know how long you'd be around to reinforce God and the other stuff, so you asserted them ten times as hard at the outset.

The other night I was taking my typical route around campus and I found myself pausing outside the chapel. I went inside to warm up, but I found I could not be still. I sat in the very back pew for a minute, and then moved up a few and sat for another minute, and then moved to the first row, and then finally got up and walked around, looking at the lecterns and the stained glass and the odd restraint that went into making it a nonde-nominational place of prayer. I felt an irrational anger toward this place, which should have been either stark and monastic or rich and Catholic, but instead was some in-between nothing, spurring nothing in me but more nothing.

I'm not totally sure but I think Tea Rose might be seeing someone. I've seen him with her twice, and I have to say, they look ridiculous. She's this blond giant. It seems like an experiment. In what, I don't know. Something.

Yours, literally.

Agnes

Chapter 7

I go to the fireplace room in the library, the room that everyone believes they have discovered. It's in the basement behind an unmarked door, and at first you're not sure if you're allowed in. Above the fireplace is an oil painting of a generic general, and lining each wall are shelves filled with ancient books that don't seem to be part of the library's main catalog, titles like *Captain Gilchrist's Maritime Adventures in Nova Scotia* and *New England Winters*, plus almanacs and wildlife guides. The books don't seem rare, or if they are, they're not valuable enough to have made it to the "rare book room" on the library's top floor. I like to imagine that this was the private collection of the man in the painting, and while nobody reads them, they have occasioned this room, this place apart, and so I feel a strange tenderness toward his doughy, forgettable face.

I sit down in one of the high-backed chairs at a long table and try to take notes on a reading assignment but something keeps flickering through me, a radio frequency whining against my ability to concentrate. *How lonely,* I wonder, *is it possible to get?* I imagine passing out, an actual concussion of loneliness.

But then the door to the fireplace room opens and Tea Rose walks in, looking over his shoulder as though he's worried about being followed. He looks surprised to see me, and I am so relieved to see him, and there is a flash between us of soft recognition, like each of us knows, if not in any pronounceable way, the other's frailties.

He takes off his jacket. From it comes a smell of soap, coffee, and something like damp leather, although the jacket is not leather but canvas. He sits at my table and opens a book.

"Hey."

"Hey."

I feel my body do its thing—racing pulse, clammy hands. I focus on my notebook, my pen, my hand, but my eyes keep pulling toward Tea Rose as if by a magnet. He is like a big translucent wolf, caged, breathing visibly. Making me, I guess, a poacher?

"What are you working on?" he asks.

I look at my notes. "English homework."

He nods. "It's quiet in here." He looks at me, directly into my face, and his eyes are such an impossible blue, a creepy blue, that I almost flinch.

I manage to read a page or so. I study each word as if I am a translator. I study the font. I make a couple notes in my best handwriting, which stand out from the rest of my notes, which pleases me because I would know in the future, by looking at them, exactly when this disruption occurred. I would know that this Tea Rose sighting fell between "characteristics of the Industrial age" and whatever happens tomorrow.

Tea Rose reads from a history book and occasionally uses a highlighter. He seems unperturbed, but his physiological activities—blinking, breathing—are pronounced. Or my feelings are pronouncing them. I sit for as long as I can take it, and then I start to pack my books. Something needs to happen.

Tea Rose sits back in his chair and watches me gather. "You leaving?"

Now I'm not sure. Is he asking me to stay?

"Yeah. I'm . . . pretty tired."

"Where do you live?"

"Halsey."

In an instant, his coat is on. "I'll walk you."

I stop myself from protesting. I am filled with the molted skin of protest, following compliments, offers of help. It has never gotten me anywhere.

We leave the fireplace room, the library. The night is cold and clear and dark except for halos of light from the library and the lampposts around campus. Tea Rose walks with his hands in his pockets. His angular body seems to unfold and refold with each step.

"So how do you like philosophy?"

I am looking at him so intently that I almost forget to answer. "It's okay. I don't like writing papers. But I don't mind the class." I watch him sideways. He is so beautiful, all lit up by the moon.

"It's so boring sometimes. I'm good for the first twenty minutes but then I just mostly think about other things."

"Same. But I usually take notes while I do that, and when I read over them later, they're pretty interesting."

"Do you think I could borrow them sometime? For the midterm?"

He is using me for my notes. That's all. Or maybe that's just the beginning. Maybe he will use me for everything I have. First he will use my notes. Then he'll want money. Then my roommate. Maybe he'll take my social security number; maybe he is a thief, maybe a murderer. I try to imagine how I would feel if I knew for certain he was a murderer. Would I see him differently? Would I deny him access to my notes, to me? No, I don't think I would. I pretend to be horrified with myself for a moment, but I'm not really. People murder for all kinds of reasons.

"Sure. Anytime."

"Cool. Thanks."

We walk quietly the rest of the way. Outside my dorm, we stand facing each other. A few people leave the building, a couple more walk in. It is a certain time of night of leaving and coming back.

"Thanks for walking me. I'll see you in class?"

He grins down at me. His height is prominent, in charge of the situation. "Yes. Definitely. Take care." He sort of high-fives my shoulder.

When I get up to our room, the lights are on. Surprise is lying on her bed with a bag of gummy bears, eyes closed, a magazine open facedown on her stomach. Her pajamas have turkeys on them.

She starts to sit up but changes her mind. "Hey!" She rolls over onto one side. "Where'd you go? I think I'm getting cavities."

There are also cornucopias on her pajamas. "Just the library. I think I'll go downstairs and do a little more work. I don't want to keep you up."

"Okay." She yawns and pushes the hair from her face. "What time is it? You okay? Don't stay up too late! You're still coming for Thanksgiving, right? Oh, your dad called."

Dear Mom,

The Thanksgivings that I remember best are like silent films, you wearing some seasonal-colored dress and lipstick, laughing with a leaf-printed dishtowel in your hand, Dad manning the bar, putting ice into the blender for one of his concoctions, me walking around with a small glass of unspiked eggnog, trailed by warnings to not drink too much or too fast so I don't ruin my dinner, the house filled with what felt like a hundred people.

In these memories, Simon is always framed by a doorway, as though he, too, was always leaving, which is maybe actually accurate. His girlfriends seemed always to be there, too, changing from year to year. I wonder what their own families thought of them celebrating Thanksgiving with us, assuming they had families.

You must have been a very good organizer. The younger people would be helped or help themselves to the buffet first, and then we were to disappear down to the table in the basement, already set with juice and napkins and silverware, a stack of videos on the TV. And then the adults would "have at it," as Dad would say. They'd sit in the formal dining room, and from downstairs we could once in a while hear chairs scraping and uproarious laughter. Who were the other kids? The second cousins from Milwaukee? The children of your friends? Simon and whichever girlfriend would eat on the couch, a blanket spread across their laps. Dad would save us the wishbone. Simon would pull very hard but somehow I always wound up with the bigger piece, which is one of the reasons why I know, despite everything, he was nice.

Lately I've been thinking there should be an official place, like a polling center, where everyone has to go once a week to get their memories wiped clean.

This year, I'm here at Surprise's house. I'm staying in the guest room, which is multi-plaid-themed, with some golf trophies up on a shelf. We ate around 4:00. It felt weird to eat so early. Poppy and Lowell, Surprise's parents, dressed in sync, with her skirt matching his bow tie. Did I mention that we are in a town that is also called Lowell? Lowell from Lowell should be a trademarked brand of Dad. Surprise's two younger sisters are very sweet and girly. I'm tired of being enthusiastic, though. Last night we did the thing I didn't think girls actually did—listened to horrible crap like the Spice Girls, played with hair and makeup stuff, looked at magazines. Surprise's sisters begged me to let them do my lips and nails a bright red and I let them. It felt good to just surrender, to be a native.

We're going back to school tomorrow. I'm not in a hurry to get back, but Surprise has some kind of study group in the afternoon. I think Poppy has been dying these last few days to ask me questions about my family, but her manners are preventing her. I have a new respect for manners. This is a very manners-driven household. Everyone is very polite. I, too, have been polite. Even my thoughts have been less impure, even late at night. When I first met Surprise, I thought she was faker than a Christmas tree. Turns out, she's got exceptional breeding.

Somehow,
Agnes

Chapter 8

Lowell helps carry our suitcases up three flights of stairs to our room. "They oughta get you girls an elevator!" His temples are flushed and slicked a little with sweat.

He hugs Surprise goodbye, briefly but tightly, and kisses her forehead. "Miss you already, cupcake. Call us tomorrow." He turns to me and extends his hand, but then leans forward stiffly and pats my back with his other hand in an embarrassed embrace. "It was great having you, Agnes. You are welcome anytime."

When he lets go, I feel a fizzing around my sinuses, the distinct warning that I might cry. "Thank you. Thanks a lot." I manage to hold it together. As soon as he leaves, pulling the door shut behind him, Surprise turns to me.

"I don't really have a study group. I'm meeting Steven tonight."

I blink. My first reaction is a hazy kind of anger, for having been lied to along with Surprise's family—although there is something pleasing about this—but then also for having been taken away from them prematurely, away from my safe, plaid haven.

"Who is Steven?" Which is my second reaction, the one I decide to go with.

Surprise is racing around the room, practically panting, unpacking her suitcase and rifling through her jewelry box. I watch her put her tissue-wrapped clothes away and then fold the tissue together neatly and place it in the assigned drawer. She unzips her makeup case and puts each thing back neatly on top of her dresser, pausing to apply blush and lip gloss vigorously.

She turns from the mirror and faces me. She looks possessed. "Steven is super hot. And sweet. He's in my chem class. We've been studying. We made out. I'm staying over tonight."

I look at Surprise's body. I've seen her nearly naked dozens of times, getting dressed discreetly in the threshold of our shared closet, towel around her waist as she pulls on a shirt, her spine long and rippling as she bends and arcs. She hasn't told me, but I know she is a virgin. She is telling me now, with her freckles and bright eyes and pink cheeks, willing me to give her permission or judgement or something. I have the desire to bring her to bed and hold her close, to rid her of the quivering, wild expectations emanating from her like electricity.

I can't think of anything to say. What do I say? *Stop, no, don't do it, do it, have fun, be careful.* Because I want to know: "Are you sure?"

Surprise is now staring into our closet. She pulls a skirt off a hanger, holds it up to herself. "Am I sure? About what? Do you like this? Should I change? I think you'd really like him. You've probably seen him before."

How private we all are. How alone. Sex is a way to be less alone. I think about Surprise's bedroom at home, all the framed pictures, the stickiness of her little sister's fingers when we clasped hands around the table to say grace, the four matching aprons on hooks, Poppy's look—I saw it—as we said goodbye, a look of sheer terror, a war-send-off look that said, *Please let her be okay, or I will die.* I feel entrusted with Surprise's happiness, or at least her virginity.

"You look really nice. You don't have to have sex with him, you know."

"I know I don't!" Surprise's eyes get wider, her cheeks pinker. "I want to!"

34

For a minute I contemplate following her, trailing her to his room and then somehow getting inside. For a minute it makes sense to volunteer myself to sleep with him in her place—let her have the flirting and romance. I'll do the dirty work.

Surprise is facing the mirror again, smoothing herself out. "I have to get going. I'm sorry I lied about the study group thing. I just...didn't want you to try to talk me out of anything. By the way, my parents love you. I think they want to adopt you."

You can't adopt something with a mother, I want to say. There's a pit in my heart, the overripe stone fruit that is my heart. I give Surprise's elbows a fatherly squeeze as she hugs me and darts out the door, her toothbrush sticking out from her purse.

Dear Mom,

I'm coming home for Christmas. I hope you'll be there. If you don't come, it will mean something. You've always been there, even after Simon died, even if you spent a lot of the day in your room. Dad and I lured you out with those "festive" cocktails with vodka and whole cranberries. Remember how awful they were? Pretty, though, and neither of you noticed that I had two. We listened to Elvis's *Blue Christmas* record about seventeen times. Our gifts were modest, as though to have gone all out would have been disrespectful to Simon, or more specifically, would have been too great an interruption of grief. But I think he would have wanted us to go all out. Maybe we should consider that this year.

But I need to tell you what happened last night, which is what has made me decide to come home and not split the time between Surprise's house and the apartment of some off-campus people who asked me to watch their cat.

I went walking and couldn't stop thinking about Surprise, who was about to get deflowered. I was remembering my first time, with Phil from the next street over. Did you know that? It was clumsy, quick, but sort of tender overall. It was the fall of last year, and we kept at it off and on until the summer, when we both left for school. He asked how I felt about long-distance relationships and I told him I thought they were pretty silly (ironic, huh, I mean, look at you and me and you and Dad). Anyway, I was thinking about Phil, remembering his parents' basement and his Rolling Stones albums and the two candles he insisted on lighting and how he'd held me afterward, exactly like they do it in the movies, and how the best part, for me, was going upstairs when we were eventually dressed and eating from their extensive ice cream collection, flavors I haven't seen before or since, like vanilla cardamom and orange pistachio.

By this point I'd reached the playing fields, where people go to drink and watch the sunrise when it's late enough and I guess play sports during the day. I was thinking about Phil with an intensity verging on longing when I saw someone walking on the path toward me, backlit by a lamppost, and for a moment I believed I had conjured Phil, beamed him here from his soggy campus in the Pacific Northwest.

But perhaps stranger than if it'd been Phil, it was Tea Rose. He was a long way from his dorm, and it was still technically Thanksgiving break. What was he doing out here? I think a psychic transfer must've happened—Phil became Tea Rose. I see no other explanation.

Anyway, the rest of the night was no less surprising. We talked a lot but also did a lot of not-talking. When we met on the pathway, we both laughed a little, as if embarrassed, which I was, because I kept feeling like he'd caught me doing something, and then from the pocket of his jacket he showed me two tiny bottles of gin, the kind they give people on airplanes. He handed one to me.

We hopped the fence and sat in the middle of the field, which might as well have been Pluto. It was freezing. I was fully layered, sweater, coat, scarf, hat, gloves. After the first few sips, we both stopped shivering so much. He told me, with a kind of ease, about his girlfriend, the towering blonde from philosophy class that I'd seen him with, and how he liked her a lot but had been feeling a lot of pressure. That despite her "party girl" looks (?) she's really naïve and inexperienced and was "getting too attached." He was home over Thanksgiving trying to drum up the courage to break it off when they got back, trying to figure out what to say and how to say it so as not to hurt her, when she called him at home, hysterical because her grandmother had unexpectedly died. She told him she needed him and asked him to come to the funeral, which was held earlier that day, yesterday, in her town, a few hours' drive from his town. And here he was instead.

"I was on the bus, in a suit, and I just kept going. It took a really long time to get here." I was enjoying his solemnity, how much credit he was giving himself.

"Are you going to try to talk to her before you see her in class?"

He sipped. "I probably should. Actually, it's probably best if she just hates me. Cleaner."

I wasn't sipping the gin so much as putting the bottle up to my lips, wetting them, but still it was working. I felt heavy, stilled.

We did what you might expect—looked at the stars and commented on them, though I told him I'm not so much for stars anymore. But he touched me in unusual ways. No kissing. Very deliberate. He looked into my face and touched my shoulders, legs. We were sitting as close as was physically possible in a way that now, when I think about it, seems to defy having limbs. I took my gloves off and finally did what I'd always wanted to do, touch his face with my fingers. My body throbbed with no-relief, which is the best feeling. Better than relief.

After the girlfriend/grandmother part of the night was over, we didn't return to it, didn't really talk about our families or childhoods or relationships. We talked about ideas. Like the different vibrations different people give off. I told him that I never understood how a pound of gold and a pound of feathers could weigh the same. He told me that precious metals are measured in troy weight, whereas most other materials used the avoirdupois system. I laughed at him. It's peculiarly satisfying to laugh at the boy you're smitten with. He told me that Ayn Rand fucked him up in his early teens. I told him that when I was twelve I ate nothing for two days because I'd read that some saint had fasted for weeks and I wanted to see what it felt like to be holy. He asked, laughing, "Where were your parents?"

We stayed intertwined, holding hands, touching, leaning, rubbing, until the sky started to lighten and the first streaks of day made our position seem awkward, ridiculous even. He kissed my mouth quickly, his breath a mixture of alcohol and no sleep, and we disentangled ourselves and walked in our opposite directions. I looked behind me, only once, and he was walking backward, grinning.

I've been in bed all day, going over the night's events. I was here when Surprise got home from her tryst but I pretended to be sleeping. She took a shower, got dressed, and left the room, all in a hurry. I hope she's okay. The thought of asking makes me tired. I feel I've run out of places to go. I just want to be back in that empty field with Tea Rose.

See you at home in a few weeks?

Maybe?
Agnes

Chapter 9

It's a long train ride from the middle of a New England nowhere to the middle of a New Jersey nowhere. It is longer still when the latter nowhere also happens to be your home. And when home is a word you can't encounter without deep perplexity and dread. And when all you have is the landscape to look at and an Amelia Earhart biography.

I have romantic ideas about trains like most people. It's one of the places where I look at each person and wonder what it would be like to have sex with them. But you can only do that for so long. The rest of the time you're just sitting there, counting down stops or hours, your mythic sense of freedom gradually being replaced by pins and needles and mild bathroom anxiety.

Eventually, I sleep. When I wake up, it's dark. We are two stops from my town. I stand, stretch, pick the Amelia Earhart biography up from the floor where it had fallen. I take my bag and move to the front of the train, feeling the locomotion beneath my feet. Something is happening inside my body. My body is trying not to go home.

I decide to walk the roughly two miles from the train station to my house instead of calling my dad to pick me up. I pull my suitcase through the underpass tunnel, narrowly avoiding a few puddles of piss or water or both. There is new graffiti, none of it interesting. My old favorite, WE PINCH OURSELVES AWAKE UNTIL WE DIE, has been scribbled over with the cuneiform of coupling, initials and plus signs and hearts. Back on street level, I stand for a minute, facing the cheese shop and the hardware store.

It's at least a couple hours before midnight but the town has that midnight feeling. It's cold. I stop for a minute to wrap my scarf tighter and pull my hat down over my ears. I pass the Chinese takeout place and the five and dime and the deli and the pharmacy and the movie theater. My suitcase has started to squeak, its little wheels unused to such a workout. I am willing it to keep going, to toughen up, and I am willing myself to do the same. How will it be when I walk in the door? No Simon. No mother except for in traces. My father, living off of traces.

I pass the Laundromat—"Bachelor Service"—whose lights are still on. No one is inside, but I can see a washer in motion, possibly the loneliest image in the world.

The hill leading down to my street is steep, and my suitcase stops squeaking. It bangs against my boot heels all the way to the bottom. At the opening of the cul-de-sac, my cul-de-sac, I pause. A car passes, flashing its high beams as if to remind me that I'm standing there.

I am at the front door. There is the sound of no sound, which is different than the sound of silence. I look at our bent mailbox, my dear pine tree. I look at the lamppost in whose shadow I'd been tongued, groped. I find myself unable to choose between bell, knocker, my own knuckles.

I ring, I knock, I rap. My father comes to the door. His beard looks upset.

"Where have you been? How did you get here? Why didn't you call? I would have picked you up. I was waiting."

We're standing in the doorway and I know she isn't here, isn't anywhere inside. I don't answer my dad's questions. I enter the house and he takes my suitcase and carries it upstairs. His pants are baggy and his shirt is tight. I walk into the kitchen, feeling so many things at once that they cancel each other out. I open the refrigerator without seeing what's inside. My dad comes downstairs and we face each other across the butcher-block island, him in his ocean and me in mine.

"How was your trip? Are you hungry?"

Something, at least for a moment, clears in me. That sensation of a sudden and unexplainable happiness, a happiness-for-no-reason, a rescue. And in that clearing, the body with its simple pangs. Sore feet. Hunger, thirst.

"The trip was good. Yes, I'm a little hungry, actually."

My dad takes the loaf of bread from the refrigerator—a hallmark of our family, cold bread—and the butter dish and makes me the first snack I ever learned to make for myself—butter daubed across untoasted bread, inevitably torn in a couple places from the uncomfortable effort of spreading something too cold and hard to be spread. A simple, ravaged thing. He sprinkles a teaspoon of sugar across the top and puts it on a plate and slides it across the counter to me.

"Thanks, Dad."

I finish and put my plate in the sink. My dad moves to immediately wash it.

"Do you want to watch some TV? Or we could play backgammon? Or are you tired?"

"No, I'm not too tired, I don't think. But maybe I'll just read and go to sleep."

My father looks relieved. "Tomorrow will be a good day. We can do whatever you want."

"Good night, Dad." I hug him, his beard against my ear. I wish it could talk.

I go upstairs. I stand at the closed door to Simon's room. I put my hands against the door. I push on the door and it creaks in place.

I put my forehead on the door. I put my mouth on the door. I put one cheek against the door, and then the other. I press my torso against the door. I lift my arms and hold them against the door. I don't want to open the door; I want the door to absorb me. I can't open the door. I can't open the door.

Dear Mom,

I'm here. I'm here at home with Dad. I want you to be here when I wake up. It's been almost five months since I was last here and this house has turned into a museum. If I ever thought I wanted to live in a museum, I know now that I don't. Why did I ever leave? If I had stayed, would you have stayed?

I forgot pajamas so I'm wearing one of my old nightgowns. It's too small, and it feels like I'm in a cocoon. It smells like you folded it.

It's useless to sleep when you know tomorrow will be the same as today.

I want tomorrow to be different.

Agnes

Chapter 10

I wake up to a room filled with light. It's so bright that I forget where I am. I can't see anything. As my eyes adjust and the room comes into focus, I assemble a plan. I will take a shower. I will get dressed. I will ask my dad if he wants to go Christmas shopping. I will channel Surprise in order to know what to do. I'm sure she is going Christmas shopping today. Maybe in the evening she will see her old friends. Maybe she will drink hot chocolate with her sisters. I may not have many friends or any sisters, and I may not like hot chocolate, but that doesn't mean I can't be busy.

Our failure as a family is the result of planlessness. We have been adrift. We are slowly going under. Today I am taking it upon myself to build a dam. Today I will fuck with nature. Today I will revoke the irrevocable. I will not succumb to the sad house.

When I get downstairs, the clock says 10:09. There's a note from my dad: *Hi Agnes, I have to stop by the office and then run a few errands. Maybe I'll see you later for lunch? Have a good dad.*

Have a good day, [Love,] Dad, is what I can only assume he meant, but the error throws me off. It's Saturday and he's at work. My first day home and he has already run away. I write "OK" with a smiley face underneath, put on my coat, and head out for a walk, not sure where I'm going, my plan thwarted just like that.

43

Dear Mom,

Dad wants me to be home but can't seem to be here while I'm here. We are the house of leaving. Leaving begets leaving. I took a two-hour walk just to not be home.

And if he knows where you are, he doesn't want me to know. But I think he doesn't actually know where you are. He told me you left shortly after you both dropped me off at school, that you didn't even unpack your bag—just added more stuff to it.

Yet every time I picture you, I can only picture you here, among things familiar to me. Maybe you're at that house where Aunt Ingrid died, the house she bought to die in when the cancer was so bad her signature on the deed was a line and an X, the place she kept secret from nearly everyone but you. Maybe you're there, thinking about Simon every day, and your sister, and you just won't be ready to think about me and Dad for another few years. Maybe you won't be ready to think about us ever again. Sometimes things change and can never change back. "Changing back"—what does that even mean? Nothing changes "back." Things only change.

I saw my first sex act at Aunt Ingrid's house, the other house, the main one. When we visited that year, just you and me, remember, and I got sick on Ethiopian takeout? She said, "Well, if she doesn't like Ethiopian food, she's as dull as I suspected." She was teasing, but not really. She hated kids. When she was at work and you were resting in our room, that terrifying guest room, I snooped. I found the *Kama Sutra* in Ingrid's bedroom, not concealed, just out on a low bookshelf. I paged through the whole thing, touched myself quickly, and put it back exactly as I'd found it. I remember thinking, if she actually knew me, she wouldn't think I was dull. I wanted her to like me so badly. You, your sister—there must be something in the bloodline that makes people forever seek your approval.

When I came home from wandering around town today, Dad was making sandwiches. A lot of them. I asked if he was expecting anyone and he gave me a funny look. I ate two sandwiches to make him feel better or something and then I got a stomachache and went to my room to lie down. Always too mayonnaisey, Dad's sandwiches.

Since we're being honest, I'll say that I never bedded a boy in my own bed. Times when you and Dad were out and Simon was getting drunk with a girlfriend in the basement, I'd tell one to come over. I'd break the "no boys on the second floor" rule and we'd sit on the floor in my room and listen to CDs and mix tapes and then make out, also on the floor. But something about a nervous, leaky, spurting boy in the sheets that you washed every week seemed wrong, that much I knew.

Now, though, I don't know. I don't know when these sheets were washed last. They smell like nothing.

I haven't gone in your room or Simon's room yet. I feel no rush. Now that I'm here, I can't imagine going back to school. Now that I'm here and you're not here, I do actually feel like I can do and not do whatever I want. And as someone who's sort of fond of consequences and punishment, you should know it's pretty torturous. Also tortuous, a word I just learned that means "winding" or "twisted."

Tortuously,
Agnes

Chapter 11

One evening the phone rings, and it's a jarring sound because the phone rarely rings here. Dad and I are watching *Jeopardy!* He has just smoked the Civil War category and I have done well in Before & After. When the phone rings, we are both torn between wanting to ignore it and wanting it to be my mother. My dad moves quickly to the kitchen, trying to keep an eye on the TV.

"*Yes I Can*," I'm saying. "What is *Yes I Can*."

"It's for you, Agnes. Someone named Phil?"

"Oh. Coming."

"What was the answer?"

"The title of Sammy Davis Jr.'s autobiography. It's *Yes I Can*. Hello?"

"Agnes, hey." His voice is deep. "How've you been?"

"I'm pretty good. How are you? How's school?"

"School's the best. Tons of fun so far. Listen, a bunch of people are coming over tonight to hang out. You should come."

The final category is Broadway. "Okay," I hear myself say. "I'll come by later."

"Excellent. Oh, and if you have anything to, you know, *imbibe*, that you could bring along to share, that'd be even better."

The *Jeopardy!* theme is playing and the contestants are writing down their responses. I missed the question and I can't read the words on the screen from where I'm standing.

"I'll see you later. Bye." I hang up with Phil and rush back to the TV, but not in time. Stupid Phil.

"I want to say it's *Annie Get Your Gun*," my dad says.

He's right, along with two-thirds of the contestants. We shake hands, our custom, and turn off the TV. My dad goes back to the H–I volume of the Funk & Wagnalls encyclopedia. He bought the set from a door-to-door salesman the year I was born, and every few years vows to read all of them.

"I'm going to meet up with some friends a little later," I say.

"Do you need a ride? Or do you want the car?"

"No. It's just down the street at someone's house."

My dad looks at me for a long moment, as though trying to think of the most essential thing he could tell me in this scenario.

"Don't get lost."

Through the window I see flurries swirling, lit seemingly by their own light, tiny filaments falling from the giant flat bulb of sky. I change my clothes and try to fix my hair. After I hear Dad go to bed, I enter his study quietly and unlock the pull-down cabinet with the key he keeps right in the lock. The pull-down door is mirrored on the inside and opens flat, as if, as Simon said once trying to shock me, for doing blow. The entire inside of the cabinet is mirrored too.

"You ever see someone do it?" Simon asked. I was about eleven. And then he took a dollar bill from his pocket and rolled it into a tube and held it to his nose and leaned down and snorted and laughed wildly. I laughed, too, though I had no idea what he was doing.

On the right side are bottles of liquor that were given to my parents over the years, hostess gifts for the parties they used to throw or thank-you gifts from the friends they used to have. On the left side is a row of small drawers containing things like passports, social security cards, the deed to the house. I carefully pour some whiskey from an opened bottle into my old Strawberry Shortcake thermos, which I found in the back of my closet and which still smells, inexplicably, of strawberries.

Outside, the air feels alive. I stand still, dizzy with atmosphere. My breathing feels like it's being done for me. I sip from my thermos and walk lightly, feeling a strange equilibrium with everything around me.

I walk uphill to Phil's, and I knock on the double front doors, one of which is slightly ajar. I push it open and enter the dim foyer. The house smells exactly as I remember it, like soup and potpourri. Faintly from the basement I hear The Doors. Briefly, I consider leaving. The music stops, then starts again—another Doors song. Maybe I can just stay up here and eat some ice cream. But I clutch my coat around myself and descend into the basement to the fanfare of those stupid keyboards.

The last time I was in Phil's basement I was wrapped in an itchy afghan on the couch. Now there are seven or eight people milling around, a few of whom I recognize. The door to the outside opens and closes and a boy and girl walk in, red-eyed, coughing and giggling. Phil walks over to me from the record player.

"Agnes! You made it. Can I take your coat?"

Still clutching my thermos, I take off my coat and hand it to him. He tosses it on the chair behind him. *I could've done that,* I thought.

"Do you know everyone?" he asks.

"No. But that's okay."

"What do you have there?" Phil has gained weight. His face is jowly and stubbly and moist. Tea Rose pops into my head and I miss him, the smooth planes of him.

"Oh, just a few sips of whiskey. Sorry I couldn't bring more."

"Can I get a taste?" He moves closer to me and puts a hand on my wrist.

I don't want his mouth on my strawberry-smelling thermos like I don't want his mouth on my body. I can't stop thinking, *This is the first boy who went all over and inside me.* The thought is mildly revolting.

"I think maybe no. I've had this sore throat thing."

He looks at me, grinning. "That's too bad. Though if I'm gonna get sick, I might as well have fun doing it." His other hand goes to my hip.

A boy comes over and slaps Phil's shoulder. "Jason's here with beers."

Phil tries to wink. "Guess you're off the hook for now, Agnes." He squeezes my hip and goes to the door leading outside, where most of the party has congregated to welcome Jason, who's trying not to look like he's struggling under the weight of two cases of beer.

I sit on a sofa. I consider going home. But home to what? I am home.

Dear Mom,

So here's what happened last night. I went to this party at Phil's from up the street and either got ignored or leched on. The other females in the room, it was like they had no faces. I can't remember what any of them looked or sounded like. Why is that, when the boys are so vivid? Does this make me a terrible feminist? I think it's because they were all looking down, which, I mean, I don't blame them, when looking up could've been construed as an invitation. The boys, on the other hand, were begging to be seen, announcing themselves with every gesture.

Anyway, I brought my own whiskey and sat on a couch for a while, maybe feeling bad for myself, maybe feeling nothing. The only person, I realized, who would feel sad if I died is Dad. Which made me irrationally angry at him. Like, why should he be the one to be trusted with all the grief? And would it ruin him, or would he just slide it into the next empty drawer in his sadness vault? Are there even any drawers left? You and Simon take up entire rooms within him, within me. I kept thinking, "At least Simon is dead. That's something. It's a start. The pain can start there, circle around a few times, and end there." With you, there is no beginning and no end.

All of which is to say: I sat there for a while, sort of invisible but not invisible enough. I kept wanting to leave but I kept not leaving. Finally I went outside to see if anyone was smoking. I only smoke when a night becomes irreparable. It was no longer snowing. Everything looked lit by everything else. This boy Jason was out there, talking to a girl who was smoking. Without meaning to, I guess, I was standing there, maybe three feet away, watching them. The girl's eyes kept shifting toward me, and it felt so weird to do nothing, to just stand there and watch two strangers up close, like watching someone else's dream. Maybe I was feeling the whiskey a little at this point. Jason took a cigarette from the girl and told her he'd meet her inside and she put her cigarette out and openly glared at me for a moment before going back in. "This is just the kind of boy I need right now," was the thought I had as he sauntered over. This kind of lying, cheating boy!

I asked him for a cigarette, which felt like an insult to the girl he'd left. He gave me the one he'd taken from her. He asked me how I knew Phil and where I went to school and a bunch of other questions, some of which I didn't answer because I didn't see the point in him knowing anything about me. I didn't want to know anything about him. He asked if I was cold and I said "I don't know" and then he asked if I wanted to warm up in his car. Amazing. The gumption of boys. The ease with which they ask for what they want, only thinly veiling it behind something else, whatever else.

I did go with him to his car, Mom. I half hoped he'd kidnap me, drive me to the middle of that nowhere, where you are. But he only did what you'd expect, and I complied because it was the next best thing. I do hope, though, that the other girl gives him a harder time.

When I got home from the party, I had that raw feeling between my legs and whatever fortitude or emptiness I needed to go into Simon's room. I just went right in. I opened the front door of the house with my key, and I shut it and locked it and I took my coat off and threw it on the piano bench and I went upstairs and stood in front of his closed door, and then I pretty much hurtled myself inside. I left the light off for a while. Then I turned it on, and the wincing began. I wanted to burn everything I saw. I wanted to burn the rest of the house and spare only this room, and live in it, alone, forever. I sat on the double bed with its blue flannel blanket and stared ahead at the long, wide desk he'd made from our old kitchen island. The karate trophies. The Ramones poster. The corkboard with Morrissey tickets, never used, from the week after. And in the closet, shirts hanging, shoes in a row. He was always very neat. It wasn't crying, exactly. It was all the water in my body coming out of my face. It was my body, coming out of my face.

I took a flannel shirt from his closet and put it on over my clothes. It smelled like grass and air, like boy. It was the only thing, besides his bed, that I touched.

I'm still wearing it,
Agnes

Chapter 12

Two days later, Christmas Day, it is exactly noon when I open my eyes to my Sony Dream Machine alarm clock, which I got for Christmas when I was ten. Only twelve more hours until it will no longer be Christmas. I close my eyes to see if there is any sleep left in me, but there is none.

Downstairs, my dad sits reading the paper at the table. The smell of bacon and coffee is strong.

"Merry Christmas, Agnes," he says. "Are you okay? I was starting to worry you were sick."

"I'm okay," I say. "Merry Christmas to you too."

"I made a fresh pot of coffee—the other one sat around for too long—and there's bacon."

"Thanks."

Outside, the day has the gray cold look of early morning.

"It might snow today," my dad says. "That would be nice. White Christmas."

We take our mugs into the living room. The fireplace is empty, rarely used because of a chimney defect, and today its emptiness seems especially prominent.

Yesterday, hungover from the stupid sex I'd had and the emotional weight of Simon's shirt, I drove to the big mall and sat in traffic for twenty minutes before turning around and going to a strip mall on the other side of town. I needed something for Dad and my options were Spaghetti Warehouse, Auto Parts Plus, Dee's Pet World, Perfect 10 Nails, or Book Shack, which seemed to sell mostly magazines. On one shelf misleadingly labeled "Current Events," I found an anthology called *The Most Fascinating People of the 20th Century*. I figured it was better than an iguana, and I could actually see my dad reading it. He liked compilations, taxonomies, greatest hits. The idea, I suppose, that some ruling body makes the tough decisions and does the tidying into groups so that we don't have to. But I did debate the iguana. Something to keep him company, something he could care for.

I found last year's wrapping paper in the attic and wrapped the book and put it under the fake tree, which we'd put together and halfheartedly decorated a few days before. Today there are two boxes next to the wrapped book.

"Go ahead and open your gifts," my dad says now.

The first box is light and contains a handsome wool tartan scarf. I'm touched because I can't imagine him shopping for it. Maybe he found it in one of my mother's drawers? But the tags are still on, and I, for Christmas's sake, decide to believe that he went out and bought it himself.

"Thanks, Dad. I love it." I wrap it around my neck, the ends trailing over Simon's shirt, which I am wearing like a robe. Dad sort of cringes and beams at the same time.

The other box is smaller and heavier. I unravel a tissue-wrapped thing and it is a framed photograph of my parents and Simon and me from my freshman year of high school. We are standing outside the front door, all dressed up for Easter, Simon wearing a blue knit skinny tie and white-framed sunglasses, me in a knee-length floral dress with a sailor bib. I hated that dress, though I loved those white patent-leather pumps, my first pair of heels. Dad stands behind us and Mom stands next to Simon, her arm around his shoulder. She is wearing a baby-blue dress and red lipstick, her hair big and frothy, and she is smiling widely—a unique event. Dad looks, apart from the tie, exactly the same as he does right now, today.

"Who took this picture?"

Dad tilts his head and looks at it, as though he's never seen it before. "Neighbor, maybe? I can't recall."

"No, it was a timer. Simon set up the tripod. I remember now." I wrap it back in its tissue. I feel like I can only look at it in glimpses.

Dad unwraps his book. "Wow," he says. He turns it over, opens it, flips a few pages, as though what he is holding is a book artifact and not an actual book. "I love it. I'm going to start it today. Probably will learn a lot."

We sit there on the couch, a small moat of wrapping paper between us. "Do you like your gifts, Agnes?"

"Oh, yeah. Yes. Thanks, Dad. I love them."

"Just because . . . ," he starts, then clears his throat. "I know it's just us for right now. But try to always remember you have a family who loves you."

• • •

I try once or twice, but I do not go into Simon's room again. I continue wearing his shirt. I also do not go into my parents' room. I think, if I see it half empty, I will feel a new level of feeling, and I'm not ready for a new level. I'm not even ready for the level I'm on.

One night we are eating a wordless and noiseless dinner of pizza. I reach for a napkin and I see my father crying. He is holding a limp piece of pizza up to his face as though to cover it, but I see that his eyes and chin are wet.

"Dad."

He bows his head, still holding up the pizza.

"Dad, it's okay."

Minutes pass. I don't know what to say, what to do with the

murderous way I feel toward him, toward my mother and toward Simon, for embarrassing us like this, for offering no protection against these unbidden moments of feeling. I get up and leave my father at the table, slumped behind his slumping pizza. I go upstairs and sit cross-legged on my bed. I think about writing a letter. I think about leaving. When I can't do the second thing, I tend to do the first.

Dear Mom,

I finally called Jenny and Sadie back and wound up at Jenny's on New Year's Eve. There was talk of some big party downtown, but it either didn't exist or the correct details were withheld or they weren't actually invited, so we had a sleepover at Jenny's like we used to in high school. They'd gotten all dressed up, but I was happy to be in jeans, and eventually, when it became clear that there was no party in our future, they put on sweatpants, Sadie borrowing a pair from Jenny.

We talked about college. They were roommates, and they took turns painting a picture of Greek life and formals and football games. I sat on the floor in Jenny's disaster of a room, facing them on the bed, feeling half there and half not, lapped over like shoals by the soft water of their chatter. They'd been very smart in high school, if you recall—we took all the same classes. College seems to have dumbed them.

Also, they'd had crushes on Simon. They used to come over a lot, peering down the hall or into his room, trying not to look disappointed if he wasn't home. When he was around, there was a lot of giggling and futzing with bra straps. I remember one time Simon took his baseball cap off and placed it lightly on Sadie's head as he was leaving to go somewhere. She turned beet red but tried to play it cool. She ended up taking the cap home, and Simon got mad at me for letting her. "She thought you were giving it to her." "Why would I give my best lid to some kid?" I got it back from her in school the next day. After everything happened, they stopped coming over. Our house became foreboding, I think—inhospitable.

At some point, Sadie pulled a small bottle of warm, cheap champagne from her bag, and we passed it around. Jenny went downstairs—her parents were glued to Dick Clark in Times Square—and came back a couple minutes later, a third of a bottle of Ouzo under her shirt. We passed that around too. We talked about ordering pizza but figured no one would deliver on New Year's Eve, and we talked about how we would always be friends, no matter what, and we talked about if I was okay or messed up—I said both—and we talked about Sadie's parents' divorce, and we talked about all manners of things in our lives, but through the fog of alcohol and our liminal sense of togetherness, our words sort of slid around the sides of us without any traction.

I woke up early the next morning with a crick in my neck, having fallen asleep on the floor amid shoes, magazines, and clothes. Jenny and Sadie slumped together in the bed like a fallen cake, faces fudged with makeup, a thin line of drool stringing from Sadie's mouth to Jenny's shoulder. I used the bathroom, and when I came back in, Jenny was up, and so we poked Sadie awake and said our goodbyes, hugging into our hangovers, creaky mouths sour as we promised to keep in touch better— as I promised to keep in touch better—and then I left, my head buzzing, but beneath the buzz, a weird tranquility.

The rest of my time at home was hazy and disjointed. I spent a lot of hours in my pajamas watching daytime TV, trying to precipitate a rock bottom, to depress myself into some kind of action. One morning I woke up in a film of sweat, a low, striated pain emanating with such force that I felt halved. I finally stood up and realized that I had bled through my pajamas and all over the sheets, the brightest red I've ever seen. So that gave me something to do—laundry and bleach and showering and driving to the drugstore for Advil and tampons. Faint stains are still there, no longer red but the color white would bleed if it could. I feel strangely proud of it, a commemoration of my time at home: a little bit of blood spilled, but at least nobody died. On the contrary, a reminder that I'm still very much alive.

Dad offered to drive me back to school but here I am—it's been a few days since I started this letter—back on the train. I wanted our goodbye to be at home. He gave me some extra cash and told me how nice it was to have me there. He drove me to the train station in light snow, but it stopped as soon as the train started moving, as though even the weather was demarcating home from not-home.

From not-home,
Agnes

Chapter 13

Back at school, the force field is real. Tea Rose and I inscribe circles around one another. I find myself walking by his dorm on my way to class, which is not on my way to class, and then knocking on his door, and then staying, instead of going to class. We sit close together on the floor and watch shitty TV, our hands wandering, our eyes straight ahead. I leave my shift at the dining hall and he is there, sitting on a bench. He picks me up off the ground so that my legs wrap around him and I can feel his heartbeat through his cold neck, where I hide my face. We want to do what we are doing without talking about it. We do what we are doing and we avoid each other's eyes, as though our faces are suns neither of us can look at directly.

By the beginning of February, I am lying in Tea Rose's bed more and more often. We have started to look at one another more, our faces close together on his flat pillow, our bodies intertwined below. I have most of my classes on Tuesdays and Thursdays and I go to them most of the time. In this semester's philosophy class, I write about how my sense of duty is a handicap. I don't know why I am taking another philosophy class. It has nothing to do with anything.

His roommate has left. He does not have a new roommate. The room feels two times its regular size, once for having lost someone and twice for not having gained someone. The bed where the roommate used to sleep is stripped and empty. The desk where the roommate used to study is bare. We do not use the new vacancy. We sleep in Tea Rose's twin bed and when I get dressed, I stand in the midst of his clothes and piles. He watches me. He drinks me in, but it's me who feels intoxicated.

"Agnes," he says now, as we lay facing one another.

"Yes."

"Nothing. Just thought your name and said it."

He runs his fingertips over my arm patternlessly. I practice using my eyes like a zoom lens, staring into the different parts of his face. There is so much symmetry. I remember those "check double-check" games from when I was a kid, where you had to find the subtle differences in otherwise identical photos. It would be impossible, I think, with Tea Rose's face. Even his eyebrow hairs are indistinguishable.

"What should we do?" I say. We are naked.

"When?" he says.

"I don't know. Now. Tomorrow. Overall."

Tea Rose uses his limbs as a simple machine and hoists me on top of himself. He kisses my neck, my shoulders. His hands are busy. "We should do this," he says.

"Yes," I say. "This."

After a while, it is night. After a while, it is day.

Dear Mom,

I guess the body is a ruinous place or it is a comfort. I go to Tea Rose like going to church, or therapy, or the ocean, and I just surrender there, floating, bobbing. Is this love, or is this oblivion, or are they the same thing.

Surprise is seeing someone. Not the boy she lost her virginity to. This boy is working hard for her. He's homely but fastidious, always pressed and tucked. She knows a lot, already, about his family, his three sisters, his surgeon dad. She comes and goes with a new air now, of someone knowing who she is and what she wants and what she expects of the world. Within the scope of this way of being, this mild transformation, she seems happy. Surprise is a person who can seem happy and also be happy.

The other day we went to lunch. She wore makeup and a little jewelry and I wore a ponytail and one of your big coats. I felt like my aunt from the city had come to pick me up at the youth home for a day among civilized society. I even found myself walking a half step behind, until Surprise said, "Hurry up, I'm starving," and grabbed my arm.

We went to the place on campus where they have a deli and a hot bar and ice cream cones and got in line at the deli section. Surprise chattered away, telling me about her boyfriend, how different it felt, how he was a grown-up, responsible, how they liked the same things.

"And he's such a gentleman too," she said. "Holds doors, stands up when I get up from the table, doesn't try too much when we're, you know, alone together."

When we got to the front of the line, Surprise ordered a turkey sandwich, dry, with fruit instead of chips, and a diet soda. I basically ordered the opposite. When Surprise's stuff came, she took one look at the corners of the bread and stepped back into line, cutting off someone else midorder.

"Excuse me. This sandwich has mayo on it. I'd like another one, please, per my original order." She smiled sweetly. I stood with my tray and watched, riveted. She wasn't being obnoxious. She was, I guess, being correct. And I saw, in that instance, that it wasn't about the sandwich or the mayo. It was about expectation. She expected something to be a certain way, and when it wasn't, she used her will to change it. Today, it was lunch. Tomorrow it would be a job or marriage. "Per my original order": Surprise's life philosophy.

She told me, while we ate, that she was dropping psychology to become a business major. "I like math, I like that kind of thinking, and most of all, I'll be able to do something with it when I graduate." Her boyfriend, she added, was a great tutor.

Lest you think, though, that Surprise has become some up-tight bitch, she sensed, despite my nodding and laughing where appropriate, that how I was feeling was light-years from how she was feeling. She moved a piece of hair from my forehead and asked if I was okay. She said softly, "Agnes, you don't have to be sad, you know. A lot can make you happy, if you let it." (Per my original order, I'd love to be happy!)

The nights that I'm not out late prowling and she's not sleeping at her boyfriend's, we still sit on her bed together, close enough for legs or shoulders to touch, and look at magazines. I'm not sad—that's what I told her that day. I'm just waiting for . . . something.

Agnes

Chapter 14

Winter is losing some of its resolve. I start loosening my scarf. My neck, when the cold air wraps around it, feels like a new neck. Frequently I am reminded of my body—the weather and Tea Rose taking turns exerting themselves on it. Tea Rose meets me after work. I am standing around back with Terrence, smoking one of his cigarettes. Mr. Figgs's handwritten No Smoking sign is taped above our heads. Terrence is telling me about his youngest brother who moved to Texas.

"Hi," Tea Rose says.

"Hi," I say.

"Hi," Terrence says. He looks at me and lifts his eyebrows gently as if to acknowledge something but not judge it.

It does not occur to me that Tea Rose would want to be introduced until he introduces himself. Terrence shakes his hand but looks mostly at me.

"Go on, Agnes," he says. "Get to class."

I put my cigarette out on my shoe and drop it in a trashcan. We say goodbye to Terrence. Tea Rose takes my hand as we walk away. We skip class and go to his room, practically skipping. It's a growing need, to be with him, to be undressed with him. But the need is starting to feel better unmet, and I never somehow remember this until we meet it. What I want is one need, on its eternally protracted way to being met, and to have it met moments before dying. I say this, more or less, out loud.

"Always with the death and dying," he teases. "This is so much more fun." He kisses me. He is ready to go again. He is never not ready. I let Tea Rose kiss me, and I let myself enjoy it. I touch his hair. What he lacks in mystery he makes up for in beauty.

"You're so serious all the time," he says.

I pay attention. I'll never turn down a chance to hear what someone thinks of me. "I don't think I'm that serious," I say. "I just...I don't know how else to be. What would an unserious person be like?" I lie on my side, propped on my elbow.

Tea Rose turns on his side too. "I don't know." He laughs a little. "I like the way you are. I don't mean it in a bad way."

"Is it because I like to talk about cults?" I ask, deadpan. He had teased me about this once before, when he "caught" me reading a book about Jonestown at the library, a few days after I'd mentioned that I'd been glued to the Waco coverage as it unfolded last year. "Don't you think it's fascinating," I'd asked him, "that nobody ever *knows* they're in a cult until it goes bad? Like, it has to get really appalling—suicides, pedophilia, all kinds of abuse—in order to be a cult, right? Up till then, it's just a religion."

He'd looked at me, bemused, so I'd carried on. "Did you know that David Koresh's mother had him when she was only four-teen?" "No, Agnes, I didn't know that." "Did you know that one of the child Branch Davidians who died was stabbed in the chest by someone inside the compound? He was three." "Jesus, that's horrible." "It's true. And before all hell broke loose, they wanted their phone fixed. I always think about that detail. They wanted to call someone. But who?" Tea Rose humored me for a while, then kissed me to make me stop talking. I didn't get to tell him that the final day of the standoff, April 19, also happened to be my parents' anniversary. They were supposed to go out to dinner that night but sat with me on the couch instead, unable to turn off the news.

"You do enjoy a good cult," he says now, lightly.

"I think," I say, inching closer to him, "that it's a safeguard. I'll never be, you know, susceptible."

Tea Rose closes the narrow gap between us. "What about me? Do you think I'm susceptible?"

I imagine Tea Rose in loose white garbs, haloed by a radiant light and surrounded by pretty young girls. It's not hard to do.

"No," I lie. "You could maybe start one, though."

"I'll be in your cult if you'll be in mine," he says, pressing on me with his full weight. I succumb, obviously.

Dear Mom,

What day is it, what day was yesterday, etc.? Do you know? I can't get a grasp on myself, where I'm standing, where I'm going. I feel a general lack of volition. Being filled with emptiness is its own kind of being full. Tea Rose and I are together a lot. I have been spending many nights in his room. I bumped into Surprise on campus and I'm amazed by how different she looks every time I see her—older. We made vague plans to meet for breakfast one of these days. Funny how you can live with someone and not live with someone, but I don't have to tell you about that.

Tea Rose and I are changing in ways I don't know how to name fully. This has something to do with time. In the beginning, there was no time. Time did not exist when we were not together and then it did not exist when we were together. I was the clock and he was the clock. We missed class. I missed a couple of shifts, which got me in minor trouble. Now we are aware of the time, almost constantly. A few days ago I woke up in Tea Rose's room. It was early, just before first light, and everything had that purple, paused look. Tea Rose was not in the bed. I squinted at the piece of paper on the nightstand, which said "Gone for a run" with maybe ten hearts scrawled all over the rest of the page. I lay there, processing the information, never having known that Tea Rose ran, for sport or necessity or any other reason, having difficulty, actually, picturing him midrun, all of his cool smoothness blurred by exertion, his pale face ruddy. I didn't know he owned sneakers. I could only imagine his barn jacket, flopping indecorously, books and Discman spilling everywhere.

I lay there on my back, and my thoughts went to Simon. There is a certain kind of stillness that invariably leads to sadness about Simon. The ceiling became a screen for my memory to project haphazard images onto: Simon in his car, Simon in his room, Simon at the dinner table, Simon with the puppy you made him return, the happiness on his face beforehand the purest thing I'd ever seen. I wonder if he ever forgave you. Eventually, the room brightened, and though I wanted it never to end, the movie faded out. Naked in my boyfriend's bed, thinking about my dead brother. I guess that's one way to start the day.

I was leaving the dorm as Tea Rose was approaching, his face a marbled pink, like the sun had risen within it, and the hair around his temples was wet with sweat. He wore a pullover fleece and mesh shorts and sneakers, just like any guy who ran, and I felt some combination of admiration for how different this was, how far from my clumsy speculations, and disgust for how much he looked like anyone.

Still, Simon came to his room. That's enough to make me go back. I avoided kissing him and headed straight to work, my clothes soft with being worn for the second day in a row.

I wish you'd let him keep that dog...

Agnes

Chapter 15

I'm at a party, drunk. Tea Rose is talking to someone across the room. It seems everyone on campus is here. Surprise is sitting next to her boyfriend on a plush, oversized chair, him squarely in it and her angled halfway up on the armrest. She looks uncomfortable in various ways. I'm standing against a wall, trying to determine how drunk I am. Someone spills on my shoe, apologizes. A boy comes over and asks if I'm in one of his classes. I do some combination of nodding, shrugging, and shaking my head, for which he puts his hand up to high-five. I touch his hand with my cup-holding hand and he leaves. These strange transactions.

I'm trying to get Tea Rose's attention, which consists of willing him to look over here. I don't feel capable of doing more. The person he is talking to was originally a boy but now it's a girl, much shorter than him, the back of her head facing me and her hair bobbing and rippling like a pond getting hailed on. Whatever he is saying is creating a lot of movement in her. Someone turns the volume up and it's one of those two awful songs by Tone Lōc and I know all the words, and the girl's hair starts moving ferociously, and I see her step closer to Tea Rose and thrust forward a little, supposedly an invitation to dance.

I'm too drunk to compute the jealousy I feel. I move toward the bathroom. There is a line. Two people in the line are making out. I wait behind them and indulge in the pleasure of staring openly, because they are too enmeshed to notice, and I am too drunk to care. A boy comes out of the bathroom and a girl goes in, and I keep staring. When the girl comes out, I bypass the kissers and slip inside. I use the toilet, clumsily, and wash my hands. I cup my hands under the cold running water and scoop some into my mouth and over my face and feel almost instantly steadied. I spend a minute, maybe two, maybe five, looking at myself in the mirror, this crooked face, this truculent hair. What, I think for the zillionth time in my life, do people see when they see me?

I hear loud banging. I barely realize that I am lying on the filthy tile, my head on my arms, my arms on the damp bath mat, my knees tucked into my chest. I am so comfortable. The door opens and I open my eyes and it's Tea Rose, bending over me, hoisting me up and over his shoulder.

"I'm fine," I say. "I'm totally fine."

"I know," he says. "Let's just get out of here."

We weave through the party like a wayward float in a parade. I hear some laughter and murmurs and feel the fabric of some bodies as we brush past. Then there is a hallway and stairs and finally, the street. I remember that we're off campus. Tea Rose asks if I can stand and puts me on my feet gently when I say I can, wrapping my big coat around me. I don't remember where I'd left it but he did, apparently.

"What happened?"

I laugh. I can't help it. He squints at me. I continue to laugh. I laugh and laugh, until my body feels incapable of gurgling up any more sound, any more anything. It feels good to act insane some-times, to act as insane as you feel.

"Are you okay?"

I nod. "Are you?"

"I am if you are."

I can't decide if he'd rather be back inside, upstairs, getting thumped on by that girl. I want him to be where he wants to be.

"I want you to be where you want to be."

"In general?" he says.

I move a step closer to him. "Yes. But also right now."

"I want to be with you."

"In general?"

"Yes. But also right now."

We are holding each other on a street in this depressed city. This much I know. He asks if I want to go home, and for a minute I think he means home-home, to my mostly empty home and my mostly empty father. Quickly I realize he means home-here, to his room or to mine. We are near the diner, so we walk there. A waitress tells us to sit anywhere. We take a booth in the back. We order coffees. I ask for home fries. That word seemingly everywhere. Tea Rose asks for cherry pie. It occurs to me that we somehow have never seen each other eat. It's just not how we've spent time together.

Our coffees come and he douses his with cream and sugar. I put a couple drops of cream in mine and watch them diffuse. It's okay, us sitting here. Our food comes and I watch Tea Rose for a minute as he sips and chews, as he sits rather haplessly and indulges this business of being human. I pour salt on my home fries and eat some. He takes a forkful from my plate, casually, like we do this all the time. He offers me some pie. I decline the pie. I tire of eating and watching him eat and I turn my attention back to my coffee. The waitress comes to refill our cups. People, I realize, do this.

As a way out of this eating situation that feels suddenly interminable, an endless sequence of forking and scraping and refilling and chewing, I tell Tea Rose, with the last of the night's alcohol churning through me, about Simon coming to me in his—Tea Rose's—room.

Tea Rose's face stops its eating for a minute. "Who is Simon?"

The question hits me hard. How can he ever know me if he doesn't know this?

I take a deep breath. I have to start somewhere.

Dear Mom,

Last night I cracked. A little tiny fissure, but enough for my favorite memory of Simon to leak out. It pooled around us, me and
Tea Rose, and it felt good to be there, in it, with him, to show
him my big brother at his big brotherest, instead of at his most
tragic. I was maybe seven, a couple of years into a period of
nighttime terror, fear of sleep due to fear of dreams, bad dreams
or good dreams that end, but mostly bad dreams, and I had fallen
asleep finally after hours of rigid stillness in my twin bed, and in
the dream I was looking for you and Dad, calling you, and you
were nowhere. You were gone. I woke up but I was still with the
dream, the dream still clung, and the house felt like a different
house than the one I fell asleep in. I got out of bed and moved
toward your room. The door was ajar, and through it I saw the
shape of your made bed, covers pulled taut. I panicked. Where
could you be, if not in your bed? I thought I was still dreaming.
I treaded along the hallway, down the stairs, past the entrance of
the shadowy living room, into the empty kitchen. The teakettle
gleamed. The dishrag was folded neatly over the divider between
the two sinks. The refrigerator gave no hum. All was mute.

I felt nauseous because I didn't know if I could wake up from
it or not. I tried hard to remember if there was a reason for your
not being home. I wanted to scream I told you so, because this
was precisely why I hated sleep, because sleep takes away, it
thieves. It stole my parents. It will steal everything. I must have
been crying. I was so scared, Mom. Next thing I knew, Simon
was lifting me up, carrying me to his room.

"I had a dream they weren't in their room and then I went in
there and nobody was there. Where are they? Why aren't they
here?"

Simon did the unthinkable for Simon: he tucked me in his
bed, in his room where I was never allowed to go. He

smoothed my hair. He told me that Mom and Dad had gone for a late drive. That Mom wanted to go and Dad didn't want her to go alone. He told me to calm down, that they'd be home any minute. I asked why you wanted to go for a drive, and I'll never forget what he said: "Why do people want to do anything?" Then he pulled the covers up to my chin and kissed me lightly on the forehead, a kiss that felt motherly, brief and cool and activating the same longing. He snapped off the overhead light and sat at his desk with the small desk lamp lit, his back facing me. He put his earphones on and I can still hear the bass and tin of whatever he was listening to. From time to time he tapped his highlighter against the textbook in front of him. Slowly, because I was trying to savor the rarity of being there, of being Simon's ward, I found my way to sleep, to fearlessness, to no-dreamland. I was disappointed to wake up in my own bed, to find that everything had been restored.

If there were a pie graph, it would probably show that I spend the most time talking about things that mean very little to me. Avoidance. So it felt good to share something real. Tea Rose didn't push me to say more than I said. It felt like I was alone, talking to myself or to you, but he was there, lightly around me, hemming me in. Afterward we had this tempestuous sex that seemed like the best response, I guess, to all the high emotion. I woke up before he did, before 7:00, and left him sleeping, his face and body emanating a warm tranquility.

I'm in my room. I have to go to class soon. I don't think Surprise came home last night either. I feel like everyone is just knocking against everyone else, spinning like the clothes in the industrial-sized dryers downstairs, all of us afraid of what will happen when we stop.

Stopping, for now—
Agnes

Chapter 16

The music building is going to close soon. The lights have been flickered, and outside my practice room I hear doors being clicked shut and locked, feet and paper shuffling down the halls. I pack my things and return my sheet music—a Mozart sonata I know well, because I felt like being good at something today—to the music library. Dreadlocked Joan Baez is standing by the main entrance, one hand on the light switch, the other holding a ring of keys. She wasn't at the front desk when I got here. When I got here, it was also, I realize, still daytime. Now it is dark.

"Oh, hi," I say.

"Hey, Agnes. I saw your name on the sign-in sheet."

I move my bag from one shoulder to the other, for something to do. "Are you waiting for anyone else? Is everyone gone?"

"Technically I'm supposed to check all the rooms. But everyone who signed in has signed out, so I'm going to leave it at that."

"I haven't signed out."

Joan laughs. "That's okay. I can see you're leaving."

I imagine being locked in. I imagine walking by and hearing someone else who got locked in, someone playing the piano at some illicit hour. I don't know if I'd rather be the one playing or the one listening.

Joan opens the door for me and follows me out. I watch her lock it in three places and test it to make sure, pushing and pulling as though she were trying to break in.

"Well, if there is anyone in there," she says, "they're definitely not getting out tonight." She laughs again—nervousness?—and tosses the keys in her messy bag. "I always tend to do at least half my job really well."

It feels too late to ask her name. Too late in the day and too late in our affiliation. We walk together for a few steps, although my dorm is in the opposite direction. I am not far from Tea Rose's.

"Where are you headed?" she asks.

I stop. I don't know if I want to see Tea Rose. I want to see him as though the other night never happened, in some untapped before. And yet I am also anxious to survey the after, to find out if anything will feel different.

"I'm not sure," I say honestly.

Joan laughs. She definitely laughs a lot. "I know that feeling. Do you want to come over for a drink or something?"

This is what people do, I realize. They seek friends and make friends and hang out with those friends. They plan things in advance and they do things spur of the moment. They don't wait until circumstances force their togetherness—like being assigned a roommate, for example—or until the need to be pressed into another body that needs to be pressed overtakes them. I knew how to do this once. I might learn again. Being around Joan feels liberating, fortifying.

"Yes. I'd love to." It feels like a triumph to say that, and to mean it. The only thing troubling me at the moment is that I still don't know her name and still don't know how to ask.

"Where do you live?"

We are walking toward the main campus gate, me on the walkway still patchy with snow and ice and her in the road. The lampposts cast evenly spaced shadows of themselves. A loud group of two girls and three boys passes us going the other way, red cups in their hands. Behind us, a shout followed by a gale of laughter—one of the girls has fallen. Joan is a few steps ahead of me now, hands in her pockets, head down as though heading into a great wind. Her back suggests that she has seen nothing and felt nothing.

"Drunk kids," I joke, catching up to her. She looks at me and smiles, as though just remembering that I am there. "I barely notice anyone at this place anymore."

"I know what you mean."

"It's rare for anyone to stand out."

"Yes." I think about Tea Rose. He is expecting me, I feel convinced, and a bit of guilt creeps in, but then I unconvince myself with surprising ease.

"My house isn't too much farther. It's on Church Street."

If she lives off campus, she must be a junior or a senior, I reason. The house is typical of the student rentals adjacent to campus: tall, narrow, ramshackle. We go up some stairs and then some more stairs and then we are in a kitchen.

"Do you have roommates?" I ask.

Joan plops her bag down on a chair and puts her coat on top of it. I do the same. The kitchen table is 1950s style, Formica and chrome, with mismatched chairs.

"I have two. They're both on the track team. We're almost never here at the same time—we keep opposite hours, pretty much. When they're not at practice or in the library, they hang out at the rugby house. I think their boyfriends live there." She laughs. "It's like living alone, but because I know they're here, I don't ever really get lonely. Their rooms are on this floor. Mine's upstairs."

She opens the refrigerator and lifts out a jug of wine. With her other hand she opens a peeling cupboard door and takes out two mugs, clinking them together by their handles. "Come on. Let's go upstairs."

I follow her up more stairs, these very narrow, opening to a small landing with a slanted ceiling and an ancient-looking heater in one corner. On the far wall, a door whose top edge slants along with the ceiling. I recall my favorite childhood books, all of which prominently featured garrets. Was this a garret? Did the house have a scullery too?

I realize Joan is looking at me. "What's wrong?" she asks.

"Oh. Nothing. This part of the house just reminds me of a storybook or something. It's very cozy."

"I think so too. Neither of the other girls wanted anything to do with being up here, so I didn't even have to fight for it." Joan pushes the door open. "You want to see my room?"

I duck my head—some sudden but wrong feeling of tallness, the door frame still five or six inches above me—and go inside. A twin bed with a faded quilt. A small dresser hidden behind a rack of hanging clothes. An old stereo flanked by cinder-block-propped shelves crowded with cassettes and CDs.

"You don't have a desk?"

"Nah. I do my homework out here on the floor or at the music library when I'm working." Joan hands me a mug of wine. It's cold and tastes like cough syrup. Joan puts music on. The Pixies. We sit on the floor of the landing and she turns a dial on the ancient heater. It thunks, shudders, and then starts to rattle, its orange warmth a kind of final destination, a place we earned. We talk about our roommates and what classes we're taking. We talk about the class we took together last semester, about the Chinese boy who raised his hand constantly and never got the answer right and one day left the room in sobs. She asks me questions about the dining hall. She laughs at a lot of what I say. I wonder if I am funny. We look at the heater more than at each other, its metallic glow as mesmerizing as a real flame, its presence a real presence. We fill our mugs a couple more times, each cup less cold than the last.

In the warmth and rattle and talk and music, I have no thoughts. I feel blissfully erased. Joan is saying something about how she used to ride horses with her sister. I am reminded, amid this polyphony, of my body. It has to pee.

"Downstairs, right off the kitchen," Joan says.

I drift downstairs and locate the tiny bathroom, its door a plastic accordion-type thing that clicks shut with a magnet. I pee for what feels like fifteen minutes and take a long time washing my hands. I let the water run while I flip open the medicine cabinet. It is crammed full with makeup, Band-Aids, tubes of toothpaste, deodorant, hair ties, and various over-the-counter drugs. I anticipate needing aspirin later, so I help myself to two, swallowing them down with tap water. I still don't know Joan's name. If Joan's name is not Joan, I will be, I fear, upset.

A powerful need to find out propels me, quietly, around the house. On the other side of the kitchen is a small living room whose large windows face the street. Light from the streetlights streams in. A car passes by on the street below, its headlights briefly striping the room. In the corner is a low bookshelf, a few purses, and what looks like Mardi Gras beads hanging over the sides of it, various books, papers, and odds and ends filling its meager spaces. On the top shelf is a stack of mail. I hiccup loudly, almost losing my balance. The wine is all at once upon me.

I can steal the mail. I can steal anything around me right now— the beads, a lamp—because I am alone and because these mugs of sugary wine are good facilitators. I don't know what I'm looking for but I want a souvenir. I hold the slim stack of envelopes in the line of light converging from the kitchen and the street.

Ashleigh P McGill

Ashleigh McGill

Ashleigh McGil

Joan Gertzman

Nicole Zigler

Nicole Zeigler

Joan S Gertzman

An index card with ELECTRIC BILL DUE TUESDAY/ TRASHCANS scribbled on it in blue marker. I can barely believe my eyes, don't believe them at first. Somewhere in this house lives a Joan. The person upstairs, I know, is Joan, because I knew she was Joan before now, before knowing she was Joan, on paper, on something as incontrovertible as mail. She is not Ashleigh. She is no more Ashleigh than I am. She cannot be a Nicole, because of her face, which is not the face of a Nicole. The face of a Nicole is not at odds with the hair of a Nicole, not at odds with the world. The Joan I felt was Joan is an actual Joan, and I want to scream that I am, that I must be, as I always suspected, a true psychic with true psychic powers. What a gift it is to be right about something!

I put the mail back carefully and practically run up the stairs. Joan is lying on her back, eyes closed, face somewhere between sleep and a smile.

"Hi," I say. "Sorry."

Joan opens her eyes. "Oh, hey. What time is it? I was starting to fall asleep."

She doesn't ask where I was or what I was doing. She doesn't say that line I hate, the one people like to say, about falling in the toilet. I look at my watch. "It's almost midnight. I should probably get going."

Joan stretches her arms overhead and points her toes, like a guitar string being tightened. She sits up and rubs her face, attempts to smooth her fuzzy hair. "Thanks for hanging out. This was fun."

"Thanks for having me over." I pause. "Joan. And for the wine and everything. I had a great time."

"Want me to walk you down?"

"No, no, don't bother. I'll be fine."

"Sure you'll be okay walking home? Where do you live?"

For a minute, I forget. I picture my house. I picture my dad sitting alone at the kitchen table, drinking a glass of milk. I picture Tea Rose's room, his bed. I picture my dorm, finally. So many places to go and nowhere to live. "I'm on campus. Not far."

"Which dorm?"

"Halsey."

Joan sits lotus-style and puts her hands on her knees like she's going to do some chanting. I am very aware of her movements, each one very intentional. "I used to live there! What floor?"

"Third."

"Ha! Me too." She gives herself a little hug, squeezing hard for an instant before letting go. "Okay," she says, "I'm going to get ready for bed. You're welcome to stay here if you'd rather not walk back. Up to you. I've got a sleeping bag and plenty of pillows."

Another place to sleep. Maybe the goal is to sleep in as many places as possible, and not just one.

"That's all right. Thanks, though. I'll see you soon, I'm sure."

"Bye, Agnes."

"Bye, Joan."

Dear Mom,

Remember that trip we took to the mountains where Simon and I were kind of "against" you and Dad? We complained about the music in the car on the drive there, and the food we ate when we stopped, and the cabin when we finally arrived? Thinking about it now, it was a fascinating thing that happened. Where I felt this opportunity to be close to Simon, and the only way to do it was to ally myself with him and against everyone else. I know it was probably a shitty vacation for you and Dad. I know we were probably insufferable to be around. But it was like Simon and I tacitly pledged our loyalty to one another, like away from home, without his friends or my friends or whatever other factors pronounced our differences, our different ages (12 and 20) and our different stations in the world and in our family, just disappeared, and we became brother and sister, blood-bound in a way we'd never explored. Or in a way he'd never permitted me to explore.

I think Simon enjoyed it as an experiment. I enjoyed it as an omen, which it turned out not to be. Back at home, things went back to usual, us on our separate floors, keeping opposite hours. The day after we got back, I remember talking to Jenny on the phone in the kitchen when Simon came upstairs, took the phone from where it was wedged between my cheek and shoulder, hung it up, and called his girlfriend, all within the space of about 4 seconds. I stomped up the stairs to my room and slammed the door, half hoping he'd call after me or follow me when he got off the phone. He did neither, and a few minutes later I heard the back door open and shut and the car roar out of the driveway—your car, since he had totaled his 2 months before.

But when we were in the mountains, he laughed at my jokes. On our last night there, we sat outside behind the cabin in the dark for a long time. There was no moon and the stars were less bright than you might imagine, for the mountains. We could barely see. We took turns making faces and trying to guess what face we were making, smiling or frowning, opened eyes or closed or winking.

He told me something that I still have a hard time believing. Before I was born, he said, he had an imaginary friend. Daniel. He said he talked to Daniel under the covers at night and outside when he was playing by himself—anytime he felt alone, he said, he talked to Daniel. He said that on his first day of kindergarten, you told him he was not to speak to Daniel or even say his name. He said one time his teacher caught him in the bathroom, chatting quietly with Daniel with the faucet running, when the rest of the class was having nap time. He begged her not to tell you. We wondered if she did or not—did she? Anyway, he said that when I came into the picture, there was a tiny part of him that was disappointed I was not a boy, a real live Daniel. It made me sad. If I could have been a Daniel, I would have been. Maybe then he wouldn't have given up.

He talked about you and Dad. He said you were a melancholic and Dad was a regular guy, which was a good combination. He said his girlfriend was a melancholic and he was one, too, which was not a good combination. I asked him what I was and he said, "You're happy and smart. Don't let anything ruin that." It's funny to be told that you're happy. When he said it, I felt it. If anyone else had said it, I would've probably been suspicious. He also clearly had no idea how much he had to do with my happiness, how easily he was able to make me happy.

Nobody wants anything to be ruined. But ruin still happens. Ruin does not seek permission. How could he not have known this, him of all people? Did he believe in the idea of the chosen few, that some people were destined to be happy and would be, no matter what befell them, and some people would never be? Or that some people have predetermined abilities to control disaster, to save themselves from too much pain, and some people do not? Did he say goodbye to himself before he did it, look at his own face in the mirror?

Not rhetorical questions,
Agnes

Chapter 17

"So you're interested in setting, the physical circumstances?"

I'm sitting in Professor Donald's office and it is the middle of March, the longest March I can remember, a month that has always felt like one eternal middle, thick with no narrowing. Outside is bright, the snow glinting patchily with ice.

"Yes." With some effort I force my eyes to move from the window to the open book in my lap.

Professor Donald gives off an almost tiring sense of length: long legs and arms; long face; long, unkempt black and gray hair; long teeth; long fingers; long skirts. She is less body than line and brain, her face a display monitor for the ideas that seem constantly to afflict her. Now she is reaching up to her tallest shelf to pull down a book. Her office is a mess of books and papers, except for her desk, which is oddly bare save for a few pens, a pristine blotter, and a closed daybook.

"Miller has some interesting things to say about that. You might start here, in your research." She pulls a Post-it from somewhere and marks the page before handing me the book.

"Okay, I will. Thanks."

She slides between her desk and the bulging bookshelf and sits across from me. "Do you have a specific angle? Have you worked out a thesis yet?"

I cringe at the question. I cringe under the specific. I know this about myself. I will get the details wrong. I will get the aura exactly right but the details wrong. I fight the urge to lift my shirt up and scream, a thing I've always felt like doing in the middle of church.

"Well. Not exactly. But it just leapt out at me right away, how the house and all of the items in the book are described more in depth than the characters. Like the people are secondary, like what the author really wanted to write about was the house, but I guess there can't be a book about just a house, with no people."

"Couldn't there?" Professor Donald asked, a smile idling somewhere beneath her long face.

I think about my house. Everything in it belongs to someone or is an expression of someone. So the house is everyone, all of us, but most of us are no longer in it. What does that make it? A collage? A ghost?

Professor Donald's smile surfaces. "I don't mean to put you on the spot, Agnes. I like where your thoughts are going. With some fine-tuning and narrowing in, you could write a very provocative essay."

I realize that it is my own house I'd been picturing as I read the book for class. I realize this with some embarrassment. Do I read anything, see anything, hear anything, or only myself? My self, the shoebox for a thousand dioramas. My self, the only book ever written. I am going to end up writing a paper about myself, again. Poor Professor Donald.

I do the thing where I thank her and say goodbye and thank her again and leave the room awkwardly, sort of stepping backward, only to get to the front door of Stein Hall and realize that I forgot the book she wants me to use. I hurry back to get it. I pause for a moment outside her door, still ajar as I'd left it. She is sitting at her desk, erasing something from her blotter, though I had not seen any mark on it whatsoever.

"Sorry—I forgot the book you gave me."

She looks pained to see me again but says, not unkindly, "Ah. It's there where you left it." Her hand is covering the place she was just erasing. I take the book, thanking her and apologizing some more, and leave her brushing eraser dust from her desk and lap.

Dear Mom,

Joan, my friend who works in the music library and actually reminded me of Joan Baez before I knew her name was Joan, tells me that when she wakes up, she lies in bed until she gets a clear vision for the day. She says that she can always tell what kind of day it will be. She says she likes knowing that it will be a shitty day, for example, because then she can spend all of her resources trying to fight the shittiness, or she can just give herself over to the shittiness, confident either way that she's communing with the soul of the day. She can be prepared. She says because of this she is rarely surprised by any outcomes. And because she is rarely surprised, she is rarely disappointed. Saddened, maybe, when she can't reverse the shittiness, but not given over to the "why mes/why nows/life is so unfairs."

Joan meets me after my work shift ends or I meet her at the music library. The other day we had a bona fide picnic, the grass's dampness leeching through the blanket she'd brought, us shivering over our sandwiches and bags of chips. Joan grew up on an organic farm and was homeschooled until college. She told me that her parents taught her that it was relatively useless to call life any adjective—unfair or beautiful or unpredictable or anything else. Life is just life, they'd say. There is nothing it is not. She uses a lot of nature metaphors. Like, plants don't console themselves if they die of late frost. They just die. There's nothing to feel too bad about. Feeling bad implies that the frost and the death are somehow our responsibility.

82

Yeah, I said. But plants don't have feelings. People do. You can't blame people for exercising the feelings they've been given. You can't attach to nothing. We're meant to attach.

I guess, Joan said. It's just that any happiness that comes from that always gets fucked up. The only lasting thing is solitude.

I think Joan has a crush on Tea Rose. And I think Tea Rose is mesmerized by Joan. I think Surprise would hate her. They haven't met. I still barely see Surprise. I can't keep track of whether she's fighting with her boyfriend, or if everything between them is swell. Their status seems to change a lot, but he is still her main focus, like a second curriculum or a marathon that needs to be constantly trained for.

Tea Rose and I are back, more or less, to where we were before the Simon floodgates opened. Neither of us has spoken of it since. We have gone over to Joan's house a couple of times, to drink wine and listen to music. I like being around her when he's there and being around him when she's there. It's like our relationship or whatever it is has another dimension to it. Or another person in it, I guess. All of us conductors, sparking.

I am trying to decide what to do for spring break. Tea Rose is going to London with his family and told me his parents would probably pay for me to come, which seems insane but also incredibly sweet. What on earth, I wonder, has he even told them about me? Joan is staying here and told me I could stay with her, since her roommates are going home and the dorms will be closed. So far that seems to be my best bet.

Dad has not been pushing me to come home. He asked me on the phone the other day, "Will you come home?" I said I wasn't sure, and he said to keep him posted. He sounded distracted, like he was watching TV, but there was no noise in the background. I pictured him hearing something and thinking it was you pulling into the driveway, you putting your key into the lock—I imagine one of his ears is always listening for such sounds. I feel so sorry for Dad that it's hard to even think about him. It's much easier to wait for you from far away.

From far away,
Agnes

Chapter 18

Joan's house is quiet. Spring break is quiet. Campus is empty, buildings locked, trees weary with the rain we've had for the past two days. The streets are beginning to lose the snow they've been lined with for months. Surprise's boyfriend is spending part of the week with her and her family. I am sleeping in one of Joan's roommate's beds, using Joan's heavy, sticker-covered laptop to work on my papers.

It feels a little like we are married, playing house. In the evenings, we make dinner. While we cook, we drink shitty wine. And after dinner, we drink more shitty wine and listen to music up on the landing outside Joan's bedroom. Despite having the whole house to ourselves, we tend to cluster together up there, lying on the floor or leaning into one another or sometimes, inexplicably, holding hands.

During the days, we do different things. I work on my papers. Joan goes for long early morning walks and takes heavy naps in the afternoons. Sometimes she makes food from scratch that most people buy at the store: yogurt, bread. She says she misses the farm.

"There are things you learn on the farm," she says, "that you can't learn anywhere else. Not college. Not through, like, jobs or whatever. Not 'on the street.' It's constant life and death. Things blooming or being born, things dying." She is drinking from a big mason jar, lemonade she made earlier. She takes a big swig. "And everything has a purpose; everything can be used. Nothing gets thrown out. I mean, even animal shit has a purpose. My mom, she keeps apple cores, uses them to make vinegar."

I nod. What she's saying seems familiar. Things I know but never learned or experienced. What is that called? Intuition? Still, I want to be encouraging. "I loved *Little House on the Prairie* when I was a kid," I say. Joan laughs so hard she gets tears in her eyes. I laugh too. There is an ease between us, and the shape this ease takes most often is laughter. To be with her is to admit a certain obsession I have with sameness, no matter how I might deny it. I want my double, and Joan's essence is a gentle and surprisingly satisfying refusal of that need.

I don't mention my birthday until the evening of my birthday. I wake up feeling nothing, and then, remembering my birthday, force myself to feel something. Last year of my teens, I tell myself. My favorite number as a kid, I tell myself. The number that always sounded so far off, so exotic, so sure of itself. Here I am—it. I shower and attempt to do something with my hair, which has grown long and scraggly. I find an eyelash curler among Joan's roommate's things and use it. We spend the day busy and parallel, reading magazines, doing schoolwork, puttering around. I am not keeping it a secret but I'm finding it hard to say. When was the last time and place, I wonder, where nobody knew my birthday? It seems significant, like some kind of hallmark of adulthood, or an anti-hallmark maybe, some shrug from the universe: "So what? Everyone's got one. Move along." When I finally say something, we are in the kitchen, I at the table on Joan's computer and Joan peering into the pantry.

"So, it's my, ah, birthday today."

Joan looks at me, puzzled, and then a smile breaks across her face, dimples and crinkles unabashed. "Get out! For real? Nineteen?"

"Yep."

"Let's go out! I'm taking you out for Chinese food. I was just trying to figure out if we had the stuff to make some kind of lo mein but forget it, we're going out. We're getting a scorpion bowl!"

We walk to Ming's, which takes a long time, and by the time we get there, we are numb with cold. Joan orders a scorpion bowl and our server, who looks no more than fourteen, doesn't flinch. We are, the triangle of us, nonchalant—Joan twirling her hair; the boy, expressionless, with no pad to scribble on; and I with my head down, staring at the faux ornate menu, a red binder embossed with gold, the plastic pages inside covered with all-caps English, Chinese characters, and overly lit, garish photographs of slick food tangles. The description for EGG ROLL reads EGG DOUG FILL WITH MINCE VEGETABLS PORK & DEEP FRYED.

A few heads turn as the scorpion bowl is delivered to our table, snapping and popping with a lit sparkler and festooned with skewered pineapple and drink umbrellas. The bowl is huge. The outside of it is made to look like a pineapple. Inside are ice and bright red punch and four straws, along with the various other accoutrements. Joan eats the pineapple chunks while she orders food for us—vegetable dumplings and vegetable lo mein "and some of those crunchy things, what are they called? Those crunchy chow mein noodles. Those are free, right?" The boy nods just slightly, not writing anything down. He leaves, disgusted or entertained or just purely apathetic, we will never know. Joan puts two straws near her mouth and taps the other two my way. "Cheers," she says, "but first, make a wish."

The sparkler has stopped sparkling. A tiny bit of orange glows for a second, then stops. I wish for my mother. My brother. For Tea Rose, that he will not fail me. For good grades, to make my father happy. But mostly, I wish for my mother.

Before going to bed, I call my dad. "I was hoping you would call," he says. "I didn't know how to reach you." I don't know what to say, so I say nothing. I feel dizzy from booze and MSG.

"Happy birthday, Agnes," he says.

"Thanks, Dad."

"I love you very much and hope all your dreams come true."

"Thanks, Dad."

Dear Mom,

Okay, so you missed my birthday. Let this letter serve as the of-ficial record—the first birthday, to my knowledge, you missed completely: no card, no call, no show. I guess I don't know how to feel about it. It's like...a newish feeling tossed onto the pile of other, older feelings. A special kind of disappointment. Limited edition birthday disappointment.

Early morning, hungover, Joan told me about her sister. In re-turn, I told her about Simon. We were in Joan's bed, making a transaction—trust for trust. Sometimes somebody's story curls up around your own and bears it out of hiding. What we have in common is not on the surface, but underneath, we are reach-ing for the same things, bracing ourselves in the same way.

Turns out, Joan's sister, who lives with her parents on the farm, is severely anorexic and has been for seven years. It started with a diet, and then a stricter diet, and then it went from there. At some point she overheard the doctor talking about the minimum number of calories necessary to stay alive, and for the past several years she has eaten that many, not a single one more. Occasionally a few less. She was hospitalized for a while but it seemed to make her worse. For a brief spell she lived in a treatment center, but she refused the therapy and group stuff and her parents could not afford to keep her there.

"She lies in bed," Joan said, "or she sorts food. She convinces my parents to buy her certain things from the grocery store, promising she'll eat them, but she never does. In her closet are bags and bags of food. There is one garbage bag filled entirely with those condiment packages you get at fast food places. I

88

have no idea how she got them. Mustard, mayo, ketchup, relish. I found a few whose corners were torn or bitten open. Like she sucked on them a little before putting them back."

Joan said it finally dawned on her one day last year or maybe the year before that her sister was not trying to be skinny. "She's trying to die. But she wants to see how long she can stay right on the edge. It's like this prolonged prelude to the main event. She thinks she's doing it alone but she's taking all of us—me, my parents—with her. It's been a seven-year suicide. I think she'd be proud to make it a ten-year one, or more. Twenty years. The rest of her life, like this, half dead."

Then she was done talking, and it felt so naturally like my turn. I told her about Simon more fully than I've ever told anyone, even myself. I told her how you nearly went crazy trying to find out who'd given him the oxycodone—you never did, right?—and how the doctor said that the alcohol was just as much at fault. I told her how I'd wanted to scream that the pills and the booze hadn't marched into his mouth like an invading army, that the fault was his alone. I'd wanted us to be madder at him, to rage at him together, but you couldn't, and Dad couldn't, and I'm beginning to understand why it was necessary for you to look for blame everywhere else before turning it inward. Blaming him accomplishes nothing. Blaming yourself accomplishes nothing, but it's juicier; there are infinite layers, infinite places to find failure if you look. I know this. I get it now.

I told her about my memories of him, his laugh, his temper, his love of skateboarding and drawing and music; the times, which I've catalogued and canonized, where he sought me out, to talk to or mess with, how cool it felt to be, for those brief moments, his peer, the eight years between us simply dissolving. I told her how now whenever I think about Simon I get an acrid taste in my mouth, the taste of pills melting, as though through some Sisyphean transfer, I have been fated to forever partake in his final deliberate act. At some point Joan brought me a glass of water and held my hand because I was crying, and I told her how you found him in his bed the next day, peaceful as if just asleep but with the note—I LOVE YOU, I'M SORRY, I CAN'T—written on a piece of smudged paper from one of his sketch pads. I told her about the smells and sounds of the house in the weeks that followed, the food people brought over that rotted because no one ate it, the hoarse screams and sobs from behind closed doors, the stringency of ammonia that seemed to be poured everywhere, on everything.

And then at a certain point I felt quiet filling me like smoke, blacking out whatever words might have been left. "You can't say it all," the silence reminded me, and it was a relief to just lie there in the midst of all that was said. Joan squeezed my hand and I squeezed hers back, like an erratic heartbeat between us, or some type of Morse code. The Morse code of just not being alone. Eventually, she fell asleep. In the dim light, her blond dreadlocks looked like fabric, like the tattered yarn braids of a doll.

It's crazy to think that every day of life puts us closer to death. I mean, it's life that kills us. Living is a slow suicide. Time is the pills we take, the calories we refuse to eat. Choosing to stay alive or choosing to die—in the end, the only thing that separates them is a handful of years and the questions we ask that never get answered.

Right?
Agnes

Chapter 19

Tea Rose calls Joan's house from London. I detect a faint accent. I imagine him testing it out privately, quietly, but decide he probably did not do this. The British tilt is probably genuine; he is absorbent.

"I miss you," he says.

I want to think and answer honestly. There is a long pause.

"You there? I miss you."

"Yes, I'm here. I heard. Thanks."

Another silence. I expected to miss him. But I realize that hearing his voice now, I am thinking about him for the first time all week.

"Do you miss me?"

It's funny, I think. I want him to be desperate for me. I have not missed him because I have been content. With Joan. A tiny shiver inches down me, like a bead of condensation on a glass, when I think of his body, his hands, his weight. But mostly, I have savored this newish sense of safety, the assurance of being an accounted-for person. There is something I have with Joan, I realize, that I don't have with Tea Rose. Maybe it's because with her our bodies stay out of it. Maybe it's because both of our families operate under a baseline system of fracture and duress, both of our siblings have tested the outer limits of pain. Maybe we really love each other. Maybe she is the first person I find myself loving in this post-Simon, post-mother world. But he is in London, and this call must be expensive.

"Yes. I miss you."

I can hear some movement, the phone being switched from one ear to the other.

"The week has gone so slowly. I can't wait to get back."

I hold back a noise. The conversation is getting impossible. My week has flown, but I don't have the energy for another round of this quilting of half-truths from little scraps of guilt.

"When will you get here?" I will just ask questions, I decide. "Tomorrow?"

"No, actually. Day after, since I don't have class."

"Okay. I'll see you then? We'll hang out?"

"Definitely. Should I come by your room? Or do you want to meet at mine?"

My room. Another thing I have not thought about until now. I picture it, dark, my ratty bathrobe hanging limp on the back of the door. Surprise's left-behind perfume bottles like faithful little soldiers, the whole room waiting to be useful again. I wish I could stay at Joan's. The thought of going back to Halsey seems devastating.

"Yes," I hear myself say, without knowing which option I'm saying yes to. "What time, do you think?" I want to know how many hours I have left of this other life I've so quickly come to prefer.

"Probably not until late. Eleven, maybe?"

"I guess come to my room? We'll figure it out from there."

After I hang up the phone, I go once more to the bathroom to check for blood. For days I have been feeling that low churning and, afraid to ruin Joan's furniture or her roommate's sheets, I yank my pants down anytime I get behind a closed door. My relationship with my period is like a child's relationship with losing her teeth— no matter how many fall out, each one is a shock, somehow exciting and a bit disgusting. I know, while having it, that I feel oddly happy, an emotion not neatly capitalized upon by the period industry, which seems hell-bent on reminding women how much there is to be miserable about, urging them to cheer up by smelling better or looking thinner. But I love when the blood comes. I love curling up in a ball on my bed, feeling the ebb and flow of cramps, the intense hugs of pain followed by the succor of no pain. The entire human experience, as performed by my body.

I look at my watch for the date, but the date is irrelevant because I am, in this regard it seems, among others, irregular. I bled right after Christmas and felt extra relieved, because I felt like, up until that moment of bleeding, that stranger I'd had sex with at the party was still inside me somewhere. So that's something.

I get up from the toilet now, stiff from having sat for so long. I wash and dry my hands for a long time, enjoying the warm water and the satisfying little bubbles and the soft towel. I go up to the room where I have been staying this past week, a week that has felt vast and timeless, like an ocean. I think about being back in my own room. I think about seeing Surprise again, seeing Tea Rose, working in the dining hall. It feels like August, like I will have to learn everything all over again.

Dear Mom,

When I was eleven, I was mucking around in the woods behind our house and came across the torn-off cover of a dirty magazine: one naked woman posing in a shower with another naked woman standing outside of the shower holding a towel out nimbly by one finger and behind her, a naked man, his erection partially visible. It was a very busy cover. And there was so much to take in—not one big-breasted naked woman's body but two pubic regions almost bare and practically identical, and then the man, his hairless muscled body and forgettable face, his sex somehow dominating the page, despite it being the least interesting part. I was afraid, against all logic, since I was very much alone in those woods, of being seen, convinced you were watching from some up-high branches, worried that my face would bear evidence of what I had been staring at when I went back into the house.

I scuffed at the dirt with my sneaker and a stick until I had made a shallow grave big enough for the page, took it gingerly between thumb and forefinger and laid it down, covering it over with dirt and leaves. I ran home, washed my face and hands, and resolved to put it out of my mind. But that night, I closed my eyes and thought about the cover, allowed the narrative of the cover to unfold in my mind and imagined what might have been in the rest of the magazine. I shuddered out my guilt and revulsion from where I touched ever so lightly between my furry skinny legs, reasoning that the more sparse the stroke, the less it counted—toward some overall filth score, toward my moral decay.

For many days in a row I would go back to the woods, dig out the page, and hypnotize myself with it before returning it carefully to the ground and running home. After a couple of weeks I had effectively memorized it into submission; thinking about it had no effect on me. At night, under the covers, my hands stayed at my sides. And then one day I went to the woods with a lighter, to say a final goodbye. It had rained the previous night, and the ground was still wet. When I unearthed the page it came apart in my hands, mud covering the women's breasts and the man's penis, a certain modesty suggested by dirt and paper, as though the hole itself had known my shame. I tried to ignite it but it didn't work. I left the soggy page where I'd found it and almost forgot about it, until now.

Maybe this would be an allegory if it didn't actually happen. But there's something masturbatory in every sex act, isn't there? Something intensely solitary and alone, despite the presence of another. I still feel, every time, like I'm in those woods, guarding a secret. Like every time I do it, I'm possessed by every other time I've done it, until the day comes when I'll want to take a lighter to my whole short history with boys. Speaking of history, I haven't had a period in a while. Wouldn't it be funny if I were pregnant? Not banana-peel funny, but I don't know, like, death-rattle funny.

Haha,
Agnes

Chapter 20

It is the day before classes resume. The dorms are open and campus, like a cat waking up, is arching and stretching back into motion: hedges are being trimmed, walkways swept, windows washed. Joan's roommates will be home in the afternoon, as will Surprise. Joan stands in the doorway while I pack. We are both amazed by how much stuff I brought with me, as though I were planning on staying for much longer than the week. Clothes, books, CDs, my high school yearbook, four pairs of shoes, my pillow, my bucket of toiletries, the framed family photo Dad gave me for Christmas.

"I wish you didn't have to go," she says.

"I know. Me too. Or, me neither."

Joan is wearing baggy linen pants under a loose patchwork dress. Her feet are bare and her toenails are speckled with orange polish. She stands with one foot crossed on top of the other. Around her neck are five or six necklaces—some silver, some hemp—and around each of her wrists are bracelets of various textiles and metals. Her hair is wrapped up in a wide blue scarf. I memorize her. I feel certain that we will never be this way again, that our togetherness this week, fierce and easy, was created by some small rip in the cosmos.

I hesitate but decide to ask. "Have you ever taken a pregnancy test?"

Joan laughed. "Um, yeah."

"Really?" I don't know why I am surprised. It's not the sex part. I am picturing Joan in the throes of sex and it's not difficult. I wonder if she keeps all that jewelry on. "Haven't you?" Now it's her turn to seem surprised.

"No...I..." I feel the need to try to qualify my response, but there's nothing else to say. "No, I haven't."

"I've taken a dozen pregnancy tests. Taking pregnancy tests is how I don't get pregnant."

"That doesn't make sense," I say, "but I get it."

"Because people who get pregnant don't seem to worry about getting pregnant until they're pregnant. I worry a lot about it in advance, and then I take a test, and I'm never pregnant because I think I've, like, worried the pregnancy away, you know?"

I feel my gut spasm, a peristaltic nervousness. "I haven't really been worried," I say now, worried.

"Oh, come on, you are *not* pregnant," Joan says, still a bit giggly. "I mean, you're careful, right?"

I am not always careful. Tea Rose and I, we have not always been careful. We have not been reckless, but we have been swept up. I am trying to remember specific moments and they are getting jumbled—him fumbling with a condom, so that's a good sign, right? If I can recall a condom? Me pushing upward on him, telling him with my body to exit before...but did he mistake my bucking for passion, for permission? Both of us gluey deep in the afternoon, with sweat, with each other, the late sunlight illuminating wheat-colored hairs on his stomach, neither of us sure where each of us began and ended, whose stickiness was whose. Panic is rising in me. Joan is still talking.

"...not seem like the type of guy who would mess around with that kind of thing. And you—I mean, you're, I don't know, so controlled? I mean in a good way—like, I can't see you losing your head. There's no way!"

I begin to believe I am pregnant. To know I am pregnant. My body feels dumb, like the whole of it is being stuffed with cotton. I did not think Tea Rose could get me pregnant because I did not think, not really, that I could get pregnant. That I could be a mother, when my own mother is somewhere. When my own mother, simply, is. There is only one mother, and I am not her.

I shake my head a little, trying to clear it, to put a full stop to the cavalcade of thoughts and questions. Joan is saying something else about fear being the most effective birth control but she stops now, giving an awkward cough. After a moment she asks quietly, "How late are you?"

"I don't know."

"Just... come with me, okay?"

She takes my hand and I follow her to the bathroom. She opens the cabinet doors beneath the sink and from the back pulls out a brown paper shopping bag. She sets it on top of the sink. Inside are boxes and boxes of pregnancy tests, several different brands. I feel too sick to laugh. Joan's face looks stuck between several emotions. The whites of her eyes are very white, webbed in the corners with tiny pink vessels. The fluorescent light makes her skin seem translucent and I notice some freckles I'd never seen before. And wedged between all of these stark micro-observations, the mossy thought grows: *Who has Joan been sleeping with?*

"Go ahead," she says. "Better than making yourself crazy. The instructions are right on the box." Joan leaves the room. I take a box from the top of the bag.

- ONLY TEST THAT TELLS YOU SIX (6) DAYS BEFORE YOUR MISSED PERIOD!
- TOP-RATED FOR ACCURACY!
- EASY-TO-READ RESULTS: PLUS (+) MEANS PREGNANT, MINUS (–) MEANS NOT PREGNANT!
- RESULTS IN THREE (3) MINUTES!

The instructions are six pages long and include warnings, diagrams, and frequently asked questions. I look at the drawing of the female reproductive system. I look at the image of the lower half of a woman holding a stick between her legs. I can hear Joan breathing on the other side of the door, or maybe it's my own breathing I'm hearing. I feel many things, but the need to urinate is not one of them. I unwrap a stick and wonder if it's true, if this thing can know what my body has yet to find out. I put the faucet on a low trickle, pull down my pants, and sit on the toilet, sidling the stick between my legs. The whole process feels ridiculous, galaxies removed from the thing it is purporting to determine, the thing being the possibility of a life-changing reality, a fleshy reality. There are theoretical babies and there are actual babies. I will narrowly escape one for the other. I try to focus on the sound of the water and let go of my body. I close my eyes.

But what does sex have to do with babies, anyway? Babies should only come if they are invited. Like anyone else. Why are they an exception, planting themselves so unapologetically when they haven't even been summoned? Sitting on the toilet, coaxing myself to pee, knowing I am involuntarily holding back my pee out of a desire to not engage in any of this, I am mad at babies. I have nothing to do with babies. Babies have nothing to do with me. A knocking.

"Are you okay?" Joan sounds like she is somehow part of the door, like the door itself is speaking.

"Yes . . . fine. Sorry. Just taking me a little while."

"Oh, no, take your time. Sorry to . . . interrupt. I'll be upstairs, okay? Do you need me . . . for anything?"

Funny how politeness imposes itself in situations that feel dire. Like, the nicer we are to one another, the better the outcome will be.

"No, I think I'm okay. Thanks, though."

I stare ahead of me at the shower stall, the soap-filmed Plexiglas door. I hear water meeting water and realize that I am finally peeing, first in stutters that splash my fingers and then in a disciplined stream, the test stick getting thoroughly doused. If there were a test for taking this test, I imagine I would do very well on it, following the instructions, as I have, to the letter, as though that will give me the better outcome.

I finish, wipe myself, and lay a strip of toilet paper on the back of the toilet. I dab the bottom of the test stick and lay it on top of the paper. I figure neatness might help eliminate the chance of error. And, superstitiously, the chance of a plus sign. I wash my hands, careful not to upset the stick, careful not to even look at it. I count to one hundred, putting "Mississippi" between every number. I do it again. I consider leaving the bathroom, maybe getting something to drink, and coming back when I'm sure the five minutes have passed. I put my hand on the doorknob but I do not leave.

And the plus/minus thing, what is that supposed to mean? Being pregnant is a plus, a positive? That seems presumptuous. Or is it plus-one, like a date to a wedding? Is the minus meant to signify negativity? Less than? Minus one person, which, if there was only one person to begin with, means you are nothing? You are zero? The plus makes you two but the minus makes you none?

When I am sure five minutes have passed, I pick up the test and shove it in the front pocket of my jeans, where it's concealed by my long sweater. On my way out of the bathroom, I grab another of the test boxes and slide it up my sleeve. Back in Joan's roommate's room, I pack both tests in my bag and zip it up tightly. I jog up the stairs and find Joan lying on her bed, reading a book.

"You were right!" I say brightly.

"Phew!" Joan says. She comes over and hugs me. "I knew it!"

I hug her as best I can. "Thanks so much for everything. I'm so glad I stayed here."

"Me too."

"I'll see you soon, okay? At the music library, or we'll get lunch or something." I leave before anything else can get said.

MOTHEREST

Dear Mom,

Or should I say Grandmom.

This is not a joke,
Agnes

Chapter 21

I have learned about unwanted pregnancy from television. I have struggled through my thinking that I was not wanted. That it is me, and not Simon, who made my mother go away.

I have spent the better part of six hours pacing my small room, holding two positive pregnancy tests, one in each hand. If asked, hypothetically, Tea Rose would not want a baby. We are not in this for love or for babies, I have been thinking to myself, pacing, my two test sticks like relay batons I have forgotten to pass off. We are in this for bodies and for loneliness.

But maybe, maybe in trying to be more substantial, more *here*, we have lost all ability to float. Maybe, in trying to stay above water, we have thrashed ourselves into exhaustion, into drowning. If Tea Rose knows about the baby, it will be harder to extricate myself. He will feel a heightened responsibility to save me, which will make us sink faster. All three of us. Or will the baby be the thing that makes him let go more readily? Will he be the guy from TV who "can't handle it," or will he be the "my baby too" guy, indignant? Pacing, I try to determine which guy is better. Both seem bad.

I expect flowers or a drawing or something when I see him—Tea Rose has presented little *cadeaux* for a lot less than a week's separation. There is a shoebox under my bed that's filled to overflowing, all trinkets from Tea Rose, some scribbled on notebook paper while we've sat in the fireplace room of the library, or on napkins from the dining hall, or on cutouts from magazines or books. Tea Rose has no problem tearing pages out of books. The first time I saw him do it I actually gasped—such a small but wild transgression. "What are you doing?" I'd said. "What? This is a good page. You'll like it."

He has said that he misses me even when I am around, because he anticipates missing me when I leave, to go to class, or to go back to my room to shower, or to go to work, or once in a while sleep in my own bed. The more I leave, the more he wants me. And it is the frequency of leaving that occurs here in our little shoebox of a world—moving from one building to the next, from one class to the next—that intensifies the missing.

But apparently it is not a matter of duration. Apparently, for Tea Rose, the longer we are apart, the easier it becomes to be apart, the less I may be missed. I learn this immediately, without being told, when I hear Tea Rose's signature knock—a rapid, low thrumming with his knuckles—and open the door to find him empty-handed, his face absent its usual flushed excitement. Usually it is his face that tells me everything—his desire to touch me, his desire to be alone with me, his desire to absorb as much of me into himself as he can.

In Tea Rose, for a while, I had a mirror of my own longings, and the reflection was enough to keep us enthralled. But here, now, with him standing before me in the empty hallway, his hands heavy at his sides, his body resolute, I see that the mirror has gone dark.

"Hi," he says, and then steps in, too quickly, to hug me across the shoulders. "Hi!" he says again, more brightly, before straightening back up. He leaves his hands on my shoulders briefly, like a father having a talk with his son.

"Oh," is all I manage to say. *Is this his baby too?* I wonder. *Is it his right to know?* I am distracted by these thoughts and distracted by how distracted he seems to be. I thought seeing him would be all I needed in order to know what to do, to know how to tell him or how to stay quiet. I thought any confusion would be mine, coming from me. I did not count on him being so strange. Like a stranger.

"Do you want to go for a walk or something?" he says in the same bright tone.

"Sure. Let me just put my coat on."

We walk wordlessly down the hall, down three narrow flights of stairs where no parts of our bodies touch, and out into the night. There is the smell of rain but no rain. We walk in the direction of the track and practice fields. Campus exudes a barely contained glee, a collective relief to get back in the swing, to have spring finally beginning to take hold and summer just around the corner. We pass the library, whose lights in a month's time will still be on at this hour, whose carrels will be filled with anxiety and the students producing it, whirring like turbines, like generators in a power outage, cramming for the mandatory emergencies known as final exams, so close to the end they can almost taste the first celebratory beer on their lips.

I think about what Professor Donald said once: that however you try to make writing a paper or studying a fun event—surrounding yourself with other studiers or going in groups to the library or computer lab—in the end, it's work you do alone. Walking now with Tea Rose, I feel acutely what she meant. There is no *us*. There is him, and there is me, and there is the work of being alive. My relationship to everything around me feels more precarious than ever, now that time has been newly minted onto my body, now that my biology has been reincarnated as a ticking bomb. The world looks different.

We pass the student center. Several people stand outside talking, making plans, their voices carrying high and glad. Tea Rose takes something from his jacket pocket. I know what it is before seeing it—an airplane-sized bottle, just like we had that night at the very beginning when we huddled on the field until sunrise.

"Do you collect those or something?"

Tea Rose grins. "Nah. I nick them from my dad. This one's from the London trip, but he always has them since he travels so much for work. He'll order three drinks at a time, drink one, and pocket the rest for his hotel room or whatever."

"Does he know you take them?" This is nice, I'm thinking. Maybe we'll just talk about this kind of thing. His parents. Their quirks.

"I think by now he has some idea. He never says anything, though. You can pretty much always find at least one bottle in all of his coats and suit jackets. I don't think he keeps track."

"Is he an alcoholic?" I don't necessarily mean to ask this, but there it is.

Fortunately Tea Rose laughs. "I think if he were an alcoholic, he'd keep track."

He sips from the bottle and passes it to me without touching any part of my hand or arm. I hold it loosely. We have reached the bleachers and I follow him a few rows up, our shoes sending clanking echoes into the night that has become thick and dark, a much heavier night than the one we set off in. We sit next to one another, the coldness pressing through my jeans and jacket. I put the bottle to my lips. The bit I can taste tastes good. I take a sip, a tiny one, and then a bigger one. A gust of anger sweeps through me, and I gulp deeply before handing the bottle back. It is now a little more than half empty. Or, if I were a different sort of person, a little less than half full. *Take that,* I want to say to the cluster of cells in my basement, *see how you like having something crammed into your existence.*

I am warm now. I feel ready.

"So," I begin, not entirely sure where I'm going, "this week, at Joan's, I—"

Tea Rose interrupts, like the words had been beating against his mouth with every step we took to get here. Now they rush out. "I'm in love, Agnes."

We are angled toward one another. In my booze-headedness, I

wonder if he is about to propose. I wonder if he somehow knows I am pregnant and wants to, I don't know, do the right thing, as it's been called on TV. Did he say, *I'm in love with you, Agnes?* Did he say *you?* Didn't he say that? Wouldn't that kind of announcement explain the oddness of tonight? I thought we were going one way, but we're going the opposite? The moon, eavesdropping through a bit of cloud cover, now nudges closer, and by its light I can see Tea Rose clearly, the smooth marble of his face carved into a grimace. He takes a small sip and hands me the bottle once again. This time I just hold it, the defiance I felt a few minutes ago gone. In its place, a whispery fear.

"I met her the day before we left London. I can't explain it. I mean it's just one of those freak things. I went into this tourist trap shop near the hotel where we were staying—I was looking for something funny to bring home for you actually—and she was in there, and we just kind of kept looking at each other..."

I feel like I might throw up. Tea Rose is talking to his hands. I take a few deep breaths, hoping the night air will steady me.

"It's okay. You don't have to—"

Tea Rose puts one hand on my thigh without looking at me. "No, I do have to. I have to tell you this. Because it's crazy to me. I need you to know that I guess it's only something this crazy that could make me ever want to not be with you. Like, it's scaring me."

"I have no idea what to say to that," I say, swallowing down more air. "You want my blessing? You want me to feel bad for you right now?"

"No! No, just listen." He takes his hand from my thigh and rubs his face. "So I notice her and she notices me and it's like we kept noticing each other, over the racks of crap. I mean, like, the second I saw her, I couldn't not see her. We didn't even say anything. I went back to the hotel and paced around and that's when I called you, because I thought hearing your voice and making plans to see you would just, I don't know, set me straight. But you were weird on the phone, and I was, and when I hung up I still just felt crazy. Like that girl put a spell on me or something!"

Oh, but I hate him right now. I hate being made to endure this. Has he always been this stupid? Am I actually pregnant with his baby? I fight the urge to run to Joan's house and swipe another pregnancy test. If this isn't a dream, maybe it's just a massive mistake, a multitudinous mistake.

"After we got off the phone, I went for a walk. As I'm walking, I see her again, a block ahead of me. And for whatever reason she stopped and turned around and saw me, and waited for me to catch up, like we were, I don't know, old friends. Agnes, we just talked. We just walked and talked for maybe five miles. Like I can't even describe it. We just fell into conversation like, yeah, like I said, we were old friends, but more than that, like we'd known each other in another life! We like all the same bands—she's just as obsessed with Nirvana, maybe even more so than I am. She's seen them three times in concert. It's like we . . . we're—"

"Oh my God, please don't say soul mates. Just spare me that much."

Tea Rose takes a hit from the bottle. Even in the almost-dark I see that he is fuchsia from having actually almost said *soul mates*.

"Okay, whatever. The point is we talked all night. We went to a pub and talked. When I realized that my parents were probably out of their heads worrying, we went back to the hotel and talked. Even they were like, who is this girl? Like they felt something special too. I mean, I'm telling you, this kind of thing doesn't happen. And if it does, you have to, I don't know, go with it. I mean, I barely even feel like I have a choice here."

At this I start to laugh. I laugh like I haven't laughed in a long time. I watch his face go from sincerest choirboy to hurt, hurt in a way I've never seen him be, and I take some paltry satisfaction in it.

"You don't have a choice?" I say, the irony almost too dense to be shaped into words. "That's really hilarious." But under my laughter I feel something else. Relief? At not having to find the words for something I don't know how to talk about. At not having to tell this most hidden, most frightening, most unreal secret. At not having to weigh his reaction against my own. At not having to fit him into a world I cannot fathom, whether this thing, this baby, stays in it or not.

"Agnes, I'm sorry. I'm trying to be honest. No, I'm not trying—I am being honest. I guess I'm trying...not to hurt you. I don't want to hurt you."

We are quiet.

"So where is she?" I ask, trying to make my voice calm, neutral.

"She's still in London. She's studying there, finishing a year abroad. Then she'll go back home to Canada, where she's from. Montreal. We'll visit this summer—I'll go there and she'll come here. We are...I don't know. We're making plans. Plans I assumed I'd be making with you." Tea Rose rubs his face, his hair, as though drying them with a towel. "It's just so nuts."

"You keep saying that, how crazy it is. But...you're...happy. You're happy, right?"

His look is pleading. "Yeah. I'm happy. I'm—"

"You're in love."

"I am." He sounds relieved, like I have given the right answer. "I love her."

We sit. I take the final sip from the bottle and hug my knees to my chest, needing to hold something, needing to cover myself. Tea Rose hunches forward, arms crossed around his middle like a player who's been sidelined. Now he moves to the row below us and sits down facing me, looking up at me full in the face, his long legs between us.

"You don't have to say anything," I say. "It's good. We're good. We don't have to do some dramatic thing."

"I just wanted to look at you," he says.

"Okay," I say.

If it were a play, I'm thinking, this would be the last act, the last line of the last scene of the last act, and the curtain would come down on us just like this, facing each other in partial moonlight. But it's not. I get up after some moments have passed and pause just long enough to squeeze his shoulder on my way down the bleachers. I hear the brief clinking roll of the tiny bottle before it drops off into silence. I walk back to my dorm, heavy and light.

Dear Mom,

Today I went to Planned Parenthood, which I really think should be renamed Unplanned Parenthood, under the circumstances. Or is it like a piece of advice? Half a statement: Planned Parenthood (is better than the alternative)? I don't know. But I went there after my last class. I walked down to the Texaco and called for a cab. I bought a Coke while I waited, drank half, and immediately felt the need to throw up. I don't know if it was because of the pregnancy or because of my nervousness about the pregnancy, about the little field trip I was going on. Whatever the case, I managed to make it to the bathroom, puke pretty cleanly, and be back out on the curb by the time the cab was pulling up. I felt funny telling the driver where to go. It felt the same as telling him that I'm pregnant, which I've said aloud to exactly nobody. And writing it to you feels even less like I'm sharing—if anything, it feels like I'm pushing the secret further inside myself.

Outside the clinic, practically blocking the entrance, a skinny, visibly pregnant woman was smoking. I didn't mean to meet her eyes but I did, which I think felt automatically to both of us like I was judging her, and she met my stare full-on as though daring me to say something, until I looked away. I mumbled "hello" as I stepped past her to get to the door. I could feel her behind me, feeling like she'd won. Inside, a woman who looked kind but tired (probably tired of being kind) sat behind an ancient computer inside a glassed-off cube. She gently pushed a clipboard through the small tunnel and asked me to sign in.

"I don't have an appointment," I told her.

"Oh," she said. She straightened her back and patted her thick curler-ironed bangs absently with a pudgy hand. "Well, you might be waiting for a while. What are you here for? Dear?" she asked, her eyes hooded by her heavy lids and her concern, which, however practiced, sounded genuine. "What are you here for? Birth control? An exam...?"

"I'm..." and I found I actually forgot the word. I stood there openmouthed, my eyes starting to ache from not crying, and gestured dumbly toward my lower half. "I'm having a...but I'm not sure if I'll actually, you know, have—"

"Okay, honey, that's fine," she said, actually rising in her seat slightly to touch the top of my hand where it rested, like somebody else's hand, on the clipboard. "Why don't you just fill one of these out and take a seat. The nurse will call you back and you can just have a talk with the doctor or nurse-practitioner, okay? You don't have to do anything else today."

I filled out the form as best I could. I didn't know all the family health history stuff. The section about smoking, drinking, and number of sexual partners might as well have been called "the reasons why you're sitting here, you reckless slut." Then it asked if I had health insurance. I think I do—it's yours and Dad's, right?—but I checked no. If I could have, I would have just written a giant NO over the entire page. No to being here, no to all of this. I stuck the pen back behind the clip of the clipboard and returned everything to the receptionist. She was talking to the smoking girl, so I just put it on the counter and sat back down.

I looked around. There were a few empty seats but most had

bodies in them. Female bodies. Three women, including the smoking girl, had pregnant bellies straining against their shirts. One woman's belly button made me wince. "I should not be able to see that," I kept thinking as I kept looking. Seems like the best example of "insult added to injury" that I can think of.

A woman sitting diagonally from me took a large bag of chips from a plastic bag she had with her. The bags were noisy and she ate noisily, milling her food with her front teeth. I again felt the need to throw up and made it to the bathroom just in time. When I was done vomiting, I sat down on the still-flushing toilet and cried silently, just for a couple minutes. I didn't want to miss my name being called.

When I returned to the waiting room, another woman had taken the seat right next to mine. Her arms and legs were thin, but her breasts were enormous, and a layer of belly flab hung over the waistband of her pants. At her feet, sleeping in a blue car seat, was a tiny baby. I was fascinated by her body more than I was by the baby. Clearly she had just given birth. She still looked pregnant, her body sort of overflowing with what was no longer inside it.

The baby's eyes fluttered briefly and its mouth yawned a perfect little O. The woman sat staring down at it with a perfectly blank expression. Maybe it was her look or the fact of the baby being in that room—a place where babies felt sort of forbidden—but whatever the reason I opened my mouth and words came out.

"That's a cute baby."

She looked at me and half smiled. "Thanks." She rubbed at the corners of her eyes. "He sleeps like an angel during the day but at night, my God."

"What's his name?"

"Quincy. After my granddad."

"How old is he?"

"Six weeks. I'm here for my checkup." Her eyes went to my body for an instant and then back to my face. "What are you here for?"

I still honestly didn't know. "Oh, just a checkup."

She smiled and laughed slightly. "Ask for some extra birth control, just in case," she said. "Unless you're ready for one of these."

I smiled. Amazing how nobody will assume you're pregnant if you don't look pregnant. I thought about how many women I've seen in my life who might have been pregnant. I looked around the room again. Was everyone pregnant? Was the whole world pregnant? Do you only think about pregnancy when you're pregnant? Is it the only thing you think about when you're pregnant?

The baby started to cry. His face turned beet red. He sounded like an angry lamb. I'd never seen anything so tiny make so much noise. The woman unbuckled him with one hand and reached her other one underneath her shirt, unsnapping something. She swept him up, gently and swiftly, to her breast. He stopped crying and started making sucking and gulping sounds. I tried not to stare but I glimpsed her nipple, huge and dark brown, as the baby expertly tugged it into his mouth. I can't stop thinking about that nipple.

I don't know if it was the actual nipple or the whole waiting room epitomized in that nipple or what, but the next thing I knew I was blindly grabbing at a stack of pamphlets with worried-looking girls on the front and fleeing the building and calling for a cab from the pay phone outside. I wanted to tell the driver just to drive, just to go until he felt like stopping, but I didn't have the guts, nor the money to see such a thing through.

What, Mom? What now? More than anything I want that superpower that the girl had from that old TV show, where she'd touch her fingers together and time would stop. Not because

I want to extend this moment but because I need time. Every minute, every day, this thing inside me is growing. Right? Isn't that how it works? It only has nine months or whatever to become a person. Nine months to become a person and a lifetime to be nothing else, nothing more. That seems insane. I should have more figured out by now, if not everything. I should have something to show for myself, one success or foolproof theory at least. Maybe the one thing I can do in this measly amount of time is forgive you. Would that make a difference? Would it make you want to be here for me now, at last? Because I'm starting to believe that if it's not for this, it's not going to be for anything. I only ever want you, but now it finally feels like I need you. I need you to be real, which is to be here.

HOW DO I KNOW YOU'RE REAL IF YOU'RE NOT HERE?

Agnes

Chapter 22

Lately I'm obsessed with trying to pinpoint how long the other body inside mine has been there. Was it that night in January, or that night in February, or the dozen nights around those nights? I wasn't paying attention. I mistakenly thought Tea Rose, with his incandescence and his discombobulating effect on me, was exempt from real-time, real-world consequences. I know that I thought this because I never paused, not in the fumblings of midnight, not in the library at high noon, to wonder if we were safe.

Now I am in a strange fog. I have made no decisions other than to do nothing, which, I'm realizing, is a most certain kind of something. In the moments when I allow myself to ponder this, I feel indignant. It seems unfair. There should be some kind of alternative, some something-else. I consult my pamphlets. I keep them in my bag and pull them out when I am alone, like they are tarot cards:

Prevent Teen Pregnancy: Practice Abstinence. I never open this one, just stare at the image of an iconic-seeming jeans-clad blond couple underneath an autumnal tree, facing each other and holding hands. Something in me does believe in them and their endangered chastity, although I feel like if the so-called worst happens, they will probably just get married and have a wonderful family life, graduating from cautionary pamphlet to lifestyle brochure.

You May Not Be Ready to Have a Baby. Close-up photograph of a young-but-not-too-young woman's face carefully arranged into a concerned expression, eyes slightly squinted, lips slightly tensed. This is the one that talks about abortion in vaguely medical but mostly layman terms, highlights adoption as a "potentially therapeutic alternative," and emphasizes the importance of talking to one's partner, parents, trusted friends, counselor, and/or clergy before making any kind of decision—as though eventually, with enough talk, the pregnancy might just disappear on its own.

Abortion: What You Need to Know. In high school I attended the huge "Right to Life/Pro-Choice" rally—since both were happening simultaneously, one begetting the other—in DC, taking notes for an article I was writing for my school newspaper. There were words on signs and things in jars. A lot of anger and pageantry and statistics. I imagine being there now and announcing into a megaphone from some high-up vantage point, loud enough for both sides to hear me, I AM PREGNANT. WHICH OF YOU WANTS ME? and being wrestled over like the baby King Solomon, threatened to be cut in half. As far as medical intervention goes, it looks like I have eight options: suction aspiration (first twelve weeks of pregnancy); dilation and curettage (D&C, first twelve weeks of pregnancy); RU-486 and methotrexate (five to seven weeks of pregnancy); dilation and evacuation (D&E, first eighteen weeks of pregnancy); salt poisoning (saline amniocentesis, after four months of pregnancy); prostaglandin abortion (four to six months of pregnancy); hysterotomy (four to nine months of pregnancy); and partial birth abortion (brain suction abortion, four to nine months of pregnancy).

All of these terrify me only slightly more than the idea of actually having the baby. I guess I am, by nature, a haver. I like having. I want to possess and be possessed. I don't like giving away and I don't like cutting out. I fold this pamphlet and put it at the bottom, underneath all the rest, but I have read it more times than any of the others and know all the words by heart.

Healthy Pregnancy, Healthy Baby. Unsurprisingly there is a chubby, smiling, diaper-clad baby on the cover of this one, as if to remind us all that pregnancy has a function. It is not just a black curtain of horror. Maybe for some it is not a black curtain at all, but rather a long-awaited thing, a joyous forty-week event, a thank-God-I'm-finally, a beautiful diaphanous veil that will, at the perfect moment, be lifted to reveal a beautiful, prayed-over, wished-for creature. I scan this one long enough to get the gist—prenatal vitamins; a balanced diet; moderate exercise; no smoking, drinking, or drugs; keeping your doctor's appointments and letting him or her know of any problems or changes. I think about the smoking woman. It seems that doing what you know is wrong would supersede most of these. Doing the right thing is such a tiny country. Doing the wrong thing out of naiveté, hope, blindness, desperation, or a moment's forgetting? That is Russia. Most of us are in Russia.

One day as I am leaving work, I trip on the low step leading to the outside exit, and instead of instinctively cradling my midsection, I attempt to rescue my bag. I fall sideways and land on my hip, hard, and my bag, despite my best efforts, spills its guts everywhere. I lie still for a minute, the pain in my hip sharp, before starting to gather my books, pens, papers, and, strewn in a little arc, like cards on a poker table, my pamphlets.

"You okay, missy?" Terrence stands above me on the step holding an industrial-sized baking sheet.

"I'm fine," I say. "Thanks." In my desperation to get those glossy, slippery pamphlets back into my bag, I fumble, flinging them farther, repeatedly grabbing, like a bad vaudeville act where I'm trying to catch fish.

Terrence just watches. "You sure?"

"Yep," I say, kneeling now. He bends down and hands me a pamphlet that has slid past me. It's the abortion one. He doesn't look at it, or at least doesn't comment on whatever he saw.

"Agnes," he says.

116

"Uh-huh?" I finally get everything back into my bag and stand up. My hip really hurts. I can feel a bruise starting to form, a slow warmth gathering beneath the pinching pain.

"I bet Figgs would let you take some time off, you know, if you needed to." He says this carefully, uncharacteristically. "Want me to talk to him?"

The kindness. It's too much. I can't look at his face. I look at his hands, my eyes settling on his worn-looking wedding band, dulled by years of bleach and detergent but still managing somehow to shine and glint shyly against his dark skin.

"Agnes? Want me to talk to him, honey?" He's never called me anything but Agnes or Miss Agnes. This "honey," it feels unfair at such a moment, gratuitous. I bite the inside of my cheek. I try not to split in two.

"I'm good," I finally say. "Thanks, though. Thank you. I'm good. I'll see you Wednesday." I walk away, feeling like it's too much; all of this is too much.

· · ·

Suddenly it is April. Kurt Cobain has just shot himself in the head, and everyone, predictably, seems to want to blame his wife. Which seems doubly unfair—to her, obviously, but also because suicide, by its very definition, suggests ownership, an irreversible self-possession. I see Tea Rose around campus, the morose version of Tea Rose, as though he is a method actor preparing to play the part of "Mourner Groupie #1," wearing sunglasses and all black and earphones. I half expect him to seek me out, and maybe quarter hope that he will, to hear Simon's story again, now that Simon shares this thing in common with his hero. I feel monstrous to even have this thought, but I have it. Tea Rose doesn't, though, reach out to me in any way, and once in a while I spend a little bit of time imagining his conversations with the new girl, picturing them crying on each end of the phone, running up five-hundred-dollar bills, listening to the same tracks and murmuring sniffy comments about feeling abandoned by their sad, blue-eyed idol. There is a vigil on campus that I walk by on my way to the library, candles and a sparse crowd and a few boys strumming the chords to "Come As You Are" over and over, and I feel sad in spite of my meaner instincts, sad for this person whose only way out was all the way out, sad for these fans who now need to recalibrate everything they thought they knew about loneliness and despair, and sad too for that baby, the daughter who will grow up in a shadow that no amount of light can erase.

As if to deflect all the gloom, nature is showing off. The dogwoods are in full bloom and my pants are too tight. I see the trees, branches outstretched like arms balancing teacups down their lengths, but I resist buying new pants. Buying new pants seems premature. I feel certain that something must happen within me, within my mind, before new pants can be bought. Instead, I loop a hair tie through the buttonhole and around the button as a makeshift clasp. I wear the same two to three oversized tops, which effectively hide my changing midsection as well as the button situation. Some days I wear dresses—long flowy things I took from my mother's closet back in August when I was packing to come here and my life was still my own. Surprise still gets dressed in the crook of our closet door. We don't pay attention to one another's bodies—at least, we don't admit to doing so. If she notices any change in mine, she doesn't let on.

A handful of times I excuse myself from class or work to vomit in the bathroom. The vomiting offers no relief. The urge comes as a kind of ray of hope amid the staggering nausea, like nothing I have ever known—flu and motion sickness and food poisoning, the last of which I've never had but can acutely understand that word, *poison*, the body trying to rid itself of a toxin. And then I wonder, is this my body revolting against this being? Is this thing inside me toxic? Or is this my body's way of protecting it from whatever matter, ideas, germs, influences I am ingesting all day long? I throw up eagerly, ecstatically even, believing it will stop. But it doesn't. It comes right back, sometimes worse, sometimes with a slightly different character. I have no appetite, except for when I wake up at 4:00 a.m., ravenous, and go down to the dorm basement, as if in a trance, to buy a can of ginger ale and a package of something, cookies or chips or cheese crackers. I sit in the chair next to the machines, my flip-flopped feet icy cold, and I gulp and guzzle and belch as though I am the only person left, a stowaway in the basement of the earth. Increasingly, this is the only way I can eat: in the dead of night, semi-cocooned by sleep, alone.

I have always skulked. I remember being young, nine or twelve or one of those years, and waking up from a bad dream, which so often happened, and scurrying to my parents' room, which I'd often done. Their door was closed and I'd hesitated there, wondering if I were brazen enough to walk in without knocking, since knocking would have been even more brazen. I finally entered cautiously and stood by my mother's bedside, my eyes adjusting after a minute or two enough for me to see her sleeping form, her mouth slightly open, her eye-lids smooth and lucent like the inside of seashells. Her right hand lay open-palmed by her head on the pillow, and her left hand rested on the mattress edge close to me. Ever so lightly, I'd touched the watch she'd fallen asleep wearing, unable, for some reason, to touch her, her body. I didn't know if I should wake her to tell her I was there, or how to wake her. I knew that just being in the room, close to her, had made my fears subside—already I was forgetting the dream—but I knew that if I left, the dark something would be waiting for me in the hallway.

After a while I'd laid down on the floor, proud that my need to be there hadn't disturbed anyone, and, with the sound of my parents' breathing like an incantation against fear, fell asleep. I'd woken up when the first light shown grayly through the curtains, less because of the light and more because of movement above me, on the bed, in the bed. I sat up and almost as quickly lay back down, having seen in that flash of a second my mother atop my father, her back curved and bare, the ridge of her spine visible, her knees bent on either side of his body, her head bowed over his and her arms along his sides. It knocked the wind out of me.

Down on the carpet, I'd feigned sleep as though my life depended on it, afraid that my wakefulness could be somehow heard. I screwed my eyes shut tightly, and then, worried that betrayed too much effort, focused on relaxing my face, gentling my eyes from the inside. I held my breath involuntarily and had to keep reminding myself to breathe without gasping. I heard more movement, murmurs, mouth sounds, that I became wild trying not to hear. It was an imprisonment, an oppression, my being there, a torture I had inflicted on myself by invading their privacy, which I hadn't realized I'd done until they went from being my parents, straightforwardly mother and father, to being woman and man with bodies who share a bed.

What have I done, what have I done? was all I kept thinking to myself, and alternatingly, *Let it be over, let it be over.* The shame of the witness is the worst kind of shame. After what felt like twenty-four hours, I heard a rising from the other side of the mattress, my father getting up and approaching where I lay on his way to the bathroom to shower and get ready for work. I heard his footsteps stop short when he saw me. I heard him tap the end of the bed, my mother's feet, possibly, to get her attention. There was a moment when the whole room seemed to draw its breath at my discovery, and I fought hard to maintain my façade of sleep, of innocence. A minute later I heard the adjoining bathroom door close and the shower turn on. And a minute after that, my mother was tapping me awake, roughly. "Get to your room," she said. "You're too old to come in here in the middle of the night." I got up and left, mortified. I never went in their room in the middle of the night again.

Meanwhile, something irreparable seems to be happening between Joan and me. The clear channel that connected us has become scrambled with static. We see each other in class and chat afterward, but it's dodgy and tense. I avoid the music library altogether. I know it's my fault, the fact and lie of this pregnancy, along with whatever chemical changes are altering my behavior in a million infinitesimal ways.

One day we eat lunch together. I have gotten used to eating alone, and sitting across from her, I am newly distracted by my body. I can't find a comfortable position, first crossing my legs and then tucking them underneath me, scooting my chair close to the table but then, put off by how my breasts almost rest against it, crossing my arms and then holding my drink awkwardly. I'm so consumed by how to sit that I miss most of what she is telling me.

" . . . refusing. I'm pretty sure this is the end."

I am too embarrassed to ask her to repeat what she was saying. This constant sense of myself is so far the worst part about being pregnant. My body is like a too-occupied room. I pick at my turkey sandwich. The pamphlet says I am not supposed to eat lunch meats but they are one of few foods I have any appetite for. I swipe pieces from the prep station at work. I like how they are cold and slick and salty. They seem very far removed from what meat is. From what flesh is. Trying now to decide how to respond to Joan's last half sentence, I open the sandwich, move the cheese, and eat the turkey beneath. I close the sandwich.

"How are you doing with it?" I ask carefully.

Joan looks at me like she knows that I don't know. Like she possibly even knows why. It is a penetrating look.

"Doing with the fact that my sister is now actively killing herself? Yeah, not so great."

I feel hot and suddenly nauseous. I so badly want to have an appropriate response but my body keeps interfering. I think of Simon, of my mother's face after Simon, how it wore an expression it had never worn before and would never unwear thereafter. The kind of sadness that engraves you with sadness.

"She's calling it a hunger strike, which is, you know, funny in its way. Seeing as how she has been hunger striking for seven years."

I try some shallow breaths, as surreptitiously as I can. "What is she striking against? Does she say?" My voice is toneless because I am trying not to throw up.

"Oh, she has a long list. The president. She reads the newspaper now and listens to news radio all day. Sanctions in the Middle East. Oil greed. The pillaging of the earth. Told my parents they were contributing to it by not being a certified organic farm, when she knows full well how expensive it is to do that and how clean their practices are. She's angry, like all of a sudden she's really angry."

My stomach roils. I imagine this emaciated, yellow girl—sallow-eyed, putrid-smelling—lying on some worn homemade quilt, newspapers strewn all around, the blinds pulled tightly. Wrongly, perhaps, I feel some peace in that image. The soft quilt. The quiet dimness, slatted with sunlight. The decision made: goodbye, misery. Goodbye, world. I don't know if I am envious or what I am more envious of—the solitude or the being done.

"Sounds like she's striking against being alive," I say, and I am about to say more, about to find within myself some words of comfort to make up for my strange and off-putting behavior, but the bile starts its meteoric rise and I throw my napkin on the table and run to the bathroom instead.

I vomit for probably ten minutes, which, in vomit, feels like an entire day. I think of Joan's sister, her pain. I vomit so hard I fear I will cast out the baby, or at least do it harm. At some point someone comes into the bathroom and quickly leaves. When the spasms finally stop, I dab my mouth with toilet paper and get up shakily. I lean against the cold enamel stall door. I slowly make my way to the sink and rinse my face, swish and spit, rearrange my hair. My eyes are bloodshot and there is a spot of puke on my top, which I try to scrub out with a paper towel. When I get back to my seat, Joan is gone, her place cleared.

Dear Mom,

I have become all schoolwork, all the time. I feel as though I
may not be back here, so I am trying to make it count, every
review session, every footnote, every article. Professor Donald
was surprised to see me when I showed up at her office to drop
my final English paper off two days early. My sociology exam
was yesterday, a mixed bag of multiple choice and long essays.
It was easy. The hardest part was how my hand and fingers
ached from actually writing the essays.

Funny how that doesn't happen when I write these letters.
Probably because I'm not aware of the clock, and I'm not having to dredge up the "right" answers or to be thorough and
correct and neat all at once. I just write what I want, how I
want. I can change the subject—hey want to talk about my
baby?—which I can't do on a test.

My philosophy paper is due at the end of the week but I
have already finished it. I'm holding on to it because I think I
might want to change the last paragraph around a bit. It's an
essay about free will. I got so confused writing it that I actually ended up writing two contradictory papers and then kind
of fusing them together. I think I've had enough philosophy for
a while, for my life, even. I feel like a person just needs the
basic tenets—life is a mystery and ultimately suffering, we are
doomed to repeat our failures, we might have everything but
everything is illusory, and there is only nothing—and can figure out the rest from there. Tomorrow is my geology exam. It's
open-book, so I'm not too nervous.

And after that...I'm done. I keep getting excited thinking
about it—my first year of college over, a whole summer off to
look forward to—and then I remember that it's me, my life, not
Surprise's or Tea Rose's, and the excitement vanishes.

Sorry, but if this baby died on its own, would I be sad? Is

123

there any way to know that in advance? I can't figure it out. There is a relief in the difficult thing being done for you. Because I think I at least know for certain that I can't get rid of it. Still, I can't imagine it's exactly thriving or happy in there. On some level it must know it's not a wanted guest, right? There's nothing I can do about that. I can't trick my body into behaving more hospitably any more than I can trick my mind. Once in a while I have the urge to poke at my belly really hard. To say, "Go away. Just do us both a favor and go away."

It's like the opposite of what I say to you.

Agnes

Chapter 23

Seemingly overnight, spring goes for it, grabs toward summer like a boyfriend making his move. The air is lush, poetic—the kind of air you remember. Birdsong is so strident it makes people pause their conversations or speak more loudly in order to be heard. Flesh is visible, yards of winter white leg and pretty clavicles festooned, as though celebrating their liberation from turtlenecks and heavy scarves. Surprise and a few of the girls from her business classes or young entrepreneur's club or whatever she is involved with these days—she went from losing me little by little to losing me at a hundred miles an hour—"go tanning," borrowing upperclassmen's cars or actually taking the bus to the tanning booth to work on their "base tans" before Beach Week, when much of the college disperses east to Hampton Beach. The freckles Surprise had when we first met have resurfaced. She has a red seersucker bikini and new jewelry from her boyfriend, and she walks like someone who has a lot of staid sex—a clenched swagger.

In contrast to all the tank tops and short shorts, I wear more and more layers. My body rejects this weather, the seasonal call to undress. I smell different. I shower earlier and earlier in the morning so there's less chance of having to share the bathroom. I miss being touched but I can't conceive of being touched, so the water's steady pulse against my skin seems like the right compromise. I make it as hot as I can handle, and when I can't take it anymore, I turn the faucet almost all the way to cold. Sometimes I vomit, quietly, right into the drain. At the end of the night the smell of me—like blood hatching, an eruption of cells in the petri dish that is my body—is so thick that I sometimes take another shower, late, soaping and resoaping every crevice. I wear an old cotton nightgown of my mother's and I make sure that when I finally pull it on and get into bed, I'm too tired to have any thoughts left in me.

In three days, campus will shut down. I have not begun packing, have not made arrangements to go home. My dad has called and left messages and I have called him and left messages. We always say the same thing: "Hello, I'm just calling to say hello. Call me when you can." My father says *convenience*—"Call me at your convenience." Not inconveniencing people is the first tenet of his religion, a religion based largely on politeness and unobtrusiveness and, yes, good intentions—but one, too, that seems to revile the dirt and grit and pus and indignity of being alive.

Surprise is all packed, her boyfriend in the hall outside our room. "Call me this summer, okay?" she says.

"I will. You call me too." We will not call one another. I know this already, but Surprise does not. She is believing in the conversation. She does not know that the conversation is an emblem of belatedness, a relic of our best intentions.

"Bye," she says, hugging me tightly with her bony body. Her shoulder blades do not allow me to hug her as properly as I would like.

"Bye," I say. And then, because it's true, "I'll miss you." I'll miss how simple things were for a moment, a moment she will continue to live in but one that discovered me for what I am: ill equipped.

"Let's go," I hear her say to her boyfriend out in the hall, like a final item has been checked off her list.

The day before the very last day of school, when almost everyone has already fled to the beach or home to start summer jobs and internships, my dad and I finally connect by phone.

"How are you? It's been a long time," my father says. "I've been talking to your roommate more than to you."

"Yeah," I say. "Sorry. It's been...busy. You know, end of term stuff, exams."

"How did it go? Are you done with all that now?"

"I think it went okay. I'll know for sure when they mail our grades."

"So...you're coming home, right? Or are you going to the beach? Your roommate said something about going to the beach?"

"I'm not going to the beach, no," I say. I try picturing my body in a bathing suit and find I cannot. Every part of me feels grossly swollen, even though, according to the mirror, I look more or less like myself, just with extra clothes and a slight paunch. "Actually I was kind of hoping you could pick me up. I think I have too much stuff for the train." My dad coughs, a form of hesitation. "Of course. I can come get you. I'd be happy to. When?"

"Tomorrow. After tomorrow everything shuts down."

"Oh, okay. Okay. Maybe in that case I'll leave today. In a little while. Stay at a hotel overnight. Since it's, you know, it's quite a drive. We can get an earlier start tomorrow that way."

Why am I enjoying this? I feel oddly powerful in this moment. "It's totally up to you."

"Well, then, I better get going," he says. "I'm just going to put some things in a bag and hit the road. It'll be late when I get there tonight, so I probably won't bother calling..."

"That's fine," I say. "Call me in the morning. We can get breakfast maybe."

"Yes," he says. "We'll do that."

A long pause. My eyes are smarting. I know that his eyes are smarting too. This is why we don't talk, can't talk. What is there to say, ever, that doesn't end in crying?

"Thanks, Dad."

"Bye . . . bye for now, sweetheart."

. . .

Dad arrives at eight the next morning. His clothes are rumpled and I feel sad that he might not know how to use an iron. I make my hug brief, which is not difficult. I make an unnecessary joke—"I'm such a good procrastinator I even procrastinated the freshman fifteen!"—which makes Dad laugh wanly. He barely sees me, let alone my body.

We load up the car in two trips. I take a stick of Juicy Fruit from the middle console.

"Are you hungry?" he asks.

"I could eat," I say. "Let's go to the diner."

My dad starts to pull away from the curb and I hear myself say, "One second. Just wait for one minute."

"Did you forget something?"

"No. I just want to look."

I stare at my dorm. It seems impossible to be leaving; it seems impossible that I was ever here. I stare past the dorm to the entrance of the quad, the same snapshot I stared at in the brochure a year ago at home: the Renaissance Revival buildings, the profusion of trees, so many trees that people visit campus from all over just to see them. The sky aches with blue. I never noticed what a pretty place this is.

"Okay. You can go."

We sit in a booth at the diner, next to the one Tea Rose and I frequently sat in. We order an obscene amount of food: eggs, short stacks of pancakes, toast, bacon, sausage, a waffle. I gulp down a large cranberry juice with ice and it tastes heavenly. My dad drinks three cups of coffee, white with cream. The crinkly little plastic cups litter the table. We don't bother trying to make conversation.

By the time we leave, it is midmorning and the day is already verging on hot.

The drive is mostly ugly and the highway makes me immediately drowsy. I SUE DRUNK DRIVERS a billboard says. TASTE HISTORY AT AMERICA'S OLDEST FUDGE FACTORY shouts another. I close my eyes against the bright sun, the grossness of America.

What good is free will, I'm thinking, if you still have to ride in a car to a home filled with ghosts?

Dear Mom,

I said goodbye to Joan pretty hurriedly last week. She asked if I wanted to come visit her this summer. I thought about her sister, vanishing in an upstairs bed, and told her yes, we should try to make that happen, knowing it wouldn't happen, and we exchanged home phone numbers. I said goodbye to the acquaintances from work, got a big hug from Terrence. There was cake and chips for us on the last day. I stood near the table and ate three squares of cake.

I figured I should check my mail one last time and when I did, there was a small card addressed to me in Tea Rose's loopy, feminine handwriting. I grabbed it and walked back here. Here's what the card says. The front is a card artist's rendering of a night scene with flowers—navy-blue backdrop, white lily-looking things, and a full moon up top. A shitty drawing. He could have done better.

Dear Agnes,

I just want you to know that you will always mean a lot to me. I know things are weird in ways we couldn't have anticipated. But I do love you and I think you're an amazing person. Being with Liz [she has a name! It's "Liz"!] hasn't changed that. Our time together will always be special to me.

129

I hope eventually we can be friends, and I know that sounds hollow but I really mean that. I hope you have a wonderful summer. See you in the fall.

Love,

[His name is an illegible scribble that seems practiced, affected.]

I pushed the card back in the envelope immediately after reading it and then flew around my room, packing. I packed everything so fast. Then I took a blisteringly hot shower and cried, hard. I couldn't tell which were tears and which was water. And I hope that's the last I cry about Tea Rose. I put on my pajamas and only took the card out to copy it down for you, but now I'm putting it in the trash. Actually, I think I'll burn it. I'm so afraid that if I hate him, the hate will transfer to the fetus. I'm afraid to love him for the same reason.

Good night, Mom—

Agnes

Book Two
The Daughter Hole

Chapter 24

Dear Mom,

My baby is due around October 21. That makes me about 18 weeks pregnant. What happened was that I told Dad. And how I told him was that I was up late one night, unable to sleep, and I went downstairs to get some water, and he was sitting at the kitchen table, just sitting there. Except for the light above the stove, all the lights were off, and I didn't see him at first. It wasn't until I opened the cabinet to get a glass that I noticed him and almost dropped the glass. I was wearing one of your old nightgowns and he stared at me for a full minute, squinting.

"Is that Mom's nightgown?" he asked, and it was. I stood and drank water from the sink, aware that he was still looking at me, aware that from the side, I probably looked soft and bulgy. Then I just said it. I put my glass down and turned to him and said, "I'm pregnant." He didn't hear me, or acted like he didn't hear me, at first. He looked at his hands for a long time. So I said it again. "I'm pregnant, okay." And his reaction was so curious. He yawned. A big, wide yawn.

"When did this happen?"

That's when I started to feel embarrassed. It occurred to me that pretty much every question that can be asked of a pregnancy is personal, intimate. That the very fact of being pregnant is personal and intimate. A biological scarlet letter, a sex billboard: I GOT FUCKED. Sorry to be crass. But what's the point now in trying to be delicate? And how unfair that Tea Rose, that any boy, bears no mark. None. So I wasn't expecting Dad's question and I didn't, of course, have a precise answer.

"I'm not sure, exactly. Sometime after winter break."

"Have you been to the doctor? The doctor can tell you."

"No. Not yet."

"Agnes. What happened? Didn't you think...Well, in any case, you need to make a doctor's appointment. Do you have a doctor? A...woman's doctor?" I told him I didn't, and that I would figure it out, and not to worry. And then he said, "Most doctors won't give abortions after a certain point. So the earlier the better, assuming..." I was surprised. Everything was surprising me. But why wouldn't it? We were operating under entirely new, unprecedented circumstances. I guess the look on my face stopped him, and I said out loud, finally, what I've known as a certainty this whole time:

"I'm not getting rid of it. And I'm not giving it away."

I mean that, Mom. I mean it as an oath. I'm writing it here, and when you put something in writing, you obey it. More real than being etched in stone, it's etched in flesh. Dad stood up and stretched. "We'll talk about this more tomorrow," he said. He walked over to me and put his hand on my head, an awkward gesture, even for him. "We'll figure it out."

I just stood there as he walked out of the kitchen, up the stairs, and out of sight. I heard his feet ascending, then stopping. That creak on the third stair.

"I love you, Agnes."

In the morning, when I came downstairs there was a note from Dad:

Agnes,

Make an appointment with Dr. Grossman today. He is your mother's doctor. He is very nice. 642-7876. I made a sandwich for you for lunch. We will talk about everything later. There is still time.

Dad

Next to the note was Dad's health insurance card. I didn't call Dr. Grossman. The idea was preposterous to me. My first time at the gynecologist, and I am introducing your doctor to your grandchild? No. A million times no. I'll tell you something, Mom. I'll tell you this—standing there in front of that note with that phone number, I really felt angry with you. It has subsided a little, only because I'm exhausted. But what the fuck, Mom. Where are you. I've tossed pretty much everything into the you-shaped hole you left, but nothing fits.

Filled with a combination of baby and spite,

Agnes

PS: I looked in the Yellow Pages and called "Healthcare 4 Women," an ob-gyn practice run by (yep) four women, two doctors, one midwife, and one nurse-practitioner. Midwives seem so Victorian to me but then again all of this seems Victorian. This whole mess that is my body feels completely unmodern and inconvenient. I said on the phone, "I'm pregnant, it was unplanned, I'm nineteen, I don't know how far along I am," and maybe I was crying a little bit, and they said they could see me that afternoon. I walked to the train in the balmy May weather, for the first time not dressed in layer upon layer, just wearing a sundress from the previous summer that was always big on me but is now no longer big and even tight in the chest and belly. I looked maybe not undeniably pregnant but definitely possibly pregnant, at the very least. I tried to enjoy the sun on my skin and the swish of air between my knees. On the train I looked at my feet but my breasts partially obscured my view. They are big now, and sexy. I felt some eyes on me, but I kept my eyes off everyone.

I found the office and signed in and gave them Dad's insurance card and filled out paperwork and waited briefly before they called my name. A nurse asked me some questions, about how I felt, about when my last period was. I gave her my best guess and told her it was my best guess. She took my blood pressure, the band tight around my arm. I stepped on a scale. I was shown to the bathroom where I successfully peed in a cup. I scrubbed my hands, filled with the desire to be one hundred percent clean. I wrote my name on the outside of the cup as I was told to do and put it in the little metal cubby above the toilet as I was told to do. The cubby seemed to have another door on the other side. A secret passageway for pee.

When I got back to the room, the nurse had a needle and a vial. I tried making a joke about giving a hair sample, too, but it fell flat. She said, "No, we don't need any of your hair." She took my blood—quickly, painlessly—and told me to wait. The doctor came in but she said she was the nurse-practitioner. I said, "So is that a nurse who practices?" and she smiled and gave me a brief description of her job. I guess I was shaking at this point. She asked was I scared, and I said yes. She asked did the baby's father know and I said no. She asked would I keep the baby, had I considered other options, and I said yes I would keep it. She gave me a card with someone's name on it and told me to call. A counselor. I told her I didn't need to be counseled. I didn't want anyone sucking out the baby's head with a vacuum. I didn't want anyone taking the baby from me to give to someone else. I told her I didn't want this baby, but I didn't want anyone else to have it either. She said it would still be helpful to talk to someone, and it was free and confidential. She said there were support groups. She gave me some water in a paper cup and I drank it and tried to calm down. I looked at her face. Her name was Priscilla. She looked like a tree—very up and down and sturdy.

She said she wanted to check the baby's heart rate. I waited for her to bend down, to press her ear against my belly. Instead she asked me to lie down and I didn't question her, I just said okay. I lay down on the table and she gently lifted my dress and pulled down the band of my underwear. The whole time I'm thinking, "She can do this because I'm letting her do this," over and over, which for some reason comforted me a lot. My underwear was white and plain, what Tea Rose called my virgin underwear. She put some goo on my belly. It was cold. She took a small box attached to something that looked like a microphone and she gently moved the microphone around the goo. Static blared, weird alien sounds. A whooshing, some squiggles. And then, through all of that watery gibberish, it came. The heartbeat. Strong, fast. Mammalian. In fact, it was as though everything I have ever known about human beings got distilled into that sound, that rhythm. It was a whisper-yell. It was not the thump-thump of kindergarten or the movies. It seemed to come from the innermost morass of the earth or from some whirlpool on the moon. I couldn't cry or speak or anything. I could only listen. Mine sounded so ordinary in comparison, cranky almost. Priscilla was saying something, something positive about the rate of the heartbeat. She moved the microphone off of me and I grabbed her hand and put it back. "Just one more minute?" I asked her. "Please." She did as I asked.

I don't know how much time passed—probably more than a minute—but I finally told Priscilla I was okay. She turned off the microphone and wiped my belly with a tissue and helped me sit up. "Everything sounds great," she said. "Are you taking your vitamins?" she asked. I lied and said yes. She said she'd like me to come back in two weeks so we can look at the baby. I asked if she meant an X-ray. She said no, an ultrasound. She said it would give a clearer sense of how the baby was developing. She said we could find out if it was a boy or a girl. She wrote some things down on a paper and told me to give it to the woman behind the desk at checkout.

"I don't think I want to see the baby yet," I sort of murmured. "But I'll come back if I can hear the heart again." She told me I might change my mind. She said if I was this blown away by the heartbeat, wait'll I see the baby, actually see him or her. It's nothing short of miraculous, she said, or at the very least, re-assuring. She seemed to really want to see the baby, or at least to prove the baby could be seen. And she'd been so nice that I didn't want to let her down. I told her I'd think it over. I thanked her. She squeezed my hand and reminded me about the card she'd given me. It had fallen on the floor near the table. She picked it up and placed it in my hand like a rabbit's foot. "You don't have to do this alone," she said.

I found myself making an appointment with the woman at the front desk, for two weeks from today. I found myself on the train back home. I found myself ordering a hot dog from the deli, thankfully seeing no one I knew and eating it in four bites while walking home. As soon as it was gone, I wanted another one, so I found myself turning around—I mean literally stop-ping in my tracks and reversing them—and going back to the deli and ordering another hot dog and eating it in the same ex-act amount of bites, finishing it at the precise spot I was in when I finished the first one. I imagined doing this forever—a quan-tum loop of walking while eating hot dogs. But I did get home, finally, and went to my room.

I fell asleep. I told Dad the gist. He seems to not be speaking to me now. I heard myself telling him that I was going to go to a support group. I thought that would make him feel better. Why am I trying to make him feel better? I wonder if I bought a stethoscope and put it to my belly if I'd be able to hear that magical heartbeat. To feel less alone.

PPS: Sorry for such a long PS.

Chapter 25

My body seems to make both my dad and me uncomfortable, so I do my best to keep it covered. The politeness of the start of summer is giving way to a heavy ripeness, the thick creeping heat like wool against skin. The day of my second doctor's appointment comes and goes. I do not go, out of fear and laziness. What if the heartbeat sounds different, or slower, or unmagical, or wrong? What if they make me look and what I see is deformed, missing limbs or vital organs? What if they say it's a boy and I want it to be a girl, or a girl and I want it to be a boy?

On a Monday morning, I wake up and go downstairs and drink two glasses of water. I eat a banana. Almost immediately I run back upstairs to vomit. I wash my face and hands, rebrush my teeth, regag. I go back down and feel annoyed by my nagging hunger. This is a new development: constant hunger, chased by constant nausea. I eat toast, staring out at the hot, flat yard, repeating *You're okay, you're okay, you're okay* after each swallow. I wash my plate and look at the clock. There is so much day left, so many ways to feel strange. I have not gone inside Simon's room. It didn't do any good last time. This house, oversteeped with absence like a cup whose tea bag has been left too long, forgotten about. A cold, bitter, tannic undrinkable cup.

On the wall near the phone are several Post-its that have been ac-
cumulating over the past week or so: *Sadie called again, call her back*;
Jenny called, call back; *Phil called*. I take them off the wall and stick
them to my fingers. I imagine myself calling back, go so far as to
pick up the phone and dial six of Jenny's digits.

But I hang up and go upstairs instead. I ignore the tightening in
my gut—not baby-related—and push into my parents' room. I kneel
down in front of my mother's nightstand and open the top drawer. I
pick up a diary, one of several, the kind with the faux-leather cover
and *Diary* embossed in gold, meant to put the owner in a mood of
romanticized solitude and to appeal to the integrity of any would-be
trespasser. But I'm not a trespasser so much as a daughter. I open to
a random page.

> …as if I am drowning. He has been more attentive but it
> feels like it's too late. I wonder if I should have ever had kids,
> whether I should have ever even married?! Every day I get
> the message that I'm supposed to be happier than I am, sup-
> posed to be feeling things that I'm not. Roseann tells me our
> kids bring us closer to God. I told her, half kidding, I guess it
> depends on the type of kid. I have the prescription but I can't
> bring myself to take it to the pharmacy. I keep hoping that
> maybe after the holidays, something will

I don't turn the page. It always surprises me when I know when
to stop.

Two days later I tell my dad that I am meeting Jenny and Sadie at
Squire Square, the outdoor mall. He seems excited that I have plans
for the day. I myself can hardly believe it, that I called Jenny back,
made small talk, agreed to meet up. I sit at the kitchen table with
him in the grayish light of early morning, dunking a tea bag into
a mug of boiling water. My dad sips his coffee and smooths his tie
again and again.

"Do you want to take my car? You could drop me at the train and pick me up later."

"That's okay. I can take the bus. Or one of them can pick me up."

"Do they, ah, know? About? Your? Situation?"

There it is. My situation. It has a name.

"No." I squeeze the tea bag with my fingers. I have always done this. My mother does this too. There is something about that quick burn to the fingertips.

"Well, I guess they'll find out soon enough."

We sit quietly, sipping.

"Dad, do you want me to get a job?"

I just want to give him an opportunity to yell at me, or express his disappointment, or tell me something that he thinks I ought to hear. He looks surprised. "Do I want you to get a job? Not...No, not necessarily. Do you want to get a job?"

"I don't know. I just feel like maybe I should, I don't know, help out more?"

He looks at me, his eyes suddenly misty. He looks like a house with a bad roof. "You're really going to have...You're really going to keep this...baby?"

He says it like that, with a pause between *this* and *baby*. As though I am the baby.

"I am."

He sighs, a deep sound. "It's not money you have to worry about, Agnes. Money is not a problem. You know we—I—will always help, however I can. But what's your plan? You can have all the money in the world but without a plan, it doesn't do any good." He pauses, as though trying to figure out where to go. Then, sounding defeated: "You need a plan."

I try to tell myself that this is good, that we are talking about it. We are having a frank discussion, and no one is leaving the room; no one is having a nervous breakdown. But my thoughts are addled by sudden crying.

"Agnes, don't . . . It's okay . . . You don't need to cry." My father puts a hand on my hand. I look at both of our hands, resting on the table. They look nothing alike. I have my mother's hands. "Or maybe you do need to cry. It's probably good to, you know, get it out." He takes a handkerchief from his pocket. My father always carries a handkerchief. I remember overhearing someone say once that a handkerchief was the most disgusting invention in the world, and I remember feeling offended. My father's handkerchiefs are spotless, fresh, smelling like some combination of soap and tears.

"Go have fun with your friends today," he says now, and his eyes are so lost, so kind, that I cry harder.

"I'm sorry," I manage to get out. "I don't know what's wrong with me. I'm not even upset. I'm just, I don't know!" I try to laugh and it sounds strangled, a bit insane. "I'm sorry."

My dad gets up. He puts his hand on mine once again, squeezes. He is not looking at me. "Try to have a good day."

Jenny calls as I am heading upstairs.

"Do you need a ride?"

"Oh. That's all right, I can take the bus."

"Don't be weird. You're right on my way. I'll leave around, I don't know, eleven-thirty?"

"Sure, okay. That sounds good. Thanks." I am agreeable. I am overly agreeable.

"Agnes?"

"Yeah?"

"Are you okay, honey?" Jenny peppers her speech with *girl* and *honey* and *sweetheart*. I once heard another girl from our high school say that it drove her crazy, but I like how it makes me feel now. Taken care of. Mothered.

"I'm okay."

"I'm glad you finally got back to me. I left a bunch of messages with your dad. I think Sadie did too. You've been kinda incognito. Or wait—*incommunicado*. I get those two mixed up."

I laugh meagerly.

"Have you . . . is it . . . have you heard from your mom or anything?"

I'm surprised she asks this, and grateful.

"No, I haven't. But thank you for asking. Seriously. Nobody asks."

"I'm sure that's really hard, girl!"

"It's okay. I mean, it's . . . it's fine."

"I mean, just, yeah. I can't imagine."

Now I'm wishing she never said anything about it. Why did I agree to this, to friends, today? In taking a breath, I realize how I'd been holding it and promptly get the hiccups.

"Well, I should probably jump in the shower. I'll see you soon, sweetie. I'm excited to catch up."

Out on the front step in the bright sunshine, I sit waiting for Jenny. The flagstone beneath me seeps heat through my babydoll dress. When Jenny's car pulls into the driveway, I stand carefully, positioning my messenger bag in front of me, across my abdomen. I walk slowly to the car and get in, my bag a shield between some terrifying moment of discovery and me. But Jenny is looking up her own nose in the rearview mirror.

"HI! Oh my God, hi," she says, still looking at herself but groping my arm with her hand. "I swear I just saw a *hair* poking out of my nose but now I can't find it! It's gonna drive me crazy." She faces me now, wrinkling and unwrinkling her nose. "Can you see it?"

Jenny is Greek with creamy skin, perky breasts, and a tiny waist. Her face is perfectly heart-shaped. She manages to be both exotic and completely ordinary, which has always made her very popular with boys.

"No. I don't see anything."

She rubs her nose vigorously a few times, in finale, before turning to face me. "Agnes! It's so good to see you! It's been, what, like five months? How was your second semester?"

"It was . . . it was pretty good."

"Damn, girl, I'm jealous!" She says this staring pointedly at my breasts.

"Oh, please," I say, embarrassed, but not really. I refrain from saying how I have been occasionally turned on by the sight of them, in the shower or the way they swell, the sudden cleavage, beneath a certain nightgown.

"Seriously, you look great!"

"Well, actually, it's—"

"Stop being modest! You look hot! Hold up, I want to play you my boyfriend's band's CD. He's the drummer. They're called the Big Littles. Isn't that cute?"

She turns the dial on the car stereo and puts the car in reverse. I hear drumsticks clicking first—1,2,3—before guitar and trumpet blare through the tiny speakers. "The trumpet player is super cute," Jenny is yelling over the music. "You would love him."

We drive past things so familiar to me. Jenny mouths along to the music and shakes her head a little. Her eyes behind her sunglasses are lined in electric blue. Something about her soothes me. I feel more relaxed here, in her loud car, hiding behind my bag, which seems to shrink with every moment that I stay silent.

I was very young when I identified a sensation that I later dubbed "the joy jab." The feeling of happiness so acute that it pierces like a knife, cuts through the smog of whatever sad or humdrum present you're in. It happens of its own accord, for no external reason, and it lasts only a moment or two. I feel it now, sitting in Jenny's car, and I try hanging on to it, squeezing myself through the aperture it creates, seeing, for an instant, my life distilled to the basics: *I have my health, my youth, my friends.* Then it vanishes.

"I told Sadie we'd meet her at Saladalley. She had to run some errands. That cool with you?"

"Sure." Saladalley is a salad-only restaurant, where "salad," as I once wrote in a restaurant review for my high school newspaper, is interpreted loosely. It consists of many tables and an eighteen-foot buffet filled with everything from traditional salad fixings to vaguely Asian preparations of noodles and meat. Also, fruit, desserts, and soups. I think of it not only as my favorite place to eat, but also objectively as 'the best' place to eat, because there are no menus and therefore no decisions to make, and no limits on how much you can eat, and because of the variety of foods represented. It's never crowded, which tells me I'm in the minority but not that I'm wrong. In my view, Saladalley is the future of dining out.

(Mrs. Steeple, newspaper moderator, circled "the future of dining out" in red on my draft and wrote "not so sure about that" with a smiley face in the margin.)

The light goes green, a song starts playing ("if you told me to/I'd move a mountain for you"), Jenny's head resumes its bobbing. We find parking close to the restaurant, a low, brown-awninged building. Through a window we see Sadie, already seated. She taps the glass, smiling and waving furiously. Jenny and I are a tangle of waving back, unbuckling seat belts, getting our bags. I am holding my breath. *I have to get out of the car,* I think to myself. *I have to get out of the car. I have to stand up, and be standing, and walk, and I can't hide behind this bag forever.*

Jenny gets out first. I open my door, keeping my bag at my middle, and swing my legs outside. I am protected from sight, for this moment, by the open door. Jenny is waiting at the front of the car, less than five feet from where Sadie sits behind the glass. They are mouthing a conversation that seems mostly to consist of "Hi!" and "You look so cute!"

Sadie beckons from the window: "Hurry up!"

"You coming, Agnes?" Jenny asks.

My dress sticks to the back of my thighs as I push the door open as far as it will go and stand up. I edge away from the car and shut the door. I face my friends, bag at my side. Sadie reacts first, her face half frozen in a smile as she stares at my middle. Jenny is fidgeting with her face again, pushing her sunglasses on top of her head, but then she takes me in, eyes roving down my body, eyebrows launching way up to her hairline.

I take a deep breath, ready to get this over with and restore, if possible, our carefree salad time.

I make myself walk toward Jenny, toward the restaurant, and Jenny takes a step or two forward, grabs my arm, to steady herself or lend support to me, I'm not sure which. "Are you . . . ?"

"Yes. I am. Twenty weeks."

Sadie is wildly summoning us inside.

"Let's go in," I say.

Jenny follows me wordlessly. The hostess, a blond whisper of a girl, whispers, "Have a seat anywhere" at the same time I say that we're meeting a friend who's already here. The restaurant is mostly empty.

We join Sadie at the table. She gets up and hugs me around the neck, her body arcing away from mine. Then Jenny says, "Oh my God, I still haven't hugged you," and does it for real, her arms around me tightly, and it feels so good that I just want to stay there. She gives me a reassuring squeeze right before we pull away and I scoot into the booth next to her, across from Sadie. I take longer than is necessary to find a place for my bag, my mind racing with my friends' unasked questions, their unspoken relief to not be me.

"Agnes, oh my God, just oh. My. God. Like, what? I mean, I'm so excited for you! Right? I mean, it's exciting! But crazy! I'll be like kind of an aunt! Who is the . . . I mean, like, are you and the father, um, together?" Sadie's horror is real, bordering on hysteria.

Our server comes over, a gangly boy with patchy facial hair and those earrings that stretch out the earlobes so they're big as nickels.

"Can I get you guys something to drink?"

"Unsweet iced tea," Sadie says.

"Diet Coke," Jenny says.

"I'll have a Coke. Or...actually just water. Water's fine."

"Free re on all drinks," he says, with either a wink or an eye twitch, I can't tell.

"Okay," I say.

"You still just want water? Even with the free re?"

Why, I'm wondering, is this boy still standing here, dangling over our table like a spider plant?

"Yes. Water. Thanks."

"Okay. Up to you."

Sadie and Jenny are giggling without actually giggling. That girl thing that's more agitation of air than sound. The waiter finally leaves.

I start talking, aware that I have been asked things, desperate to preempt any pity. I talk as much to calm myself down as to explain myself to my friends, to quell my old urge to shriek, rip off my ill-fitting clothes, and run into the street.

"I'm not with the father, no. We were together. Or...we had a thing. It was really intense. I think we loved each other. I think. But it was not, like, sustainable. It felt like it could never be sustainable in the 'real world.' It felt like we only existed when we were alone. Maybe. It just...yeah. It was complicated, or at least it always felt that way. But we—he—met someone. It's fine."

Jenny is nodding encouragingly. "So...does he not know?"

"No," I say. "He doesn't know. There's really no point. We're not gonna, like, play house."

Sadie looks traumatized. The waiter comes back and sets our drinks down, along with the bill. "Help yourselves to the salad bar," he mumbles, walking off. His job is done.

Lucky duck, I think.

"Do you guys want to get food?" I ask, standing.

We file over. I'm the first one there. There is a pressure that comes from being the first one in line at a salad bar. My choices will be seen and, especially given my condition, analyzed, however briefly. My instinct is to overload. I heap my plate with almost everything, the mayonnaise-soaked salads (Neptune, Waldorf), the oil-soaked salads (three-bean, pasta), heavy cucumber coins, tomato wedges, cottage cheese, canned fruit (where I lingered as I tried to fish out the cherry half hiding under the anemone-like pears and peaches, ultimately succeeding), sunflower seeds, croutons. I drizzle ranch over almost everything, doing my best to spare the fruit. I fill a shallow bowl with the soup of the day, broccoli cheddar, first using the long ladle to knock apart the film on top. I hold my salad plate in my left hand and the soup in my right and move slowly back to our seats. Two pumpernickel croutons fall. About two feet from the table, I feel my grip on the soup bowl start to waver, my thumb sliding in some thick wetness that sloshed around the rim. I make it to the table, spilling only a little as I set the bowl down. I am sweating. It is too hot for soup.

Sadie and Jenny sit down nimbly with their nimble, sensible plates, as I am still working on seating myself. My underwear feels tight and part of it has bunched up inside me. My thighs are moist where they now rub together. My belly seems to have grown a few inches since morning. I feel out of control, here under the scrutiny of well-meaning friends.

Sadie chews a lettuce leaf, her mouth like a rabbit's. "What did your dad say? And does your mom, I mean, like, have you heard from your mom?"

I have finished my soup and I am sweating visibly. I dab at my face with one napkin and then another. I eat a crouton with my fingers. "My dad doesn't really know what to say. He wants to have an answer but there's no answer. If he can't fix something immediately, he kind of just hides." I don't have anything to say, not here, not now, not to Sadie, about my mother.

Jenny looks nervous. "Agnes, I think you'll be a great mom. If . . . that's what you want, I mean."

"I wouldn't say it's what I want, no."

There is silence, as viscous as the stuff pooling in my plate.

"I guess I don't feel I have any, um, choices. It's weird. It was like, the second I found out, the only two options became kill myself or keep the baby. And the first one, well, *you* know. So that left the only other thing. I just want to do the least damage possible. I feel like I'm a bomb and I'm trying to figure out how to contain the blast." I'm still sweating and my face and hands feel greasy. I take a big gulp of water. "I'm trying to be a very responsible bomb."

Sadie is vigorously putting on ChapStick. Jenny is trying to be nice, and she *is* nice, dear Jenny. She has always been soft, and kind, and sympathetic. In third grade she stuck up for the boy with the speech impediment. After Simon died, when the rest of the class sent a single signed card, she wrote me a heartfelt letter.

"That makes sense, Agnes, totally," she says now. "And, like, we are here for you. If you need anything."

Sadie is smashing her lips together nervously. Her eyes dart around, not landing on me, inscribing a circle around me. "Totally," she says.

I dig into my bag for some money. We get busy settling the bill. We are using this time, this task, to steady ourselves. Finally, we get up. On my plate is the cherry I had worked hard to fish from the fruit vat, now drowning in salad dressing.

Dear Mom,

It's funny how you can tell your friends you're pregnant one moment—pregnant with a baby you didn't plan and don't want, pregnant by a father you don't even know anymore—and be in "Make a Splash Swimwear Boutique" the next. Both girls "needed" new bathing suits for their upcoming vacations, so I politely browsed with them, discreetly burping up salad and trying not to take up too much space in the tiny store. Each of

them tried on at least a half dozen suits, and I was made to offer my opinions on them, admonished to "be honest," and to
answer questions about whether polka dots flattered the ass or
insulted it, whether white was too see-through with regard to
the nipples or appropriately see-through.

Jenny ignored the little placards in the fitting rooms instruct-
ing women to not remove their underwear. "I can't see what it
really looks like! And what the hell, I'm clean! I bet guys can
get naked when they try on bathing suits. It's sexist!" Sadie's
nose stayed wrinkled for a long time. "You might be clean,
but what about other girls? It's so unhygienic! You could get
weirdo diseases!" Jenny brushed this off, saying loudly, "Vaginas are vaginas," which made us all—even me—laugh. Quietly,
as though not wanting Sadie to hear, Jenny asked me a couple
of times if I was okay.

But looking at them in their skimpy suits—each of them
ultimately chose a barely-there bikini—I felt about 300 years
old. Their jutting hip bones, perky breasts, smooth summery
skin... every part of their bodies had its sad opposite in my
own: my aching hips; heavy breasts; the rough, itchy patches
of skin, now stubbled because of how lazy I have gotten in the
shower, the effort of hunching and scraping and rinsing, just to
be hairless... as though being hairless changes anything for me.

After the bathing suit store I just felt done. They wanted to
keep going, look at shoes and sunglasses and makeup, but I
didn't feel like I could handle it. My first time socializing as a
pregnant person, and I exploited it fully—"I'm feeling a little
nauseous. I think I need to go home and lie down"—and both
girls offered to drive me but I insisted on taking the bus. I wonder what they said about me after I left.

I wish I had a pregnant friend. I don't know. I want to be
with someone who feels what I feel, that pregnancy is an oc-
cupation, a colonization. I never minded being alone before it

became impossible for me to ever be alone. Being commandeered like this—it is an inviolably lonely place. This is the only time in this baby's life where it can only be separated from me by death and not by distance. I can't escape it unless I get rid of it. And then I'd be a hypocrite, right? Choosing not to be its mother, which seems to be the same choice you've made.

I need to find some light. I need a friend and some instruction. I was never a great babysitter; I don't even really know how to change a diaper. Tomorrow I'm going to call that doctor's office again. I'm going to do whatever they tell me.

Pledged,
Agnes

Chapter 26

Priscilla from Healthcare 4 Women gives me a hug when she sees me. I hug her back as long as she lets me.

"How have you been, Agnes? How are you feeling?"

I don't know where to start. Suicidal, elated, nauseous, starving, sore, waterlogged with exhaustion, terrified.

"Pretty good."

"I see you missed your last appointment. Everything okay?" Priscilla is looking in a folder. I feel momentarily excited that I have my own folder, that there is a record of me, that at least here, if not in my own life, I am a member. I am part of a system. A system of folders.

"Everything is fine, I think," I say.

"Any complaints?"

"Physically?"

Priscilla smiles. "Or otherwise."

"Well, um, I'm tired a lot. And having some trouble sleeping, but that's nothing really new. Food doesn't always agree with me. And my skin—I mean, my belly—I'm just really itchy."

Priscilla is nodding. "That's your skin stretching. It can be very distracting. I recommend a heavy moisturizer. Some people swear by shea butter, which you can find in a lot of drugstores. Is the nausea debilitating? Do you want me to prescribe something for you?"

"No. I don't think so. I mean, I can manage."

Priscilla closes my folder and looks at me closely. "Is there anything else?"

I wish she were my friend. She knows how to look at me, how to ask. I imagine myself making an appointment every day for the rest of my life.

"No. Just, you know, going along."

She opens the folder again. "This name, on the insurance card you gave. Your father?"

I nod. "We're all—I mean I'm—on his insurance."

"Okay. That's good. Let's get you weighed and check your blood pressure, and then I'm going to send you down the hall for your ultrasound. Your insurance—your dad's—covers it."

I step on the scale. I have gained three pounds since last time, which seems to please Priscilla. She wraps the blood pressure cuff around my arm and pumps it up. The pressure feels good. "So do you want to know the sex? If not, make sure you tell Allie not to tell you. Allie is the technician."

"Do most people want to know?"

Priscilla shrugs. "It's a personal thing. Everyone's different."

I nod, easygoing, as if to say of course, of course everyone is different, as if we are two people at a street vendor talking about ketchup and mustard, as if I were not going to have to make a decision in the next ten minutes, a decision about a baby that will soon no longer be just a baby but an actual boy or an actual girl, and not in a theoretical way but in a son or daughter way.

"We're done here. Let me go make sure Allie is ready for you."

Priscilla exits the room, my folder under her arm. She comes back a minute later. "You can go on down the hall. Let's see you again in four weeks, all right?"

I slide-hop off the table, my thighs sticking to everything, to the air even. "Oh, um, last time you mentioned a group of some sort? A support group maybe? I think you wrote it down but I don't know . . . I think I lost it. Do you think I could get that information again?"

Priscilla folds in her lips and her eyes look watery for a second.

"I was hoping you would ask or say something about it, but I didn't want to pry. You know, we're not supposed to talk to patients about their personal situations. Which is a big problem, if you ask me. I mean, practicing medicine is about more than just treating the body, right?"

As she is speaking, she is writing things on a pad. She tears the page off and hands it to me. "It's called the Center for Unwed Mothers, but they're working on changing the name. A little outdated, I know. But there are a lot of resources there, and most of them are free. Call this number. Let me know how it goes, okay?"

In the other room, Allie tells me to "get comfortable" in a medieval-looking chair. This one is lower to the ground than the one in the examining room, and there are no stirrups at the end. Allie is petite, under five feet, not including the frothy blond updo like an impressive dessert on her head.

"So we gonna find out the sex today, honey?" She gives me a bright smile and turns off the lights. Her face glows from the computer she stands behind. Her half-open mouth is slicked with a pink lip gloss I can almost taste. I feel a sudden indignation that seems to come straight from the baby. *Leave me alone,* it seems to suggest. *Let me exist in this pre-personhood a little while longer.*

"I don't . . . No. I don't think so. No, actually."

Allie opens her mouth and eyeballs wide, in mock surprise. "Really? Wow! Most moms are dying to know! Aren't you curious?"

"Um, I'm not, really. I think I'm still just, you know, getting used to everything." My heart is beating very quickly.

And then I am nowhere. All around me and inside of me is silence, thick like wool, as though instead of being ultrasounded, I got taxidermied. When I open my eyes, Allie and Priscilla are standing over me. Priscilla is holding a small cup of juice.

"Well that was a first!" Allie says, touching her wrist to her forehead in a theatrical fainting gesture.

Priscilla hands the juice to Allie and helps me sit up. "You okay, Agnes?"

My mouth is dry and I feel like I've been asleep for hours. "What happened?"

"You blinked out for a minute or two, hon, gave me a good scare," Allie says. I notice she is wearing earrings shaped like tiny coffee mugs. "Here, drink this."

I accept the juice and drink the whole cup, with Allie and Priscilla watching. It tastes like straight sugar. I want to make a joke like "Got anything stronger?" but I feel too weak.

Priscilla puts two fingers lightly on my wrist and after a minute, apparently satisfied, pats my hand gently. "You're okay. I think you might've gotten yourself a little dehydrated. Make sure you're drinking plenty, especially in this heat."

"Do you want me to reschedule or should we keep going?" Allie asks.

"I'm fine. Let's keep going. I just need to use the bathroom first."

Around the corner from the ultrasound room, I splash water on my face and pat it dry with a paper towel. My eyes in the mirror look big and old, like an encyclopedia picture of an owl. My hair is a mess but I feel too tired to do anything about it.

When I get back to the room, Allie is once again behind the computer screen with the overhead lights turned off. Priscilla is gone. I settle back into the chair, slightly tearing the already crinkled white paper covering it. Lying on paper feels terrible, I decide. I would rather lie on someone's germs.

Allie lifts my shirt slightly and folds down the waistband of my already unbuttoned shorts. I don't bother trying to fasten anything anymore; I just make sure my shirts cover my waist. From a tube in her hand, she squirts some clear goo onto my abdomen. The sound of the squirt and the feel of the goo are weirdly taunting, like chastisements. *I get it,* I think, *the semen should have gone right there, on my belly.*

"I'm just going to run this wand all across you, and we'll be able to take a look at what baby's been up to. I'll tell you when I go in for a closer look at the private parts, and you can turn your head if you don't want to know, okay?"

I stare at the monitor on my right, which I hadn't noticed before now, mesmerized as the shape of a head suddenly appears, then a complete profile, an entire body. It is moving. Suddenly a hand scrunches up under its chin. The gestures are so human that I am startled—this is a human inside me. Not just a baby, but a person. Calling it a baby is somehow less threatening. But a human?

I interrupt Allie, who is narrating a tour of the baby's brain. "You can see why we call this thing a wand, right? It's magic to me every time, how we can peek into each organ—"

"Is there any way to know, like, how, or I guess, like beyond the physical features, is there any way to know other things about the baby, like, about its brain, anything psychological like that?" My heart is beating quickly and I'm afraid I sound borderline hysterical. I adjust my legs, which are sticking together and to the paper beneath.

"Ha, no. Not yet anyway! Can you imagine? 'Your baby will be an obsessive-compulsive type A introvert.' I bet we're not far off, though, the way things are going."

Allie points to the baby's face on the screen. "No cleft palate. That's good news. Everything is looking great, healthy as can be. Take a look at that spinal cord."

I don't ask what a cleft palate is; I don't want to know. I try to imagine Tea Rose being here, holding my hand like on TV, but I can't. His person, his body, is an abstraction to me, an echo.

"Good-looking kidneys," Allie is saying. "All right, my dear, the moment of truth. If you don't want to know, turn your head. I'll tilt the monitor this way too."

I turn my head so that I'm looking at the wall. For the life of me I cannot guess what this baby might be. Girl seems wrong and boy seems wrong. I focus on a smudge on the wall and try to suppress the churning in my gut.

"Well you certainly have an active baby! He—or she!—keeps wiggling around, turning away from the camera. Let's just wait a minute and see if we can get him—or her!—to flash us."

She gasps a little. I feel like gasping should not be allowed during any part of this process. "Whoops, there we go. Okay, baby. I gotcha! OKAY! Great. Alllll right. Got what I needed. And everything looks just fine. You've got a healthy baby in there. Ten fingers, ten toes, your placenta in a good place, everything is doing exactly what it should be doing. I'll just print out some pictures for you to take as souvenirs, and we'll be all done here."

Allie hands me a tissue and I wipe the gunk off my belly. I sit up, feeling heavy, twenty pounds heavier than when I first lay down. She hands me a little envelope and a strip of black and white images—baby's head, baby's profile, baby's spine, some region of baby I can't discern, baby's heart and lungs, and baby holding one hand up as if in a wave. I fold them and quickly put them in the envelope. "Thank you," I say.

"Uh-huh, my pleasure. Just go out through here and take a right at the end of the hall and you'll be back in the waiting room, where you came in. Good luck, hon!" She leaves the room.

I have that moment that I think most people have when they're left alone somewhere strange—what can I steal?—but I lurch myself off the table, the envelope in my hand already slightly damp. The door clicks loudly behind me, and it somehow reminds me of the sound a trigger makes when the gun is empty.

Dear Mom,

I saw the baby today. It was like looking at a constellation, but of cells instead of stars. I keep looking at the ultrasound pictures they gave me, a little strip of film like you get from photo booths at carnivals, and I can't believe it's such a baby already. I can't help but feel like I got tricked—like, I know I could have opted out of it or something, but I wouldn't have really known what I was opting out of. They should've told me, "Look, this is going to make it 100 percent real to you," and then I might have reconsidered. I actually passed out for a second—dehydration, apparently, or maybe I was trying not to be there? Were they forcing me to love it, by showing it to me? I mean, I don't know if I'd say I love it, but I can't deny that it's in there. What's the causal relationship? It seems all of civilization is built on this unscientific, emotional idea that we love our children, simply because they're our children.

Do you think that's enough?

Agnes

Chapter 27

When I tell my father that I have decided to go to a support group meeting, his eyes go strange for a moment. I think he forgets and remembers I am pregnant fifty times each day, the shock and disappointment on continuous playback.

"Where is it? Do you want me to drive you?"

"That's okay. I'll just take the car, if that's okay."

My dad nods, blinking rapidly and clearing his throat, as though spores of something have just flown into his face. We sit down to dinner. I have made spaghetti, which is all I seem to want to eat lately—boiled until mushy, salted and buttered vigorously, slathered with jarred tomato sauce. My dad likes it too. He is shaking Parmesan cheese from a plastic shaker onto his pile. "When is it? The . . . meeting?"

I know that my presence makes him uneasy. The conspicuousness of my body seems to downright scare him. Often I am awake when he gets up. I hear the shower, hear his shoes go down the hallway and past my closed door, hear him run the coffeemaker and take sips while turning pages of the newspaper. Then I hear the garage door open, the car pull out, and the garage door close. I hear these things from my bed, and they usher in the day with a rhythmic kind of dread. Once in a while I go downstairs and join him, drinking weak tea or orange juice since coffee still makes me throw up. We say good morning, we say goodbye. I feel from him a deep and strangled love like something I want to cure him of, release him from. Over and over I repeat my new mantra: *you'reokayyou'reokayyou'reokay*, mouthing it to myself like an incantation, some kind of a spell to ward off our mutual scrutiny, his aggrieved existence, any blame he feels.

I'm trying to remember what my dad has just asked me. I am distracted by this new silence. Every day, a new kind of silence. I always thought silence was one thing.

"Sorry, what did you say?"

My father puts his fork down—a rarity—and dabs his mouth with the paper napkin. "When is your meeting? Of your...group."

"Tomorrow. Tomorrow night. Six-thirty."

He picks up his fork, starts twirling. "Okay. Good. We can have dinner before you go."

. . .

The Center for Unwed Mothers sits in the middle of a squat, dingy strip mall, flanked by a methadone clinic on one side and a pawn-shop (*se habla español*) on the other. I park around the back and walk to the front door. A man smoking a cigarette in front of the clinic touches the top of his head, as though doffing an imaginary cap, and gives me a glassy grin. It's the first whiff of smoke I've gotten during this pregnancy that has made me want to smoke. The door seems locked or stuck. I throw a little more weight into it and it pushes open with a slow sucking noise, and as I cross through, I feel like I am being reluctantly admitted into an exclusive vortex. Where VIP stands for "very inconveniently pregnant."

The room is freezing and loud from a window air-conditioning unit set to high, a jolt after the warm summer air. Vinyl couches and folding chairs form an irregular circle on the left side of the room. The blue carpet is stained in a few places, bubbling up in others from an odorous humidity that swathes the room despite the cold. There is also the vague smell of air freshener and sugar and plastic. For a second I panic that I am not in the right place, that perhaps the right place does not actually exist, that I have wandered instead into an AA meeting or a Bible study.

But then I see. On the right side of the room, five or six women, most of whom are visibly pregnant, or even, I think, excessively pregnant, milling around a table of lemonade and packaged cookies. One of them approaches me now, but she is not pregnant, or if she is, she is approaching fifty and rail thin and pregnant.

She has crumbs on her pilled purple sweater and wears a lizard brooch. Instantly she reminds me of someone, and I am preoccupied trying to remember who. I notice that her purple nail polish is chipped as she extends her hand to me.

"Hi! Welcome. I'm Mary, the coordinator?" She points to the nametag opposite the brooch. "Must be your first meeting, because I never forget a face. Never in my life. If you just come this way, I'll get you to sign in and make yourself up a nametag." Everything she says lilts upward, questioning. She keeps one ice-cold hand in mine, gently, and puts the other one near the small of my back, guiding me. "Help yourself to some refreshments?"

I write my name and phone number on a sign-in sheet and then write my name again with a Sharpie, this time a bit more slowly, luxuriating a little in the fresh point and bold lines—I have always enjoyed a new Sharpie—on a nametag, checking surreptitiously to see if anyone has included her last name too. No. First names only. I try to find the least awkward part of my chest to stick it on and settle on the left side, up high and close to my armpit, safe from my breasts that seem to heave even when perfectly still. My mouth is dry and the thought of sugary cookies and lemonade makes it more dry. I locate a pitcher of water and pour some into a cup. I drink the whole thing and pour another one and almost immediately have to pee. A girl—or are we women? I don't know—appears at my elbow. She looks younger than me.

"Hi," she says. Her nametag says Alicia. "Is this your first time?"

For a moment I can't decide if she's asking if this is my first baby or my first time here. Either way, I figure. "Yes. You?"

"Uh-huh. My mom said I had to come. She was worried if she left me alone I'd just go see my boyfriend."

I nod. "My dad wanted me to come too," I hear myself say.

"It, like, doesn't change anything, but whatever. It's not like I'm getting an abortion at this point."

"Ladies, let's migrate to the circle and find our seats?" Mary announces, her hands framing her mouth in a megaphone gesture. I notice her tongue flicks out frequently, like a lizard.

I sit on one of the folding chairs because I know my thighs inside my thin skirt would stick audibly to the couch vinyl. Every person in the room, I notice, has erect nipples. One woman is putting on a sweatshirt. Including Mary, there are seven of us.

"I'm sorry for the cold," Mary says, as if in reply to the sweatshirt and the nipples. "It's either freezing or sweltering, unfortunately."

"It feels GOOD," says one woman, whose nametag says Gloria. She sits closest to the air conditioner and fans herself with both hands.

"So before we get talking, let's welcome AGNES, who's here tonight for the first time? Welcome, Agnes?"

Alicia reaches over and taps my knee. I feel unexplainable emotion rising to my face.

"Hi," I manage to say. "Thanks."

"Today we're going to talk about healthy ways to manage our stress during pregnancy? But before we get to that, does anyone have anything to share?" Tongue flicker.

A blond girl with dark circles under her eyes puts her hand up. "Yes, Carrie?"

"My boyfriend, he bought a crib. Like, he picked it out himself. I got home from work one night and he was putting it together. I just feel like, he is like, finally getting it. I didn't ask him to buy any-

163

thing or anything." Her voice is climbing with excitement. "I kind of can't believe it."

Mary smiles widely and one or two people tap their hands together in muted applause. "I'm thrilled to hear it! What do you think has created the change in him?"

Carrie stares at the ceiling for a second. "I don't know. I guess I feel like we're being really honest with each other now? Like after last week, I sat down with him and was like, you're either in or you're out. You can't, like, be with me and not be with this baby."

"Damn right," a girl, Megan, says, stretching her arms over her head and revealing most of her enormous belly, including, I note with relief, the same line of black hair that's starting to form on my own.

"And how did he respond after that discussion?" Mary asked. Tongue flick.

"He walked straight out the room! He went into the den and turned the TV on and I was like yelling and following him and he kept turning up the volume and I kept like trying to yell over it and finally he yelled at me, 'CARRIE, okay, I heard you, just let me be. I just need to think,' and I was like 'You're not thinking; you're watching the damn TV' and he was like, 'Fine, then I need to fucking not think,' and I was like so pissed and, I don't know, just, yeah, like, so MAD, that I just left and went for a drive. I wanted to smoke so badly but I didn't. I just blasted the radio and drove like a maniac." She laughs slightly, and a few others do too. "When I got home, he was asleep. And like the next day he told me he was going to try harder."

"Okay, good," says Mary. "So let's look at this, as a group. Last week we talked communication? How to communicate with your partner, if you have one; how to communicate with others in your life who either want to help you or might be having a hard time knowing how to help you? We even talked about, if you remember, how to talk to people who have shut you out completely? Sometimes this is the case with our parents, right?"

Most of the group is nodding. I nod.

"We all communicate differently," Mary says, and then the questions begin. "Carrie needed to yell? And Carrie's boyfriend needed to think? Unfortunately, *we're not always in the same place at the same time*, are we? Actually, we rarely are! But the important thing here is honesty. You've got to deal with these feelings, these fears. You've got to share them! And then you've got to be prepared for the aftermath. Remember the acronym: TRY: Take Responsibility Yourself—if those around you see you being responsible for yourself, accountable for your own actions, they will follow suit. All you have to do is TRY! "

I look around to see if anyone else is holding back an eyeroll. But no. Everyone appears to be absorbed, nodding thoughtfully. I shiver as an extra-large chill works through me. My nipples are actually beginning to hurt from the cold.

"Yeah, well, I told my grandmother about my fears and she won't look at me," Gloria is saying. "I was like, 'Gramma, I miss talking to you. And I am SCARED.' And she, like, walked away. She's mad because my mom had me young, and it messed her up, and now she feels like I'm doing the same thing." Gloria rearranges herself on her seat. Mary is nodding encouragingly, her eyebrows way up high. "But I'm not. I'm not my mom. I finished school. I got a job. I don't do drugs. I mean, I'm here, aren't I? And I'm gonna love my baby and be around for him. I mean, we'll live with Gramma. But my gramma will be his great-gramma, not his mama. So it's different."

"Gloria, you make a very good point here. Very, very good. One I'd like us to think about and discuss in the weeks to come. Think about, and discuss, and think about some more. About patterns, patterns of behavior. All of us, for better or worse, are linked to our own mothers and to the ways we were raised. We all need to decide what we want to bring to our own mothering experiences and what we'd prefer to leave behind. Some things are going to creep in, regardless. But as we've been talking about, being mindful, being conscious of each decision we make, big and small, will help us become our best selves and the best mothers we can be."

The group seems to hang on Mary's every word, which I find incredible. How starved we are for attention, for wisdom, such that even the most basic platitudes, when delivered expressly to us, seem holy. I don't really want to be a part of this, but here I am. Impishly, I find myself thinking about abortion. Were there women who came here once or twice and then decided, no, this baby will not be happening? Or is there a separate group for those women? Does Mary lead that group too? What about the women who are going to give away their babies? Is there a room for them?

Mary is talking about stress management, her tongue keeping the beat between almost every sentence.

"Nutrition is impor*tant*. Sleep is very impor*tant*. If anyone needs those nutritional guideline handouts again, I have extras I can give you. I also have several bottles of prenatal vitamins. If anyone needs some help or can't afford them, let me know. But beyond the things you can do to take care of your physical health are the more abstract things that can make all the difference. Positivity is cru*cial*. You want to try to minimize your exposure to negative, critical *people*? People who make you feel bad about your*self*?" Mary's eyes are shiny and her voice is growing faintly shrill. She is somewhere else now. She is on some kind of mountaintop, beckoning us toward redemption. She is being the change she wants to see in the world.

Alicia bows her head and covers her face with her hands. There is some channel of energy happening between her and Mary, something softly kinetic.

"Does anyone care to share anything?" Mary asks after maybe a minute.

"It's just really hard," Alicia says from behind her hands. "It's just so hard, like, to do this alone."

"Well, Alicia, you are not alone, are you? That's why we're here, remember?"

Maybe it's in the drawn out, peevish way she says *remember*, or the look she gives her, tender and reproachful, and how it makes their faces suddenly resemble one another, but in that moment I realize that Mary is Alicia's mother. I look around, but nobody is offering any reaction. Maybe they already know. Maybe they don't care. I'm suddenly more interested now in being here, in participating in this, if only as a witness to someone else's mother–daughter vagaries. Maybe this is how groups like this work. You feel better about yourself because other people's problems seem worse. You stop thinking, for a few minutes, about your own shit, because someone else's is more lurid, more interesting. Maybe the expectation isn't healing, but rather gaining perspective. Your problems don't get solved. They get placed. A sense of calm moves through me as I watch Alicia become more upset.

"I mean, yeah, in theory, that's why we're here," she is saying, taking her hands away from her face and facing Mary. "But come on, Mom! Everyone in this room is alone. We can be alone together, but we're all alone. I think it's my boyfriend that needs the support group. I think they should be the ones to have to figure out how to do this too. Why should they get to opt out?"

April, who looks both fourteen and forty-five, is nodding. "That's how I feel too," she says softly.

Mary's agitation vibrates through her slowed, deliberate speech, as though each word is an attempt at calming herself down. "Yes? Yes, of course? This is probably, on some level, how we all feel, Alicia! That too much is being asked of us! That the sacrifice is too great? This might not be how you envisioned your life, but life, as we are learning, does not always comply with our expectations! And so we must do our best with the situation we are in—we must do our best to TRY!"

"It just sucks," Carrie starts to say, and then clears her throat. "It

167

just sucks like how guys can have sex and not have their life turned upside down."

"I'm saying," April is saying, leaning forward a little, her voice rising, "it's bullshit. I swear the whole reason they don't have to grow up is because they don't have to worry about getting pregnant, ever. Who do they have to grow up for? They go from their mama's house to like some dumbass girl taking care of them. You don't hear about single fathers hardly at all, but single mothers? We *out here*."

I sense Mary's frustration that this session is getting away from her. I wonder if perhaps maintaining control over this, over us, is the only way she can cope with her daughter's pregnancy. I wonder how long she has been doing this, and I wonder if somehow, in that way the universe has of giving us exactly what we don't want, her role here is the precise reason Alicia's egg got fertilized. I wonder if Mary is married and if her husband is Alicia's father, or if Mary herself is unwed and Alicia was unplanned. How far back does this go?

I get up, perhaps too suddenly, and draw head-turns from most of the group. I need water. I need something. I go to the other side of the room and fill a cup. My bladder seems to instantly fill, and the pressure, as I stand there drinking, grows more and more intense. Impossible, I think idly, to imagine having to pee more than I have to pee right now. And still, I hold it, in some kind of rebellion toward my body, toward these alien urges and aches. The nature of rebellion is that it redoubles the forces of oppression, the measures willing to be taken. That is why when you pull a gray hair, four more grow in its place, as my mother used to say as I watched her up close at the mirror, tweezing gray hairs. At some point you must surrender to your body. And to the body inside your body. I picture myself peeing on the floor.

I find my way, somehow, clenched in all directions, to the bathroom, which looks like a bathroom in somebody's house. I sit heavily on the toilet and the pee struggles out, as if dazed from being held. When I return to the group, Mary seems to have regained her post.

"...which is a good way to minimize anxiety? And you should help each other with this too? Check in with one another? Share your tips? I'm giving you a list of books that you can get from your local library? And before we wrap things up, I'd like each of you to write down one thing that you're most worried about—let's call it your biggest baby-related fear, whether it's a health concern or a financial one, or if it's something as basic as changing diapers—and put it into the box? We'll address one or two tonight and then continue next week?" Mary goes around to each of us as she talks, handing out two slips of paper. One is blank, and the other is a typed list of book titles. At the top, handwritten, are the words TAKE RESPONSIBILITY YOURSELF.

"Who needs a pencil?"

I put up my hand and Mary hands me one, brand-new, sharp. I stare at the blank page and try not to notice everyone around me, heads bent, scribbling as though they have been waiting their whole lives for this chance. Mary catches my eye and gives me a small smile. "It can be anything?" she whispers. "Anything at all?"

Dear Mom,

I can feel the baby moving all around. I think it has been happening for a while but I think I was not letting myself feel it. Every time it would turn or roll or whatever, I would make a move in rebuttal and convince myself it wasn't actually moving, that it was just me who was moving. Just me. But there is no more "just me."

I have been thinking a lot about the fish I killed in third grade. Remember the one I won at the school fair? I guess I didn't really win it. I missed hitting the target with the water balloon all three times but they gave one to me anyway. At home, you gave me a bowl to put it in, blue pebbles at the bottom and everything, telling me it had belonged to Simon's fish, which was one of those moments where I found myself wondering, what else don't I know about this family, if I didn't know that Simon ever had a fish? Anyway, you'd kept the fish food, too, so we were all set, and I named mine Fishy Fishy Glub Glub, and I took care of it very devotedly for a while. I kept expecting it to die, and it kept not dying. And then at some point, I guess I got bored with it. Feeding it and cleaning out its bowl, the fish itself—none of it brought me any pleasure. I started taking care of it less. I sort of just wanted to see how much it actually, you know, needed me. It was a kind of experiment in neglect, and the day I came home from school to find it belly-up in cloudy water, I felt truly shocked.

I think you can probably see where I'm going with all of this. When Mary the support group leader asked us to write down our biggest fears, I immediately thought of Fishy. It's not so much "What if I kill my baby?" but more like "What if I don't care enough about my baby to keep it alive?" And obviously I don't mean just physically alive. I mean, the kind of alive you are when you are loved versus the kind of alive you are when you're not. I didn't write this on my little slip of paper. I felt too much shame. I thought about writing something more general and socially acceptable—"What if I'm an unfit mother?" (which might as well be the center's tagline) or "I'm scared of actual labor," which I'm guessing is a popular one for obvious reasons and which is a legitimate fear of mine, too, based on the little I've forced myself to read—but then time ran out and I hadn't written anything and I managed to avoid the whole exercise. Between us, I guess the thing I'm most afraid of, really, is love. Not having it. Having too much of it.

I'm beginning to begin to understand, or probably not understand but rather sense, or imagine, why you might be gone. I mean, I don't think me and Dad are the Fishy Fishy Glub Glubs in this situation, not quite, but maybe you got tired of looking into the same bowl every day. Maybe you knew that if you'd stayed, you would've inflicted on us the most terrifying thing of all: indifference.

Maybe you need to learn to miss us.

Yours—in solidarity?
Agnes

Chapter 28

The phone rings early, one week and one day after the support group meeting. I did not go back the previous evening, even though I planned to go back and told my father I was going back. I went to a movie instead, a "taut political thriller." The theater was semi-packed with people who were, it seemed, like me, only semi-watching. I ate a small popcorn and most of a big box of Raisinets. My attention alternated between my food and the screen and the strange sensations in my belly, or my uterus. I honestly don't know which. At one point my lower half seemed to be visibly vibrating. Could the baby hear the loud sounds of the movie? Was it cold from all the ice? I took my sweatshirt off and draped it across my middle, figuring if I could hide it I might stop thinking about it, but it didn't work. In the end, the president's good men won, by a narrow margin that seemed to take hours to play out.

I answer the phone, still in my too-small nightgown and too-small robe.

"Hello, may I please speak to Agnes?"

"This is she," I say, and then, because it doesn't sound right, "her. This is Agnes."

"Agnes, hi. It's Alicia. We met last week? At the meeting? At the center."

"Oh right, of course. Hi."

"I hope you don't mind my calling you. My mom—um, Mary—had the list, and since you weren't there last night, I just figured I'd check in . . . to make sure, you know . . . just to say hi and see if you were okay."

It didn't occur to me at the time what Mary might use our phone numbers for. For her daughter? For a friend list for her daughter? The idea creates a small swell of emotion in me.

"I'm okay, yeah. I just . . . I don't know why I didn't come back. I'm sorry." I don't know why I'm apologizing, except that I often feel the need to apologize when confronted with an observation, however innocuous, about myself.

"Oh . . . please. You don't need to be sorry! I wouldn't come if I didn't kind of have to."

We both laugh. We are being, I think to myself, exceedingly polite, as though each of us believes she is a child who believes the other is an adult.

"The thing is," Alicia says, clearing her throat slightly, "I was wondering if you maybe wanted to hang out sometime. Just like, I don't know. Go to lunch or coffee, something like that."

"Yes," I hear myself saying immediately. "Sure."

Alicia laughs, sounding relieved. "Okay. When? Do you work? Are some days better than others?"

I feel sudden shame for not working, for not doing much of anything besides occupying my body and this house. I want a friend. I miss everyone I've ever known. I miss Tea Rose and Surprise and Joan. I miss that part of my life that happened not so long ago but that already feels ancient, older than my childhood, and I do miss my childhood also, or at least the childhood co-created by my memory. I want someone who will always stay and never die and never leave and never turn into a ghost. Maybe Alicia is that person. Maybe this baby is that person.

"Any day is fine. Are you free tomorrow?"

"Tomorrow I have to work but how about Thursday?"

"Thursday, sure."

"Do you know that café, La Place? They have this chocolate pudding thing there that I'm obsessed with."

I know the place, the place called The Place. We used to go there in the first couple years of high school, when it had a smoking section, to drink coffee and smoke. Junior year they cleaned everything up, made the whole place nonsmoking, but it still bore the scent of decades of coffee grounds and ashes and damp newsprint and also alienation and angst.

We agree to meet at La Place on Thursday at 3 o'clock. I hang up the phone and feel something new, or something old that has been buried. When I'd made plans with Sadie and Jenny, I had felt trepidation, but here, now, it's a mild, hesitant gladness.

I eat toast with two glasses of ice water. The water cannot be cold enough. I lie on the couch afterward with a book, a bestseller I bought at the grocery store the other day. The house is still, perfectly still, save for the click and whirr of the air-conditioning as it kicks on and off. I haven't been swimming yet. I haven't finished a book. I haven't bought a single thing for the baby. I haven't even made a list of everything the baby will need.

A rare, galvanizing disgust comes over me and I heave my body from the couch. I go to the laundry room and get a bunch of rags and some cleaners and a bucket and a mop and a broom and a sponge. I start sweeping the kitchen floor, first delicately, with small strokes, and then aggressively, jabbing at corners with the stiff bristles. I am disturbed by how much grit has been covering the floor without us noticing it. How could we not notice? How many things have we not noticed?

I fill the bucket halfway with warm water and dump in some cleanser that smells like ammonia and something worse than ammonia that is meant, I'm pretty sure, to mask the ammonia by smelling better than it. Can cleansers expire? I wonder how often my dad cleans, if he cleans. I dunk the mop in the bucket, wring it out, and start swirling it around the floor. I feel a little out of breath but mostly invigorated. After a few minutes I get the hang of how to navigate the mop and my belly. Despite the air-conditioning, I am sweating, can smell myself. I stop to pull off my robe and drink some more water. Then I lug everything up to the Pink Bathroom and keep going. When I finish in there, I move to my parents' bathroom.

It is while I am on my hands and knees in the shower stall, scrubbing at the gunk stuck around the drain, that I start to feel woozy and short of breath. Immediately I try to assess how much the baby has been moving and I panic when I realize that I haven't been feeling much of anything. My nose is filled with chemicals and my hands suddenly itch and burn and I drop the sponge like it's scorching hot and lunge-crawl out of the shower. As I brush some hair from my face, I accidentally get cleanser in my eye and with that, I feel finished. I crouch on the floor of my parents' bathroom, on the grayish, not-too-clean-looking bath mat still damp from my father's shower. I admonish myself in silent strings of insults at lightning speed: *you worthless idiot, you stupid bitch, you have probably poisoned your baby, you have been breathing in toxins for over an hour now, you have let them seep into your skin, into your blood probably, into your baby's blood, you are trying to kill your baby and make it look like an accident, losing your eyesight is the first of many punishments that will befall you, you stupid, selfish, horrible, murderous girl.* I'm crying now, sputtering. With some difficulty I stand up, dizzy and sweaty and weirdly cold, grabbing the sink to steady myself. I rinse out my eye. I take a few deep breaths and wrap my arms around my belly. I am pleading with it to do something, to forgive me.

I leave the bathroom and only hesitate for a moment before lying down on my mother's side of the bed, taut and cold like beds in museums, for exhibit only. Dad's side shows signs of use, the sheets beneath the comforter bunching here and there, the pillows slightly askew. I imagine he has trained his body, even in sleep, to stay on his side, negotiating Mom's absence as if it were a phantom limb, so much there without being there at all.

When I wake, I am facing the other direction, the lumpy vacancy of my dad's side. I look at the clock and see that one hour has passed almost to the minute. There is an urgent sensation in my bladder, as though pee is going to come screaming out of me, and I wonder how I'll even make it to the bathroom, and as I am trying to quickly get off the bed to get there, a deep punch in my gut sits me back down. Another thump knocks me in my side. The baby. The baby is moving. I didn't kill it. We are alive.

• • •

At La Place, I watch Alicia eat her chocolate pudding.

"Are you sure you don't want to try this?" She holds out a spoonful tentatively.

"No, thank you, though. I'm probably the only pregnant person who's not into chocolate."

"I eat chocolate in the middle of the night," Alicia says. "I keep a bag of semisweet chocolate chips in my bedside drawer. I'm not even kidding you right now. In the middle of the night when I can't sleep, I pound a handful," she laughs. "Works every time."

I laugh too. It feels good. "I thought chocolate was a stimulant."

"Not for me, I guess," she says. "It stimulates me right to sleep."

I'm eating a croissant that I wish would turn into a pile of pepperoni. "I have this weird thing for meat. Like, cured meats. Which I know you're not supposed to eat."

"Yeah. Listeria. That shit will kill you."

"I was looking at this pregnancy magazine at the grocery store and there was an article called 'Listeria Hysteria' and I couldn't tell if it was supposed to calm me down—like, the writer was making fun of people who freak out—or if it was supposed to freak me out. I only read the first paragraph."

Alicia eats a large spoon of pudding. "Oh, I read that one. It was more of a 'myth debunking' article but it still freaked me out.

I read too much. I read every single pregnancy and parenting magazine. My mom subscribes to all of them so they're always around. I've read four or five books so far, on pregnancy and birth and postpartum depression and babies' sleep habits—you name it. I can't stop."

"Wow. That's . . . great . . . right?"

"I don't know. It's one way to cope. I figure if I shovel in as much as possible, a tiny bit might actually stick and, like, come in handy when I need it to."

I think about this. "I don't know why, but I haven't been able to read a thing. I've tried. It's like my brain shuts down. Nothing sticks—all the information just bounces right off of me."

"Um, I think that's called denial," she says, laughing. Her front teeth are brown.

I laugh, too, instead of disagreeing, but inwardly, I argue: no. It's not denial. Denial is something different. What we're talking about is the myth of preparedness, the belief that knowledge can save a person. I don't want to have a philosophical discussion about it, not now, when things are going mostly well. It's good for me to remember not to ruin things.

Alicia takes a sip of water. "You know what, though. Seriously, I feel like until the baby actually gets born, like actually *happens*, everybody's probably in denial. I mean, physically"—she gestures toward her crotch—"I still don't even understand how it's supposed to come out. I mean, I know—biologically, I know—but it's just, it just seems impossible."

I nod. I don't tell her how utterly terrified I am of the pain, of any pain. I don't tell her how I ran from doctors' offices as a child, blind with fear over shots or how I wept openly before getting my ears pierced, despite wanting them pierced. "Bring on the epidurals, right?" I say, trying to sound breezy.

Eventually we stop talking about pregnancy long enough to make plans to go swimming, both of us suddenly and simultaneously identifying that the other major reason this summer has felt so strange is because neither of us have been near a beach or pool.

"It hasn't even occurred to me, until just now, to miss swimming. It's as though it went off-limits, along with alcohol and, like, the soft cheese or whatever," I say, trying to remember what else I'm not allowed to eat. *I should actually read more,* I think. "Swimming counts as exercise, right? It'd probably be good for me."

"Swimming is supposed to be so good for pregnant women. It makes sense. I mean, the baby's swimming around all day. So it's like, a fishbowl in a fishbowl." *(Fishy Fishy Glub Glub! Again!)* "I read somewhere that people like the water because it's like a return to the womb."

"Yeah. And to the...I don't know, ooze? A return to whatever we were, as an entire species, before we were born."

Alicia is scraping her bowl. "Do you believe in evolution? Don't laugh! I haven't been to college."

"I didn't learn about evolution in college. But, yes, of course I believe in it. What's the alternative?"

"I mean, like, do you believe we descended from apes or whatever?"

"Well, more or less, I guess. I don't believe I'm made out of some guy's rib, that's for sure."

Alicia gets quiet. She wraps her arms around herself and looks down.

"I really want to believe in God, but I don't know how," she says finally.

"I know what you mean," I say.

"I envy people who look to God, like, for everything. Like they believe every word in the Bible. They believe God will cure them if they're sick. They believe they know exactly what's good and exactly what's bad, because God tells them."

"Do you really know anyone like that?"

Alicia shrugs and smiles a little. "My mom's like that."

"Really?"

"Yeah. I mean she does a pretty good job hiding it—she's not super judgmental in public or anything. But with me—"

I feel weirdly protective of Mary. "She probably just wants to protect you. Or maybe she's scared, and God gives her courage. I don't know. Obviously she's not doing it to harm you."

Alicia gives me an odd look, one I probably deserve. I have no idea of the dynamics between her and her mother, and I'm fully aware that I'm projecting my own desires onto their relationship, onto Mary, because she is a mother who is, however peripherally, in my life.

"You don't really know my mother at all," she says quietly.

"You're right," I say. "I don't. She just seems . . . nice."

Alicia nods, clears her throat. "Do you have a car?"

"Yes. Do you need a ride or something?"

"No. Not today. I can walk to my house from here. But can you pick me up to go swimming?"

"Sure."

Pearl Jam's "Daughter" comes on. Simultaneously we register those first few bars of acoustic guitar, before Eddie Vedder's pained, ridiculous voice begins. We seem to feel exactly the same way about the song—sheepish for liking it—and we grin and bob, listening, instead of forcing more conversation. Of course I feel that it's a song about me, and I'm guessing Alicia feels that it's a song about her, and there's a sudden gratitude and understanding between us, two strangers attempting friendship in the midst of a maelstrom.

Chapter 29

That evening, unbelievably, my dad presents me with a small chalkboard and a box half full of chalk, as well as a crate of stuffed animals and picture books.

"I was cleaning out the back corner of the garage and found some of your old stuff. Figured it might come in handy. Or I can get rid of it, if you don't want it."

"I want it," I say, reaching for the chalk. The long, cool cylinders.

I bring the stuff to my room and prop the chalkboard up on my dresser. I write TO DO at the top. I put the crate, slightly musty, in the back of my closet. Impossible, I think, that this baby will play with these toys as I once did. I can remember playing with them not that long ago. I wait until the house is quiet and Dad is in his room for the night, before taking out a stick of chalk and biting into it. For a minute I feel the urge to spit it out, but I chomp down instead. I put the box in my underwear drawer and then, realizing my absurdity—*it's not a sex toy, Agnes. It's just chalk; nobody has to know you're eating it*—set it on my dresser and get ready for bed.

• • •

At the public pool, where we each paid two dollars to get in, Alicia spreads her towel across a chaise lounge and unbuttons her cover-up, which looks like a men's dress shirt. I am watching two teenagers check the chlorine and pH levels. One of them opens a tall drum of chlorine and uses a little shovel to remove some white chalky discs. I feel a little flushed, thinking about my chalk. Do other people crave it, too?

"Agnes?"

My head is still turned so that I hardly notice the shadow of Alicia's body. She stands in front of me, her back to me, holding a tube of sunscreen over her shoulder. "Would you mind?"

I spread the thick white cream on Alicia's freckled back and shoulders. Her skin is warm and smooth, her back narrow, offering no indication that she is pregnant. Relieved that she is also wearing a two-piece, I take off my gym shorts and T-shirt and face being scantily clad in public, in the sunlight, for the first time since last summer, when I was a completely different person who was just a person.

It's late morning and the sun is intense. Earlier, I hemmed and hawed about what to wear and had all but decided on shorts and a T-shirt and just dangling my feet in the water. But something overtook me, and I tried on last year's suit. I don't know what. It entered me like a puff of frustration but left me with some weird kind of confidence. I stood in front of the full-length mirror of my parents' bathroom and said fuck it. My breasts stood out quite a bit, spilling slightly over the sides of the nylon top, but the size and shape of my belly probably did a good job distracting whomever's eye was tempted to linger there. The bikini bottom sat low on my hips. *Fuck it,* I thought again, toward the unseen audience behind my reflection.

In general I am partial to wearing lots of clothes. I have always preferred the winter and fall. Even as a child, family trips to the beach filled me with a kind of boredom and dread—the insistence of the sand, the hazard of so much exposed skin, not just mine but a whole beach's worth, all patched together in various sizes and hues like an unseemly quilt. The beach—its expansiveness, its flatness—seems like the antithesis of nudity or near-nudity. It seems like a place where one should want to cover oneself. A small dark room I could get naked in. A cave I could get naked in. On a beach I just want to hide. And pools—pools were only moderately better. But here now with Alicia, I can't deny how good the sun feels on my stretched out body.

I didn't bring anything but my towel and a few crumpled up dollar bills in my purse. Alicia has a beach bag with the works: towel, water bottle, snacks, sunglasses, sunscreen, magazines, and several books. I feel doomed. Alicia finishes lathering herself with sunscreen and insists I do the same. *She brought the provisions. She is clearly in charge,* I think to myself, so I obey. She rubs cream on my back with the strong, decisive strokes of a mother.

"I feel like you're going to be a great mom," I say, settling back in the chaise lounge and squinting out at the pool. Kids splash around while their mothers chat in clusters against the wall. A fat boy, predictably, yells, "Cannonball!" before jumping in and spraying the small crowd.

Alicia lowers her sunglasses and looks at me with genuine gladness. "Aww. Thanks. That's really nice to hear." She starts to turn back to her book and then says, a bit awkwardly, "And so will you!"

I laugh. "You definitely don't need to say it because I did."

"No, you will!"

I should drop it, I know—I've already put her on the spot—but I'm too curious. "What makes you say that?"

Alicia puts her book facedown against her chest and looks out at the pool. The fat boy is now sitting on the side, being lectured by his mom, his swim trunks bunched up around his ample waist.

"You just seem...mature. Like you know stuff."

I think about Simon, who killed himself while we slept. I think about my mother and how she quietly stole away. I think about

Tea Rose, who fell in love across the ocean. I think about Joan, the particular intimacy we shared that wordlessly reached the end of its road, no outlet, like a cul-de-sac. I think about Surprise, the girl who became like a wife in one semester, her trophy virginity recycled into jewelry and roses.

"That's funny. I feel like I don't know anything." I don't know why people keep disappearing on me. Do they know something about me that I don't know? Or about the world? What's the difference between it being my fault and it being not my fault? The result is the same. My sense about Alicia is that we both feel alone, but we feel alone in very different ways. There is the feeling alone that can be solved by others. And there is the feeling alone that can't. Alicia is rummaging around in her bag. "Here. Read this. It's fascinating. And I found it really comforting."

She hands me a book called *The Pregnancy and Postpartum Survival Guide*.

"It's a library book, so I need it back in a week. But you'll probably finish it in a couple of days." She sits back in her lounge chair and resumes reading her own book, *Newborn Nights: Healthy Sleep Habits for Parent and Child*.

It's intriguing, I realize, being around a pregnant Alicia. I can't imagine what she must have been like before. What did she do with her time? Was she as zealous about her homework, her hobbies? She is the same age that I am and a lot more goal-oriented. I am beginning to firmly disagree with Socrates and that business about unexamined lives. How can you live if you're examining your life all day long? Look at Alicia. She is marching calmly and dutifully to the next permutation of her existence. She is examining what it will take to get her there. She is not examining her examination. Only I seem to do that, and it's definitely not getting me anywhere.

I read a few pages of the book but I feel cut off from it, locked out. The tone is meant to comfort—written in second person, liberally sprinkled with phrases like *believe me* and *I've been there*. But I haven't been worrying about the things she is talking about, which makes me realize that my nebulous anxiety will soon have precise targets, and if it doesn't, I will probably need a whole different section of the library. I glance over at Alicia, calmly turning a page. Her belly is rounder than mine; even it looks more sure of itself.

I close my eyes against the white of the book, the glare of the sun, the shrieking of children. I recall the feel of Tea Rose's back, his working shoulder blades as he moved on top of me. For the millionth time I wonder what we were thinking—when, of course, we weren't thinking. Not thinking was precisely the point. All the birth control education in the world can't stop the freight train of that singular frenzied oblivion. I must have dozed a little because when I open my eyes, Alicia is standing over me, not totally approvingly. "You're going to burn if you don't reapply," she says, handing me the tube.

"What time is it?"

"Time to get in the water!"

She helps me to a seated position and once more briskly rubs lotion on my back, even though the sun hasn't yet touched it. I follow her to the edge of the pool. I'm aware of eyes on us as we walk together, eyes that make the short distance seem very long. It's not the children who pay attention but their mothers, mothers who are scornful or merely curious, mothers who share the same unspoken wish—*Please don't let my daughter wind up like that.*

Alicia surprises me by jumping in the water, like a child, even holding her nose. Her breasts bounce almost clear of her bikini top, and her belly, for a split second, seems to catch all the light of the day, glistening with sunscreen, reflecting the surface of the pool and the thousands of droplets being splashed all around it. She lands without going under but then quickly bobs her head down and does that thing every girl knows how to do, dipping her head backward, her face skyward, the underwater bubbles frozen at the entrance to her nose, and then up, slicking her hair back. "Wow, it feels great!" she says as she comes up, smiling.

I'm sitting on the side of the pool, dangling my legs. The water does feel good. I lift myself down and feel goose bumps spread over my entire body. Alicia's nipples are standing on end, impossible not to notice, and I look down and see that mine are too. I am unused to being this conspicuous on this many levels.

Alicia seems calm, happy, in her element. She bounces in and out of the water, diving down and wriggling her legs up in a move we used to call the mermaid. I count to three and go under, the chlorine sharp in my eyes, the sounds from above beautifully muted. *If I could just stay here,* I think to myself.

"That was at least a minute," Alicia says admiringly when I surface.

I resist the urge to do a backward somersault, knowing how my belly would rear out of the water like a humpback whale, and instead take off for the far wall, swimming first breaststroke and then freestyle. I'm amazed by my weightlessness and speed, two things that elude me on dry land. I reach the wall, take a deep breath, and swim back to Alicia. Maybe it's the water, diffusing our shyness or sense of appropriateness, but it doesn't feel strange when she puts her arms around my neck from behind and leapfrogs onto my back. I spin in circles. We are both laughing.

"Your turn!"

We switch spots and Alicia spins us around, our laughter now shrieky and carrying across the pool. When we finally stop, I see that Alicia's top has gotten pushed to the side, almost fully revealing one breast. This starts us laughing again. Our laughter is a kind of freedom, to be in the water, temporarily disembodied, and a relief, to be with one another and not alone. Our laughter is also incantatory, protection against the eyes, one pair and then two and then three, until everyone at the pool is staring at us, our noise drawing their attention while also repelling it.

Fuck everyone, Simon used to say, after fighting with our parents, his girlfriend, his homework. Fuck everyone.

Chapter 30

I am reproducing. All I see around me now is reproduction. The pollinating bees. The mating birds. Spores of sex in the air, all around us. We echo and are echoes. Everyone has this one thing in common: we were born. Some of us are parents; all of us are children. This fact is blowing my mind.

I keep wishing I were back with Joan, at her house. She shimmers before me like some baffling mirage of home and safety while my own home closes around me, while my body cages me in more tightly. Meanwhile, Alicia and I hang out regularly, and I regularly feel excluded from her brand of preparedness. There is an inverse relationship to how we cope: Alicia is nesting; I am trying to fly the coop.

"Agnes," she says to me one day at the pool. "Have you gotten any of your stuff yet? For the baby I mean?"

I am lying under my towel, cold from the water. "Not yet, no."

"I can give you the checklist my mom made. She handed it out at the last meeting."

"Sure, yeah, that'd be great."

"Also," she said, rolling to one side and shielding her eyes, "I'm having a baby shower. My mom's kind of insisting. I think she wants to deal with all my relatives at once."

"That's nice," I say. "Right?"

She ignores my question. "I mean, I'd be happy to take you shopping, if it's, like, too awkward with your dad."

"Thanks." I don't know what else to say. I sense there is something she wants me to commit to.

"I mean, sooner or later...," she starts, then trails off. "Just know that I'm here...if you need help." There is an edge to her voice. I decide to ignore it.

A couple of days later, I get the invitation, pink and frothy, in the mail.

Sugar & Spice & All That's Nice
That's What Little Girls Are Made Of!
Please Join Us For A Baby Shower Honoring
Alicia
Saturday August 13
10:30 a.m.

It takes me a moment to realize that the nursery rhyme is meant to announce the baby, and not Alicia herself. She did tell me she had found out she was having a girl, but for some reason I forgot until just now, until I held this evidence in my hand. She told me she would be naming the baby Hillary. Or was it Ellery? Diana for the middle name, after the princess, whom she adored, and the "Greek goddess of the moon."

"Actually," I'd said, "the Greek goddess of the moon is Artemis, I think. Diana is the, you know, Roman version."

"Oh." Alicia's face had clouded over.

I felt the need to console her. "But it works even better! Diana was associated with fertility and childbirth, too, which is, like, perfect."

Alicia still looked gloomy. "I guess. I just feel like, I don't know...it sounds so much better to say you named your daughter after a Greek goddess, not a Roman one."

"Diana is a beautiful name. A beautiful middle name. The story behind it really isn't important."

"Have you thought of any names yet? You need to think of four: boy first and middle and girl first and middle. That's a lot!"

I hadn't. I still haven't. "No. I'm hoping they'll just come to me in a dream."

. . .

That evening, Dad and I automatically bring our plates to the living room. Eating in front of *Jeopardy!* has given us a shared conversation. The kitchen table, especially in the evening, has become untenable, the empty chairs too distracting.

One of tonight's categories is Call the Doctor! and the question, a Daily Double, is "Doctor whose book *Baby and Child Care* was, for fifty-two years, outsold only by the Bible."

"Dr. Benjamin Spock. Who is Dr. Benjamin Spock?" Dad says. He is, as usual, correct. A car commercial begins, my least favorite kind of commercial, as Dad turns to me with a vaguely eureka expression and says, "You know how I knew that? Your mother has that book around here somewhere." He stands up and puts his empty plate back on the tray. The car commercial says something about "peak performance" and "pioneer precision" and I wonder if alliteration is the mother of marketing. Dad is standing at the bookshelf, the one with the encyclopedias and other various reference books bought at garage sales or mail ordered decades ago. "Here it is," he says, pleased, pulling it out from between *Famous Gardens Around the World* and *The Vietnam War*, volume I. He hands it to me.

I fight the tears that spring to my eyes, that are constantly springing to my eyes. They keep trying to fall and I keep clenching them back. The book is paperback with a laminated cover depicting a soft drawing of a Madonna-looking mother—long dark hair swirling around her shoulders—and her cherubic infant. The binding is uncreased, its pages crisp and unmarked. I can't imagine my mother possessing a book like this, let alone reading it. My father stands above me, watching me, the air between us cringing with hope.

Hope, that most violent softness, like a maw with no teeth.

"Thanks, Dad."

He sits back down, more energized now, leaning forward in his seat, ready for Final Jeopardy. The category: First Families.

. . .

Several mornings later, Dad surprises me with another gesture.

"One of the girls at the office quit. Just like that," he says, stirring another spoonful of sugar into his coffee.

I pour a glass of milk and sit at the table, my bathrobe hanging open like two hands thrown up, like it has given up trying to contain me. Alicia told me that milk can relieve heartburn and is healthier than the Tums I've been downing. There is a packet of Tums in the pocket of my bathrobe. Underneath my robe I'm wearing old shorts and a T-shirt that I found at the back of one of my drawers that says ROYAL CITY ALL-STARS. I have no recollection of it whatsoever.

"She was only part-time—part-part-time, really—but we'll definitely need to find a replacement." My dad sits down across from me. I haven't been listening fully but now he is looking at me intently.

"Okay," I say.

He takes a noisy sip. "I don't know if you've given any thought to—" He stops, clears his throat. "If you want to make some money, you know, or just, if you think it might be a good idea to keep yourself busy, while you're still . . ."

We're making lots of eye contact, his eyes trying to reassure me of his good intentions, my eyes reassuring him that I am reassured. Now he is assiduously straightening his tie. "Why don't you give it some thought?" He is talking downward, as if to the tie. "You don't have to decide anything right now. I think it's just good to consider all the options."

"Sure, yeah," I say. "I mean, am I even qualified? What did she do?"

"Filed, mostly. Occasionally took phone calls, when Nancy was out. You could do it in your sleep, I bet. It doesn't pay a lot, but it's something. Not that you need—" He stops abruptly again, clears his throat. "Not that I won't support you, financially I mean, but just, it's good to work. A job can be a good, you know, distraction." I can practically see the commas in his speech, little hooks of silence he keeps getting snagged on.

"I'll definitely think about it, Dad. Thanks."

"Sure, sure." He puts his coffee cup in the sink. "See you later, Agnes. Have a good day."

After he leaves, I get dressed and decide to walk into town. By the time I reach the top of our street, I am badly winded and already sweating. The day is overcast and humid. My dress clings to me uncomfortably and, I know, unflatteringly. I sit on the curb right next to the lip of the storm drain, into which we threw sticks and rocks and the occasional piece of trash as kids. My understanding of it was that it was some outdoor garbage system; nobody had explained that it was really for rain. I grin a little, remembering this now—I really had no idea where trash went. Underground? Deep enough down so that the molten center of the earth could incinerate it? All I knew was that it was really not ideal to ride a bike with one hand and hold a banana peel with the other.

The front door across the street from where I'm sitting opens and Jeremy, whom I hadn't seen in years, steps out. He is two years older than me and had what they called "behavioral problems" when he was younger. I have no idea if he still has them. When I was seven, I wandered up to this same spot one day when Simon and Dad were yelling at each other and Mom was in bed, and I saw Jeremy peeing in his yard. I watched him do it and when he turned around, I stared hard at the ground, in an effort to convince him that I'd seen nothing. I remembered his eyes on me from across the street and across the lawn, and when I finally looked up, he was still staring, un-blinkingly, shaking his penis vigorously with one hand and then the other. I stood, offered an awkward wave, and ran home. Truthfully the penis-shaking bothered me less than the yelling at home, but my shame for him propelled me away, as if to protect him. I stayed in my room with the door closed for the rest of the day, aware that Mom was doing the same, and I never told anyone what I'd seen.

Jeremy squints behind thick glasses and waves. He runs a hand through his straw-colored hair and then takes his time stretching, as if he'd just woken up or as if auditioning to play the part of a young man who'd just woken up. "Is that Agnes?" he calls.

"Hey! Hi, Jeremy."

He saunters over. He is lanky and looks unwashed. He stands at the edge of his yard and takes his time looking both ways before crossing, despite the fact that cars are scarce on our street. I feel vulnerable sitting down but I remain seated anyway. Jeremy stands directly in front of me.

"What are you doing?" he asks.

"I was going to walk into town, but...I guess I changed my mind." I let out a weird laugh. "Got a little tired."

Jeremy is making me nervous. I can't stop wondering if he is going to pull out his penis. I'm trying to remember the actual last time I saw him. Always from a distance, driving past as he checked the mail.

"How have you been?" I ask.

"I head upstate tomorrow. For the entire rest of the summer." He says it as if I should be impressed. "You look different."

"Yes, well." I hunch forward, trying to show as little of myself as possible. "It's been a while since we've seen each other."

Jeremy still stands directly in front of me, unmoving. If there were sun, he would be blocking it. "Second year in a row I'll be a coun-selor at Camp Lenape. It's all boys. The girls are across the lake."

"That sounds like fun," I say.

"It's a lot of responsibility. A lot. So much extra stuff falls on me because I'm naturally a good leader. Last year a kid was so homesick he was just freaking out, inconsolable, and I was the only one who could calm him down. Shit like that, you know?"

"What did you do?" I ask, in spite of myself.

He looks me dead in the eyes, his own eyes curiously dead. "I did what I had to. The senior counselors and director were all like, 'We don't know what we'd do without you. We'd probably have to close down the camp.'"

"Wow," I manage to say. "That's intense."

"Well, you can't have kids freaking out. It looks bad. It can start a chain reaction and then parents will stop sending their kids. It's a huge liability. I didn't really want to go this year because I've gotten really into the stock market and wanted to do stuff with that, but they pretty much begged me and I couldn't say no."

"No," I say. "Of course."

"I could take you to town," he says, "if you still want to go."

I do not like the idea of sitting in Jeremy's car, even for a few minutes. "Oh, thank you, a lot, but that's okay. I think I'm going to just head home. I have a few things I should probably do instead anyway."

"That's cool. I have to pack. I just came out here to see what the weather was doing. And then I saw you so I came over to be polite."

Carefully, I stand up. His eyes don't move from my face. "Well, it was nice to see you. Have a good time at camp."

He makes a noise like a snort and a cough. "Well, it's not exactly a 'good time.' It's a ton of work."

"Right, yes. It does seem like a lot of work." I turn to walk back down the street. "Good luck, Jeremy."

"Luck is pretty worthless," he says. "I learned that from the stock market. Bye, Agnes."

Now there's a person, I think to myself, who doesn't really give a shit whether I'm pregnant or not.

I put the key in the front door but it is already open—I had somehow forgotten to lock it. I pour a glass of water and sit at the kitchen table, feeling defeated but also oddly relieved. How interesting, how we put ourselves so squarely in the center of things, how we assume that we must also be at everyone else's center, when of course, geometrically, it can't work that way. I don't have to walk to town, I think to myself. There was no reason for me to be there and I won't be missed by anyone. I haven't broken any promises. The cool air of the house feels nice.

Dear Mom,

I'm going to take the job with Dad. It will probably be boring but I honestly don't know the difference anymore, between what is boring and what isn't. I think I actually prefer boredom to other things I'm accustomed to feeling (like despair, anxiety, extreme fleeting happiness).

The other day I went into Simon's room for the first time since coming back home again. I just marched right in. Dad was at work and I had spent the better part of the morning on the phone with Alicia, who was talking me through her birth plan and trying to convince me to write one. She was saying that preparation is a key part of acceptance and that the reason I haven't made any "plans" is because I have not fully accepted that I am a mother, and the reason I have not accepted that I am a mother is because I have not made any plans. Maybe she's right, I don't know. She's definitely stirring something up in me.

Anyway, so I hung up the phone and went upstairs and just walked into Simon's room. I braced myself for that moment of horrific sadness, for the emotional shrapnel to hit me in all directions. Since he left us I have tried to imagine him in those last moments, his fear right before the collapse, right before the oblivion set in, what it must have felt like as each system shut down, what bile and metal he must have tasted as he prayed for the end to come faster, to come now. The tragic ironies of suicide, the body fighting for its life, the intense pain that must happen before the end of all pain is achieved. I will never stop grieving for Simon, not just for the loss of him, but for the secret agonies he felt his entire life that I'm only just beginning to grasp.

I haven't had control over much of anything in my life and I don't really see that changing. I could have controlled this baby by aborting it, or I can control it by fooling myself (and it?) into believing that I know what to do, that I'll always know what to do. I have done neither. I met a boy named Tea Rose and I think I fell in love with him and out of that came this and I am just letting all of it be. I am trying to just quietly be with the things that have happened to me and the things I have let happen.

Anyway, for the first time, standing there with the light streaming brightly through the window, the room felt like a room and not a mausoleum. I sat down on the bed and after a while lay down on it, on my left side, my head on Simon's pillow. There was no smell there. I had this sustained calm—I can't describe it, so I won't try. I got up after a while and closed the door and went back to my own room and two decisions came to me with the clarity and tonelessness of a telegram:

1. I will start working for Dad.
2. Simon's room would make a good nursery.

So, enough about me . . .

Haha,
Agnes

Chapter 31

On a Monday just shy of thirty weeks, the first alarm I've set all summer wakes me from a dream in which I was being pelted all over by BBs from an unseen BB gun, including in my mouth, which for some reason I couldn't close. I get up gladly, opening and closing my mouth, but I stand too quickly and need to sit down again. Standing up too fast has become a new hazard. When I get my bearings, I move to the shower, brush my teeth, and get dressed in some of the maternity clothes Alicia forced me to buy over the weekend: a pair of gray trousers with an elastic waistband and a blue silky button-down top, cut to accommodate the belly. I find a black pair of heels that I haven't worn since my high school graduation and put them on, surprised they still fit since Alicia keeps warning me that my feet and ankles will swell to twice their size. I twist my hair, which has gotten thicker and longer, into some kind of bun, and put some lip gloss and eye makeup on. I find my black purse from high school—another thing I never used this year, preferring big pockets—and go downstairs.

"Good morning!" My dad, making the coffee, looks genuinely happy to see me. Happier than I've seen him look in a long time. "You look very nice!"

"Thank you," I say. I feel shy.

I sit at the table and when the coffeemaker beeps, I start to get up. "Let me get it for you," my dad says. "Cream and sugar?"

"Yes, please." I have not had much coffee during this pregnancy but I somehow don't want to do anything that will disrupt this new continuity between us.

"How about something to eat? Some toast? Or an egg maybe?"

This has been the third straight week of feeling constantly hungry but not craving much in particular. I have been subsisting mostly on buttered noodles, baked potatoes, and raw vegetables dunked in ranch dressing, along with frequent fistfuls of arugula, parsley, and fennel seed, the combinations of which allay my still-fierce appetite for chalk and silt.

"Toast would be great. Thanks."

My father moves spryly around the kitchen with the air. He brings butter and marmalade to the table. When the toast is ready, he brings a plate with two pieces over to me and sits down with his own.

"So," he says, like a father about to give a pep talk, "you nervous?" He scrapes butter onto his bread.

"No, not nervous really. I mean, you'll be there," I say. I butter my toast and spread marmalade to the edges. The rim of the jar is sticky and I refrain from asking whether it's been in the refrigerator since before Mom left. It tastes sad.

"You'll be fine. Nancy will show you the ropes. She's in the middle of trying to put all of our paper documents and files into a new database, at least from the past five years, so you'll be assisting her with that. The room where we keep the files has gotten pretty jumbled over the last couple of years, so you'll be doing some organizing and weeding out in there too. It's not the most interesting work, but you'll be paid what we've paid our temps, which is decent enough." He brushes some crumbs from his beard with his napkin.

I feel suddenly queasy. "I'll be right back," I say. I go to the bathroom and hover over the toilet. Then I sit on the toilet. Nothing happens. I take some deep breaths and return to the table.

"Are you all right?"

"I'm fine. Sometimes these waves just come over me." My coffee and toast are more or less untouched. Dad reaches out and gingerly pats my hand. "Agnes. We'll see how this goes, okay? Obviously this is not a long-term thing. But I think it'll be a good way to occupy yourself and make a little money until, you know, the time comes. And who knows. Maybe after the, ah, baby gets a bit older, we can find a way for you to work part-time and take some classes part-time. Your education is important." I'm nodding and next, crying.

"Okay. Take it easy, sweetheart. We'll figure it out."

He hasn't called me that in a long time. *Sweetheart* was always Mom's word, and she used it at the beginning of exasperated sentences. Dad's kinder, gentler appropriation of it makes me mad at her, makes me ache for her, makes me unable to look at him. Which is fine since he is not looking at me either. Our eyes can't meet because we cannot face the mirror image of our suffering, or is it the mirror image of our love, or is there ever even a difference?

I pull myself together by biting the underside of my bottom lip. "I'm okay. Thanks, Dad."

He clears our dishes and runs water over them. "Ready?" he says brightly.

"Sure."

We drive in silence and I think about Surprise; by now she is surely on the pill or outfitted with a diaphragm. Knowing Surprise, she might go for both. Surprise will not get pregnant at nineteen, nor at twenty or twenty-one. After college, she will begin to establish some kind of a career, to prove that she can, and then she will get engaged. She will not get pregnant until after the whitest conceivable wedding. She will be a mother whose children's clothes will be folded in neat rows in drawers, and these rows will significantly inform their views about the world and how it is supposed to work. My mother folded our clothes and left them in haphazard piles on her bed, for us to retrieve and put away. If we didn't get to them in time, she left them outside her closed door.

Soon we arrive at the squat tan offices with the 1950s signage that Dad chose when they moved to this location, right before I was born. It was always a thrill for me to see our last name in metal, suspended on the side of a building, visible from the street: Fuller & Gerstley, LLC. I loved the ampersand, which reminded me of a treble clef. Once inside, though, I remember all the things I didn't love—the low ceilings with fluorescent lighting; the chilly, manufactured air; the beige everything. Nancy, my dad and Mr. Gerstley's secretary for over two decades, is on the phone when we walk in but hurriedly hangs up and comes around her desk.

"Could this be Agnes? Oh my STARS! Look at you! Just look at you!" Nancy has dyed blond hair and very floppy fishlike lips that have been coated in the same bright coral for as long as I've known her. She is effusive without being warm, ebullient without seeming happy. I can't begin to imagine how old she is. Fifty? Sixty-five? She is wearing a knee-length silky floral dress with buttons at the top that gently strain against her ample chest, nude stockings, and no shoes.

"Hi, Nancy."

"Good morning, Nancy," Dad says. "I'll get Agnes settled in, and then maybe you can give her an overview of what she'll be helping you with."

"Of course! I'm ready when you are!"

I follow Dad down the narrow corridor to his office. The entire space consists of two offices, his and Mr. Gerstley's, the front desk/reception area, two bathrooms, a walk-in storage closet where the files are kept, a conference room, and a kitchenette with a small table and a few chairs.

My dad's office is exactly the same as I remember it: diploma and CPA certificate framed and hung on the wall, along with two old family photos that Mom removed from our house after Simon died.

Even now I can't bring myself to stare directly at them. One of them hangs on the wall behind Dad's desk, so he sees it when he walks in, and the other hangs on the wall in front, so that he can only avoid it if he keeps his head down or keeps the door to his office open (he does both). Two generic wingback chairs flank his desk from the front. The room feels windowless but there is a window, adjacent to the desk, that looks out onto the parking lot. On his desk are lamp, blotter, telephone, pen holder with pens, and three framed pictures: one of Mom at the Grand Canyon, taken before we were born, and then Simon's and my high school graduation photos. All three look dusty. Off to one side is his computer, looking rarely used. The room seems as though it could belong to anyone, to anyone's sad dad.

"Do you need anything?" Dad asks.

"No, I don't think so."

"I figured today we'd order take-in for lunch, but you might want to start packing yours. I usually make myself a sandwich over in the kitchenette, which you're welcome to do."

"Okay," I say. I feel a crushing despair that seems to emanate from the walls.

"I've got a client meeting in about thirty minutes that I should prepare for. Why don't you go out and get started with Nancy. She'll probably have some paperwork for you."

I go back up front and Nancy is on the phone again. Again, she hangs up quickly and gives me a bright, blank smile.

"Let's get you all squared away!"

She hands me a clipboard with a few pages on it. "This is for pay-roll. Your dad says you'll be here three days a week to start. Your pay is hourly, and you'll get your check every two weeks."

I sit in the waiting area and fill out the forms. When I bring them back to Nancy, she has just put the phone to her ear. She motions for me to leave the clipboard and holds up her pointer finger in a "one moment" gesture. "Just listening to my horoscope," she stage-whispers. I nod and smile.

"Okay!" Nancy says brightly after about two minutes. She hangs up the phone and comes around the desk. "I just can't start the day without my horoscope. Coffee and my horoscope! Speaking of which, there's a pot in the kitchen. I just made it before you got here. If you drink the last cup, please make another pot." We walk past the kitchen. "You'll see all my little Post-its hanging around in there. Mostly common sense, but you know."

"Sure," I say as we head down the hall. "So what sign are you?"

"Who, me? I'm Aquarius Sun, Sagittarius Rising, and Aquarius Mars," she says. "Very high vitality. What about you?"

"I'm a Pisces."

Nancy gazes at me sideways, still smiling, always smiling, but with just a hint of pity. "That's a good one too." She looks as though she might say something else but then just opens the door to the storage closet and flips on the light. In the corner is a beat-up desk with an old computer on it. The rest of the space is boxes and filing cabinets, with very little room to move around.

"So basically we need to enter most of what's in all of these folders into that computer."

I have been nodding almost the whole time she has been speaking. This job would probably be categorized by most people as horrible, but I am oddly excited. It seems so straightforward, so monotonous, like a long, waking slumber. The last thing I want is a challenge.

"Do you have any questions?"

"I don't think so. Not yet. Well...wait...is the computer pretty self-explanatory? I mean not the computer, but the program where I put all the information?"

Nancy grins with what seems like extra fishlip. "Look at you— nervous on your first day! Don't be. Trust me, I don't like technology either but this couldn't be easier."

"Oh, I don't mind technolo—"

"You just turn it on with this button back here and this one down here." Nancy brushes past me, skimming my belly, and starts fiddling with the machine. "It takes a minute to warm up. Okay, so here it is." She opens a file that's on the desk. "Sometimes you have to dig through these to find what to put in each of these areas," she says, pointing to the screen. "But they're almost always in here somewhere. The database is identical to what's here on paper. See?"

"Yes. Great. Thanks. I'll come find you if I have any questions."

"You really shouldn't, but if you do of course that's fine," Nancy says, pushing herself up from the desk and straightening her dress. The gaps between her buttons seem to be expanding. "I'll leave you to it. Mr. Gerstley usually comes in around ten and stays a little later in the evening. He also doesn't work on Fridays. He's retiring in very small steps, such a dear man. Okeydoke, good luck! Happy first day!"

Relieved to be alone, I grab a stack of folders from a box and sit at the desk. I wonder what will happen to the sign outside when Mr. Gerstley retires all the way. I open a folder and start typing in information. It's pleasant, doing something, as opposed to being home or wandering around town. In two weeks I'll get a paycheck. There is this folder and then the next one and then many more like it, and that thought soothes me.

When my father pops his head into the room, I have no idea how much time has passed. I have been in a rhythmic reverie and I'm sorry, actually, to see his sad, hopeful face. I want to stay in the blank.

"Hey, Agnes," he says. "Well, look at you now. One morning in and you're already an expert."

It occurs to me that it's better for him, probably, when I am sitting, and he can temporarily forget that I am pregnant.

"Just came to see what you might want for lunch."

"Oh," I say, as a wave of pressure engulfs my bladder. "Let me just run to the bathroom, okay? Sorry."

I barely make it to the toilet and pee for what seems like thirty minutes. I'm surprised to see my dad standing in the exact same spot when I get back.

"Did you think about it? How about sandwiches?"

"Sure," I say. "Sandwiches would be just fine."

Lately, in my dad's presence, I imagine that I'm dying and that he needs to choose which one of us—me or the baby—to save. I keep wondering what he would do. My father stands there awkwardly. I wonder if he can read my thoughts. I'm itching to go back to the folders, to actually crawl inside of them, live among the straight rows.

"I'll have tuna fish, if they have it. And chips, please. And an iced tea." I know I am not supposed to eat tuna fish.

"You got it. I'll have Nancy pick it all up and bring it back." He pats me clumsily on the shoulder. "Are you having an okay first day?"

"Yes, everything is good so far."

A half hour later, Nancy brings back the food and we all eat our sandwiches politely in the kitchen. I return to my desk in the storage closet and pick up exactly where I left off, as if I had never left off. I work steadily until my father appears again in the doorway, this time holding out one of those small, slim cans of pineapple juice. I take it and thank him and drink the whole thing in four gulps. It is ice cold and astonishingly sweet. As soon as I finish it, the baby starts pummeling me so hard that I have to stop what I am doing. It's impossible to do anything with this kind of activity happening from within. It'd be like trying to walk a dog while flying a kite, I think to myself, waiting for it to subside. Eventually it does, and I resume my work. Sometime later, my father appears for the third time, like some visitor from a folk tale. He tells me it is time to go home.

Two days later, a Wednesday, I go back for my second day, which is much like my first. Friday, my third day, is much like the first two. I pack lunches for my dad and myself. It feels not wholly unnatural to do this. I start playing a game at work, where I keep track of how many files I can complete in an hour and try to beat it. The most I've done is eight but usually I get stuck at six. On Tuesday I read from my mom's copy of *Anna Karenina* and do laundry. On Thursday Alicia comes over and insists on painting my toenails, a bright pink called "Juicy Melon."

Another week goes by and we are deep into summer, in its armpit, as Simon used to say at the start of every August. I feel now that I lumber rather than walk. I cannot get cool. Alicia and I go to the pool whenever we can, which feels good as long as we're in it, but lying on chairs in the sun and climbing in and out of hot cars begins to feel like too much effort.

Shockingly, I am happiest at work, in the generous air-conditioning and the beige aura of file folders and clicking keys and turning pages. I grow accustomed to the triple beep from the kitchen, signifying that Nancy's Lean Cuisine is ready, and generally go in to retrieve my own lunch a few minutes later, amid the fog of chicken-and-sauce smells. How can such a small quantity of food perfume an entire floor? Nancy usually eats at her desk while talking on the phone. Sometimes I bring my lunch back to my closet; other times Dad and I eat together at the small table in the kitchen. One time Mr. Gerstley joined us. He is a man I can only describe as a "distinguished gentleman," because of his salt-and-pepper hair, crisp suits, and shiny shoes and spectacles. He has not changed at all since the last time I saw him, several years back, or the first time I saw him, at five or six years old. Next to him, Dad looks slovenly and tired.

I know that Mr. Gerstley has four grown children and a very attractive wife. Is it possible for some people's lives to just be good? Is there a corner in the basement of his large Victorian house where he masturbates to slasher films or gambles away his life savings? He and my father met in college and he is, or was, or still is—how does it work—Simon's godfather. When he says, "You look lovely, Agnes, and you're even smarter than I remember," I feel so grateful but also know he is a liar, since I've said nothing beyond one comment on the weather and another on my sandwich. I guess it's okay or maybe even essential for men like him to lie.

On a morning in early August, Dad tells me he doesn't need a lunch, that he'll be meeting a client at a restaurant. So I pack my own and we ride to the office together in what has become an amicable silence. Nancy is hanging up the phone, as usual, as we walk in. She looks me up and down, appraising my outfit or my body or both. After getting my first paycheck, I went to the mall, alone, and bought some roughly "business casual" maternity clothes—two pairs of pants, four blouses, and a dress. I told Dad about it that evening, thinking he'd be glad, but his face looked pained and the conversation was short. The next morning, Sunday, there was a note: "I went grocery shopping" along with five twenty-dollar bills—"for the clothes you bought." I'm confused by this but I don't reject it. This is his way, I guess, of coping with me. A transactional form of coping. If he gives me money, maybe he thinks I will not expect as much emotional currency. Or at least, I will be less disappointed by that particular empty coffer.

On this particular morning, I'm wearing the dress, navy blue with an empire waist that is supposed to either hide or coquettishly display my belly. I do my best to ignore Nancy's machine-like vertical scan and say hello as I make my way to the kitchen, where I put my lunch in the fridge. I go to my desk and work for a couple of hours, at which point I begin to feel very strange.

Around eleven o'clock, when I usually go to the kitchen for a snack or tap out a palmful of fennel seed—I keep a spice bottle in my desk drawer, along with some dental floss for afterward—a sensation grips me that makes me feel like I am dying a cartoon death, as sudden as if an anvil dropped from the sky onto my head or a stick of dynamite exploded in my lap. I can't catch my breath and spots swim maddeningly in front of my eyes. I try to stand but fall to the ground, my hip painfully striking the corner of my desk on the way down. I can't figure out what to do or what is happening. For some reason I have the urge to take off my underwear, even though it doesn't feel particularly like the main problem, but I can't make my arms work or move my body in any way that makes sense. I can't shake the sensation that my blood is going to burst out of me in one giant, body-shaped blob, or that the baby itself is going to heave out, a huge sci-fi baby with teeth.

Dense with pain, I scan the ceiling, which I'd never looked at before. I notice it's covered with small, symmetrical indentations, like honeycomb. I close my eyes but still see, bubbling from the darkness, patterns of tiny holes, so I open my eyes, but there is the honeycomb ceiling again. My blood swarms and I am certain for a moment that I'm going to vomit. The next thing I know Mr. Gerstley is leaning over me.

"Dear? Are you okay? Agnes? Nancy, I need you to call 911," and then louder, "Nancy! Call an ambulance please, right now, please."

Mr. Gerstley's eyes are kind and calm. "Agnes, can you tell me what happened? Do you know where you are?"

"I was just trying to—" I say. And then Mr. Gerstley and his kind face and the file cabinets and all the smells and fears and holes and reasons go black.

Chapter 32

The first thing I hear when I wake up is Nancy saying, "If I'm going to drink it, I prefer it to be low-acid, calcium-fortified." I'm still on my back, but now on a gurney in an ambulance. There is no siren sounding; we are not moving terribly fast. The ceiling is a soothing corrugated steel. I wonder if Nancy is talking to me the way they do on TV shows, trying to break a coma as if it's a spell, recitations of lists and other mundane things. But then I hear another voice, a male voice.

"I know what you mean about the acid thing."

And then I throw up, with no warning. I jerk my head up in an effort, I guess, not to asphyxiate on it, and it sprays out of me like my mouth is a special kind of nozzle. Nancy is hovering over me, her face a mix of horror and disdain, and the EMT whose voice it must have been appears on my other side, helping me sit up. He hands Nancy a stack of paper towels and she dabs at me like I'm a public toilet she's been suddenly tasked with cleaning. The EMT takes my pulse with strong, gentle fingers. I see his stubble up close and get scared I'm going to be sick again—tiny holes following me everywhere—but I force my eyes away and the feeling subsides. When I look at him again, I take in his whole face. He is very handsome, which feels, right now, both like an impossibility and a needless indignity. I smell like vomit and I feel worse. I know I look disgusting. Fuck this EMT, I'm thinking, for making me worry about what I look like right now, when I'm probably about to die. I try to push my legs together, aware of my dress and the unflattering result of being half up and half down with a big belly.

The ambulance comes to a stop and things happen very quickly. Into the sticky summer heat just long enough for the hospital air to feel especially cold, deathly cold even, redolent with all the sterile and antiseptic smells associated with illness. *Why this smell?* I wonder. Nancy is asking me something about my insurance but I am trying to think of the term for something that's intended to hide something but that ends up further accentuating it. Euphemism? The hospital smell is a euphemism for nonhospital smells?

"I'm on my dad's," I manage to mumble. Like how a footprint denotes the foot but is actually the absence of the foot, a physical absence. Or a seashell. What if this baby dies inside of me and I become the footprint or the shell? Walking around as one thing but in actuality the absence of the other thing, the real thing.

I'm wheeled into a room by two men, who leave very quickly. I'm surprised to see Nancy is still with me, calmly checking her nails. I have an overwhelming longing to be in my own bed.

"Nancy?"

"Mmm? What's that, dear?"

My mind is blank. Nancy reaches for my hand, pats it a bit roughly. "I'm sure everything will be just fine. Maybe it's something you ate?"

My mouth is very dry. "I feel okay now. Honestly I think I'm better. Is there any way I can just go home?"

Nancy smiles tightly, her coral lips like a child's crayon line. "I don't think you're going anywhere just yet, honey. In your, um, condition, they need to make extra-certain you're okay."

"Do you know where my dad is?"

A nurse comes in and Nancy sidesteps away from the bed.

"Agnes? We gonna need a urine sample, okay, honey? After that we'll listen to baby, and I'll take your blood pressure. Can I help you up?" I sit up without help. "Good girl. I'm gonna walk you to the bathroom, okay?" She hands me a cup. "Easy does it. Let's go slow. I'm Shonda, by the way."

I take the cup and we walk ten slow yards to the bathroom. My upright body feels like lead. I can't picture myself pulling my underwear down, let alone peeing, let alone getting it in this cup, and I know none of it can happen with Shonda watching me. I assure her that I'm all right and I enter the bathroom alone. Somehow I manage to get a few drops in, more on my fingers. I place the cup carefully on the side of the sink while I rinse my hands. I imagine it falling, and me just laying down on the floor, forever defeated.

I open the door and hand the cup to Shonda. She helps me onto the examining table. The gurney is gone. "Lemme run this to the lab, 'kay? I'll be right back. Just relax."

Nancy has moved to a far corner of the room and is staring at a diagram of the heart as if it's a painting in a museum. Shonda comes back in. She moves with incredible speed. I feel like an extinct volcano in her midst.

"How you feelin'?"

"I feel okay, actually. Just a little tired."

"How far along are you in your pregnancy?"

"I was in college. I'm not married. I live at home with my dad." This seems like important information.

"That's okay, doll. We just want to keep you and baby healthy, okay? Can you tell me how far along you are? Do you know?"

Shonda has freckles and enormous teeth. I could imagine lying next to Shonda in the dark and feeling comforted. Then again, the idea of lying next to most anyone in the dark is very comforting. She is looking at me expectantly.

"Um. Thirty weeks, I think?"

"You think? Who's your doctor?"

As if not having a doctor would make me any less pregnant. I feel a burning shame, burning with the heat of the thousand shames I have been able to suppress so expertly until now. "I don't really have one. I went to a clinic a couple times."

She nods, wrapping a blood pressure sleeve around my arm and pumping the bulb rapidly. We wait, the hissing of the device like a drum roll. "Okay, darlin', 150 over 92." I have no idea what 150 or 92 means. "I'm gonna need to lift your dress so I can get to your tummy. That okay, honey?"

She squirts out the cold goo. I remember the cold goo from a couple months ago. I remember lying in that other room and feeling fine and then feeling weird and then blinking out like an appliance, all gears halted. I wonder for the thousandth time if my massive confusion and inability to sort my emotions is negatively affecting the health of this baby, altering its development in strange and irrevocable ways.

Cosmic-sounding static issues from my belly, the ferment of cells choked with blood. Then—with a relief like a jolt of electricity—the rushing of a heartbeat, steady and loud and fast. Extremely fast.

I want to keep listening but Shonda removes the wand and hands me a tissue. I dab dumbly at my stomach. "I'm gonna get you an IV. We need to hydrate you and that baby, okay? How are you with needles? This just a bitty one, okay?" She slides something onto my right wrist. I try to say something, I'm not sure what, but my mouth is dry.

"Sit tight, honey."

Nancy has moved farther away and is staring out the small window, her back to me. It seems as though she keeps receding, like the part of the room she's in keeps elongating. I have a clear, calm thought—*She hates me*—before I hear the door open and close again. Shonda wheels in an IV with a bag of liquid attached.

Quickly, sleight-of-handily, she hooks the IV up to my wrist. I feel cold almost immediately.

"You cold?"

I nod. Shonda unfolds a blanket from the foot of the bed and drapes it over me. "Doctor'll be in in a few minutes. I'm gonna take a little blood from you, okay? Squeeze this." She hands me a small rubber ball.

"Did something happen? Bad, I mean? To the baby?"

Shonda produces another needle and pops it into a vein in the crook of my arm. "Okay, relax your hand." We both watch the vials fill with my blood. I'm fascinated that anyone would want to do this for a living. She takes out the needle, tapes a piece of cotton to my arm, and wraps a label around the vial, all in about .04 seconds. "Baby's fine, so are you. Your blood pressure's a little high. Doctor wants to know what your liver and kidneys are doing—this'll tell him. He'll be in soon." Shonda smiles warmly and glides from the room. I want her to stay. I feel scared but also too tired to feel really scared. I feel scared resignedly.

I close my eyes, and it sets in. Beneath the fear. Beneath the cold. Beneath the blanket. Relief. Gratitude to be stuck here, to have what would appear to be zero control and almost as little knowledge of my situation. Why does powerlessness and ignorance get a bad rap? This, this is heavenly.

I see my mother so clearly now. Her intelligent face, each feature a brilliant idea. I feel as though she's with me, in a stronger way than she'd ever been when she was actually with me. I open my eyes and am startled to see Nancy's face peering into mine, erasing where I'd just been. Behind her is a pattern of moving chevrons, multicolored zigzags obscuring the rest of the room. I must be dreaming but I am fully awake. The IV bag is half empty.

"You should be on your left side," Nancy says. She hoists me over and moves my pillows around so that I stay put. She is surprisingly strong.

"Do you know I've had three abortions?" She looks at me with raised eyebrows. "One in my teens. One in my twenties. One in my thirties."

I nod, or try to. She hovers over me, not menacingly, but not not menacingly. Idly I wonder if she intends to kill me.

"Legally, I'm sure it's too late," she says. "But it's something you might have considered. You have to admit, this is all a little"—she clears her throat for about five full seconds—"inconvenient."

"I actually did—I mean, think about it," I say, feeling the need to defend myself from Nancy's hostility despite being at an obvious disadvantage. My judgment feels soft and wobbly, as though it has been diluted by the fluid trickling in. *What's in the fluid?* I wonder.

Nancy shrugs. "Maybe you did, maybe you didn't. But here we are. And this is exactly why women are only making seventy-one cents to the male dollar."

Just then the door swings open and a doctor walks in and the room goes still. Above me, the IV bag is nearly empty, its sides straining together. My mouth is dry. Nancy is at the far side of the room again, near the window. She fixes me with a blank expression.

The doctor is male and young and good-looking. What is with this place? Do they have to be attractive, to make you feel like an even bigger disaster?

"Hi, Agnes. I'm Dr. Lang. How are you feeling?"

I don't know, I want to say. I forget what I'm supposed to feel like. "Fine," I say. "I think I'm fine."

"This is a prescription for labetalol. It's going to help manage your blood pressure. You will also need to rest—as in, no activity at all. This is very important. We call it bed rest. Are you familiar with it?"

"Is it just, like, resting in bed?"

Dr. Lang makes his fingers into a gun and cocks it slightly with that *tch-tch* noise people do that is supposed to convey agreement, as if I have just answered correctly a question about sports. "You got it. It means total rest. Nothing physical. We need to get your heart rate down. You'll have to come back in a week, and the week after that, and so on, until we can deliver the baby, probably a bit earlier than your due date."

"What's wrong with me? And what about work?" In my peripheral vision I can now see Nancy. She has stepped closer, it seems, grown larger, the way a shadow might. I pull my blanket up a little higher. I wish—I actually wish—my dad were here.

Dr. Lang has a lot of energy. He seems to sort of rev himself up before he speaks, like a certain kind of contestant on *Jeopardy!*

"Preeclampsia," he announces.

What is preeclampsia? I think.

"Basically this means that there is too much protein in your urine. Also, your blood pressure's a little high. These things can be dangerous for you and for the baby, but in your case, I believe that some meds, strict rest, and close monitoring will be sufficient."

"I have a job, though."

"Bed rest is generally not convenient for anyone," he says smilingly. "Your boss will just have to understand. I will write a note so that he understands this is medically exigent."

"It's a she, actually," I say. "She's over there. Also I guess it's my dad, so, yeah. He."

"Oh, I'm sorry. Hi, I'm Dr. Lang. Nice to meet you," he says to Nancy, who has slid over and is standing near my bed. "I thought you were Agnes's mother."

Nancy laughs, an exaggerated, semihorrified peal, confirmation that she did say all those things after all. "Nancy Jones. Nice to meet you."

"If we were closer to your due date, we'd probably go ahead and deliver this baby, but you're still a ways off. Thirty weeks, you said? Do you remember the date of your last period?"

"Um. January." How could I have even been alive in January?

I miss Tea Rose suddenly, violently—with the same intensity that drew me to him in the first place. That got me here.

"Baby's fine, Agnes. You'll be okay. But listen—this is important: Any headache or change in vision, you need to come back and see us immediately. Okay? Otherwise, just take it easy—doctor's orders." Again he makes the gun thing at me. Like he wants to shoot me, but only to make everyone laugh.

Dear Mom,

I've been in bed for two weeks. It's awful, but some small part of me enjoys it, the punishment of it. The first five or so days I read a lot. I read three books. I even read a parenting book, as atonement for being such a messed up failure of a pregnant girl. The book emphasized the importance of having a "birth plan," which really makes me laugh. My plan is to birth this baby without killing anyone. I'm not even going to pretend I know the right way to do that. That there even are choices seems absurd. The baby is in. The baby will need to come out. I sort of don't want to be present for any of it, and this book seemed to enjoy accentuating "being present."

I've been writing letters in my head. To the baby. (Ha, like I need another pen pal who doesn't write me back!)

For example:

Dear Baby,

Do you have any thoughts yet? Just because your thoughts are untranslatable doesn't mean they're not happening.

I wish I could know your language. Like the first thing I'd want to say is sorry. Sorry for being a clueless, unprepared host. Sorry for your lack of father, for the many other inevitable lacks included therein.

Sorry that I didn't want you, didn't plan you, sorry that I routinely fear your arrival.

Love from your mother.

It feels sort of good to write it.

Dad has been really nice. He got to the hospital just as I was starting to worry I'd have to go home with Nancy. He looked terrified, and through his terror, I felt him seeing me. It was as though his fear made me real, created me.

His eyes were two puddles of worry. "Eating a lousy, over-priced chef salad with clients, of all things," he muttered, disgusted with himself. "It's okay, Dad. Nancy was there and she's been so"—Nancy appeared on the other side of me with her purse and put mine on the foot of the bed—"great, really great. Thank you, Nancy." Dad thanked her too. Nancy smiled that too-bright smile and said. "See you tomorrow—well, one of you, anyway!" before leaving the room.

There are three possibilities, Mom, no matter how I try to narrow them down: Nancy is insane, or I am, or we both are.

Dad and I stopped twice on the way home from the hospital, once to pick up my medication and then again to pick up dinner. From that point up till now, Dad has remained very solicitous. He doesn't express any concern about the baby—still doesn't acknowledge it, really, and he doesn't quite dote—but it's like he has suddenly become acutely responsible, like a kid whose dad has told him they're getting rid of the dog if he doesn't take better care of it. I guess I'm the dog in that scenario.

He brought the small TV that was in the basement into my room. He brings me breakfast every morning and comes home most days to fix me lunch. Sometimes we eat dinner together here in my room, while watching TV. I think I've gained ten pounds in the last two weeks. I was up four last week at my checkup. Honestly, I'm not terribly hungry for most meals but I don't have the heart to turn down his efforts. What does it matter? I'm fat anyway.

What I'm getting at here is something that might altogether surprise you: Dad has been sort of amazing.

Agnes

Chapter 33

Saturday morning, it's a relief to open my eyes to my cool, dappled bedroom. A beautiful day for a baby shower, I think to myself, and I honestly can't tell if it's a sarcastic thought or not. Mostly I am just happy to get out of bed, to have somewhere else to be. I shower and get dressed. I fix my hair and try to put some extra care into my appearance—tweezing a few straggly eyebrow hairs plus a bonus one on my chin. I put on eye makeup and lip gloss. I consider perfume but most strong smells still make me feel nauseous. When I go downstairs, Dad is sitting at the table, eating a bowl of cereal.

"Good morning," he says. "How do you feel? Maybe you should stay in bed until it's time for you to go . . . ?"

I pour some cereal and join him at the table. "I'm good. It feels good to be up. I think I was on the verge of muscle atrophy."

"Well," he says, "you look nice. I just wanted to ask—do you have a gift? For your friend? Don't you have to bring a gift to these things?"

Shit. "Shit," I say. A weird fear fishtails through me. Somehow I have forgotten that a shower is a type of party, and a party means presents. A party also means people, other people, whom I'll presumably be obliged to talk to. I think about lying. About using my amnesty to just take a drive, or go to a casino, or find a beach. But then I think about Alicia, how much all of this means to her, how devotedly she has studied her new fate.

"Well, actually, I just remembered—I told Alicia that I'd get her whatever she didn't get from everyone else. Like, she said that usually there are a lot of repeats, so I figured it'd be good to not risk getting her something she's getting twelve of, you know?" I am, of course, completely making this up.

I drive to Alicia's with the AC on blast, afraid of sweat showing through my dress in places I can't see, but then my nipples become a secondary problem. I leave the radio off. I check my face and teeth in the rearview mirror at every red light. *This isn't about you,* I keep telling myself. *Nobody is going to be looking at you.* But it doesn't stop me from messing with my hair and putting on more lip gloss. For the hundredth time since I learned the words, I try to remember the difference between narcissism and solipsism. Can a narcissist be a mother? Can a solipsist?

Alicia lives about twenty minutes away, on a patchy street behind a gas station. The back of the gas station sign is visible from her driveway, making it feel like the set of a high school play with a sad plastic moon waiting to be wheeled backstage by black-clad, ill-adjusted teens. Mary greets me at the door, her face a mask of pained cheer. "Hello? Thank you for coming? It's Agnes, right?"

"Yes, hi. Hello."

"Go ahead if you would and fill out a nametag over there, just inside the kitchen?"

I step inside awkwardly, my dress and shoes feeling too tight. "Thanks so much for having me!" I say to her narrow back. She ushers me to the nametags and Sharpies, all pink for the occasion. I guess it makes sense that Mary would run this shower the way she does her unwed mothers meetings. I scrawl my name on a nametag and slap it on, determined to be a good guest.

A table in the front hall is piled high with gifts, big pink boxes adorned with pink curly bows—like a cartoon drawing of a baby's hair—pink tissue poking out of pink shiny bags. Alicia, clad in pink, steps through a cluster of guests and hugs me breathlessly. Our bellies press together. It is the oddest sensation.

"Agnes, hi! Thank you for coming! You look great! Gosh I feel about twenty times huger than you!"

She does look bigger than the last I saw her. Her nametag reads MOMMY.

"You look great," I say. "Um, I have no idea how I did this, but I somehow forgot your gift at home. I'm so sorry. I will get it to you."

I see Mary frown for a nanosecond before flashing a big smile. "Not to worry? Right, Alicia? They don't call it 'pregnancy brain' for nothing!"

The group of us moves into the living room. In the adjacent dining room is a table of refreshments, all of which are labeled with descriptions: CHAMOMILE PUNCH—SWEET AND SOOTHING, ASSORTED TEA SANDWICHES—SMALL BITES AID IN DIGESTION, CHOCOLATE CUP-CAKES—CHOCOLATE IS A NATURAL OXIDANT, FRUIT—DON'T FORGET YOUR FIBER!

"Please help yourselves?" Mary cries out. "Then make yourselves comfortable, if you would, so the program can begin?"

I put a few things quickly on a plate, fill a plastic cup with punch, and sit down on a folding chair. I'm not at all hungry. I take a foamy sip and immediately regret it. The punch is sweet and vegetal and disgusting. Across the small room I recognize Gloria from the meeting at the mothers' center. A baby is strapped to her in what looks like twelve yards of fabric—I can only see its tiny foot and a fluff of hair from where I'm sitting. I try not to stare, all the while desperately trying to figure out why I feel such shock. She was pregnant when last I saw her. Now the baby is here. What possibly could be more unsurprising? And yet.

Our eyes meet and we both smile. She looks as uncomfortable as

I feel. I glance around the room, as if to appear busy, or content. There is a lot to look at: the heavy rose-colored drapes, the upright piano covered in crystal knickknacks, the china cabinet filled with tiny porcelain children, the mantel covered in photographs of Mary and Alicia, framed in gold. In none of the pictures do they appear together. The faux-Victorian ornateness reminds me not of some grand, royal drawing room but rather of a sad dollhouse.

"I'm Teeny. Aunt Teeny." A hand appears near my lap. I shift a bit in my seat. A woman who looks to be in her seventies dressed in a riot of florals has sat down next to me, a plate of four cupcakes on her lap.

"See all those Hummels in there?" She gestures toward the china cabinet. "They're mine. I never said Mary could have them. I'm not dead yet!"

"Oh," I say. "Hi, I'm Agnes."

"Agnes, that's an old-fashioned name," she says. She carefully unwraps a cupcake with two fingers that look like they belong on the hand of a much younger woman. "No ring, I see. So clearly you're not an old-fashioned girl." She winks at me as she takes an enormous bite of cupcake.

I have no idea what to say. "Ha," I finally offer. "I guess not."

"Just a joke, dear." Teeny winks some more. "Never been too old-fashioned myself." Her teeth and tongue are black with cupcake and grotesque chewing and sucking noises issue from her mouth. Briefly, she unlatches the top portion of her dentures, curls her mouth around them, and tongues them back into place, either to clean them or in a display of power or both: *You think that's gross, honey, watch this.*

"I never liked these things," she says, waving a hand across the room like a wand. "Though I'll never turn down a chance to eat cake in the morning." She starts in on the second cupcake.

I look around. Gloria's face is turned down toward the baby and she is rocking very subtly in her chair. Mary stands by the food table, cleaning drips and rearranging serving tongs. Alicia sits in a cluster of four girls, her hands proudly on her belly. Her friends' full attention is on her; they seem riveted by her talk of too-small underwear and waking up three times a night to pee and other such indignities, delivered airily, as though they are legitimate causes of envy, as though we are at a country club and she is waving around a brand-new engagement ring. *Attitude is everything,* I remember reading once, bold font on a poster in the high school guidance counselor's office, above the image of a toddler boy wearing a grown man's suit. What if I'd moved more jauntily through this pregnancy? What if I'd acted more proud of myself? Seems impossible, and far too late.

"So what are you having?" Teeny asks, dabbing at her mouth with a napkin.

"I don't know," I say. "I didn't really want to find out."

"Good." Teeny nods approvingly. "Old-fashioned, but smart. Too much technology with these babies. How do we know it isn't messing up their brains? I think kids used to be smarter. My kids, when they were kids, are smarter than my grandkids are now. I don't think that's a coincidence. My daughter wanted all the bells and whistles: sex tests, chromosome tests. All those X-rays. Her sons are dolts. Cute as hell, but definitely not bright."

I smile politely. "I think sonograms are generally safe—"

"Honey, *generally* doesn't cut it. Do you want to drive a car that's *generally* safe? Condoms are *generally* safe, too, right?" She snorts a little as she glances sidelong at my belly.

"Well, I mean, everything has its risks, I guess—"

"That's true," she says, the gleeful sarcasm gone from her voice. "But you don't go begging for risk just so you can pick a paint color for the nursery." She unwraps cupcake number three. "Alicia's always been a good girl, and pretty," she says in a not-very-quiet whisper. "Mary did her best but she had this one coming. Very tightly wound."

As if on queue, Mary appears at the front of the living room. "Hello? Before we start in on the gift opening, I'd like us all to play *a neat little game*. I will hand out some index cards and pencils. I'd like everyone to guess the date and *time that Alicia's baby girl will be born*." Her voice stretches toward cracking but somehow never does. "The due date we've been given is September twentieth, but obviously it could happen any time now, or after the twentieth, of course? It will be so fun to find out who comes the closest! Alicia?" Alicia smiles and puts a hand up nervously, as if she's just been called on in class. "You'll play, too, won't you?"

"Uh, sure," Alicia says. Everyone laughs for some reason.

I am handed an index card and a brand-new, sharpened pink pencil. Mary's face as she hands them to me is exactly the same as it was the last time she handed me paper and a pencil. I feel suddenly depressed, thinking about her life as a series of groupthinks and ballots, a tapestry of index cards scrawled with other people's handwriting, other people's gently coerced answers to questions they never wanted to be asked.

Aunt Teeny nudges me with a bony elbow. "What do we win, if we win?" she calls out.

Mary clears her throat. "Oh? Haha? Satisfaction, I guess? No prizes—just for fun, remember? I will personally call the winner to let her know. How does that sound?"

"Sounds stupid," Teeny mutters, before scribbling something illegible and folding her card in half, "but I guess everyone's entitled to their idea of fun. Mary"—she speaks more loudly now—"you remember what Uncle Bill's idea of a good time was, don't you? Bill being my husband," she addresses the room. "Excuse me, my *dead* husband. Thirty minutes on the toilet with a Q-tip in each ear. May he rest in peace."

I write *September 20, 12 noon* on my card. Alicia is a rule-follower and the daughter of a rule-follower, so it seems at least as possible as not that this baby will carry on the tradition. Following Teeny's lead, I fold my card in half and drop it into the cut crystal bowl on the coffee table.

The rest of the shower is devoted to the opening of gifts, box after box and bag after bag of pink outfits, three-packs of pacifiers, soft toys, bibs, blankets, and a horrifying-looking contraption that I learn is a breast pump. Recalling kids in high school joking about penis pumps, supposedly used to make a dick bigger, I learn from color graphics on the box that a breast pump does not have the same purpose. Rather, it extracts the milk from your breasts and sluices it into a baby bottle.

"This is perfect, exactly the one I wanted!" Alicia exclaims of the pump. "I'll be able to build up a supply in the freezer, and Mom can feed her, too, right, Mom?" Mary seems scandalized. "We'll see how it goes, dear? Remember there's also formula, which can be a *real* gift to mothers? But *thank you, Darla*. What a generous present!"

Alicia passes each gift around, and almost every guest looks genuinely awed, stroking silk-lined fabric and fingering tiny buttons. I find myself looking more at their faces than at the items plunked unceremoniously in my lap by Aunt Teeny, who doesn't even glance at them but instead tosses them toward me like she's trying to beat a record in Hot Potato. Mary records each gift and its giver on a pink piece of paper using a pink pen.

After some milling around, I see Teeny over by the china cabinet with another cupcake in her hand. People begin their hugs and goodbyes. I thank Mary and turn to Alicia, who stands by the door with a look on her face of what can only be described as maternal bliss.

"I'll drop off your gift very soon. Sorry again for forgetting. Thanks for—"

Before I can finish, Alicia is embracing me. "Agnes," she whispers in my ear, "I really hope you get to feel what I'm feeling at this exact moment."

Outside, walking to my car, I take big gulps of the hot, humid air. Aunt Teeny walks about ten steps ahead of me, surprisingly fast, and with a rolling, stuttering motion that reminds me of a beetle. I notice she is wearing nylons because of how they are bunched and sagged at her ankles. I notice, too—walking faster now, as if to catch up to her, though I can think of no reason to do so—two porcelain figurines sticking out of her purse. A boy and girl Hummel, their heads tilted slightly toward one another like coconspirators. Abruptly, Teeny turns around.

"Well, we survived it, eh?"

I laugh a little. "Yeah," I say, and then feel guilty, thinking about Alicia and her rapturous face. "It was nice, though."

Teeny snorts a bona fide snort. We fall into step, walking slowly now toward a white Buick parked across the street. "It wasn't nice. It was a crapshow. You don't have to pretend with Aunt Teeny."

"Well, I mean," I say, still wanting to defend Alicia, her face, "it seemed to mean a lot to Alicia."

Teeny shrugs. "You know what I think?" She turns toward me, gigantic sunglasses covering her eyes and most of her face. "I think you're going to have an easier time of this." She wags a finger toward my belly.

"Really?" I ask. "Why?" I don't want her to leave.

"Because you're expecting it to be bad. You're expecting to fail."

I don't say anything. There's nothing to say.

"Best-case scenario? You'll be pleasantly surprised. And the worst-case scenario doesn't matter, because you're already there."

"I guess that's one way to think about it," I say.

"No," Teeny says. "It's the only way to think about it. Poor Alicia doesn't know what's in store. All the froufrou outfits and milk vacuums in the world won't help her. They'll just make it worse. They'll just remind her of when she was foolish enough to think they would help her. Let me tell you something, Agnes, in case you haven't already started to figure it out." Teeny steps closer, puts a hand on my shoulder. "Motherhood is when you find out exactly what kind of terrible person you are. Enjoy not knowing while you can."

I feel my eyes start watering and then I am crying.

"It's good to cry, honey," Teeny says, her voice a bit softer. "Pretty sure Alicia hasn't cried enough."

We stand there together in the hot sun, a few cars passing us. After a minute Teeny hands me a frayed tissue from her purse. I take it but don't use it.

"Well," I say, "it was nice meeting you."

Teeny laughs, and I laugh a little too. Then she hugs me, her grip strong around my shoulders. She smells like sugar and baby powder. "You'll survive, dear. Somehow or other."

I want to get in the car with Teeny and drive with her wherever she's going. "Thanks," I say.

She opens the passenger side and for a moment I think she is opening it for me. But she tosses in her purse, the Hummels clinking heads, and slams the door. With a sort of wave-salute, she scurries around the car, climbs in, and speeds off, like she can't get away fast enough.

I stare after the car. Her license plate says MYTURN.

Dear Mom,

I didn't go straight home after Alicia's shower. I felt like I needed another layer, a buffer before home, something, as they say in soap operas, to take the edge off. I understand why people go to bars on their way home from work. There has to be a bridge, some kind of neutralizing force between two fraught worlds—in this case, the world of Alicia's baby and the world of my own baby, except of course that I carry the latter world with me wherever I go. I'd have gone to a bar if I could have ordered whiskey and drank it without getting in trouble or dying from shame (or, you know, I guess, hurting the baby).

I wound up at Pearlmann's, where the parking lot was crowded with the kind of people who go shopping on Saturdays, extra crowded, I guess, because of the giant signs in the windows announcing the Biggest Red Dot Sale Yet. I know I was disobeying Dr. Lang's orders, but it felt really good to move around.

I started thinking about a gift for Alicia, and I found myself staring at a display of nightgowns, some silk, some flannel, some with buttons and sleeves and others with tiny, sexy straps. I could see Alicia in any of them, which confuses me with regard to the "kind of person" she is and how much I actually know about her, know her. I choose something in the middle: cotton, cream with pink and green flowers, knee-length with fluttery sleeves. I asked for it to be gift-wrapped and I was handed the box, neatly covered in bridal-seeming paper and tied with a gold ribbon, with amazing speed. How do they do that? It would have taken me twenty minutes at least.

I was going to leave after that, drive back to Alicia's and just drop it at the door, or I guess maybe hand it to her personally, though dropping it at the door was my preference, is always my preference (actually seems like more of a "life philosophy" than a preference), but I wound up riding the escalator to the Infant and Child department, and that's when everything got hazy.

Mom, have you ever even seen the aisles marked "New Mother, New Baby"? It was like...I can't even describe it. It was like Alicia's shower in some hysterical dimension. An entire wall of nipples. I saw the breast pump Alicia got along with maybe ten other kinds. Trashcans especially for diapers. A thousand variations on the themes of googly-eyed jungle animals/half-witted teddy bears/psychotic ducklings printed on all manners of blankets, outfits, bibs, sheets. I kept walking and ran into a display nursery, a complete room with floor models of a crib, mobile, dresser, changing table, and a rocking chair (called a "glider"). A woman, probably in her 30s and at least as pregnant as me, rocked in the chair, ankles crossed, hands on her belly, a look of misty bliss on her face. I felt like I'd walked in on something, an intimate moment, and her reaction told me I had—she sort of sat upright and we both started apologizing.

Women: constantly apologizing but rarely sorry. She wasn't sorry. I wasn't sorry. What on earth did we have to be sorry about?

I think as a kid I often felt that I was interrupting your solitude. I knew you loved me, but I knew you'd rather be alone. So you want to know what else happened at Pearlmann's? I'll kill (ha) two birds (haha) with one stone and tell you both at the same time:

Dear Baby,

I figured it was time I got you some stuff, so I found a salesperson at Pearlmann's and I walked around the store with her and I pointed out all the big things, and I put all the little things into a basket, which the salesperson insisted on holding ("you've got enough to worry about," she said, and I still can't tell if she said it kindly or unkindly), and then I handed over the credit card Dad (not your dad, my dad—your grandfather, holy crap) gave me for emergencies and I tried not to faint when she told me the total.

I gave her my address and she said the big things would be shipped in a few days. The big things are a car seat and a crib and one of those gliders. The things I carried out with me are some of those snap-on undershirt things and some baby blankets and sheets and socks and bibs and a rattle, and in another bag there was a breast pump, and in the final bag was the gift-wrapped nightgown.

I forgot to get diapers.
But there is still time, I hope.
Love from your (trying) mother.

> And love from your (try-
> ing) daughter,
> Agnes

Chapter 34

Four interesting things happen, all in succession. Dad has been keeping the portable phone in my room, despite the fact that it rarely rings. I'm in bed again, bored, bored with reading, bored with TV, bored with masturbating, bored with time passing and trying to so-called pass the time, which I guess means trying to make it go faster than it does, which I now know is an impossible exercise. So when the phone rings for the first time in five days, I practically jump to answer it.

"Agnes?"

I hesitate. "Yes?"

"Hey. How are you?"

"Sorry, who's this?"

Some forced laughter. "It's me—Joan."

My heart beats faster. "Oh! Joan, hi! How are you doing?"

"Well, um, I'm okay, I guess. I actually have a question..."

"Sure—shoot!" I can't stop making myself sound the way I do.

"So, okay, well, I know things were a little...weird...at the end of last semester. I mean, I had a lot going on and stuff, but I just found out that my housing situation got all messed up— like, I was supposed to stay in the same house with the same girls, but they invited someone else without telling me, so I basically got kicked out, and so I've been going nuts trying to find an apartment—anyway, the bottom line is, I need a roommate. I can't afford anything on my own, even with a second job. I mean, you're probably all set or maybe you want to stay on campus or whatever but I'm pretty desperate. And, I mean," she quickly adds, "it'd probably be fun."

I kick my sheets off because I am sweating. "Wow, well, um actually—"

"Oh . . . also . . . you should know, because I did the math, it's actually cheaper living off campus and not having a meal plan. Seriously. Like significantly cheaper. And like our food bills would be way cheap too."

"The thing is," I start, not sure how I'm going to finish, "I'm not going back this fall. To school."

Silence.

"Really? Why not?"

There is sweat behind my knees. I'm not sure I've ever sweated there before. "I, um, I'm just going to take a semester off. I just feel like I need to be home, you know, for now."

"Huh. Okay. Is everything okay?"

"Yeah, oh yeah, everything's fine."

"Agnes?"

"I mean, you know, it's just, I think it can be hard on my dad, having me so far away, and school isn't going anywhere . . ."

"My sister died."

"Oh God . . . Joan," I immediately get the hiccups. "Jesus, I am so sorry."

"Yeah. I guess that's one way to kill yourself." She sounds mad, but something more brittle than mad. An anger she's only allowed herself to feel the surface of, a cracked surface under which oozes an unspeakable fury.

"Joan, I don't even know what to say." I can't tell if my face is sweating or if I have somehow started crying. "I mean, I should know what to say. I feel like . . . I've . . . you know, I guess, I've been there."

"Thanks." After a minute, her voice less flinty, "I should probably let you go. I need to figure out this whole roommate thing."

"I'd love to be your roommate," I say, and then I really do start crying, because I would, so badly, love to be Joan's roommate.

"Yeah. It's cool. I'll figure something out."

We get off the phone in an interrupted flurry of commanding each other, or ourselves, to hang in there, to keep in touch, to hang in there.

I get out of bed and go downstairs. I want to run away, to pull this baby out of me and just run away. I don't want to be here anymore. I don't want to be anywhere. I am sitting at the piano, thinking about Joan's dead sister, dead because she starved herself, and I can't help but feel impressed. She wanted to leave the world, but not abruptly. She wanted to fade out. She wanted to erode the boundaries between this world and the next, or this world and the void, and live in that thinnest, most transparent of places. She wanted to float too.

Things don't, as everyone is fond of saying, "happen for a reason." What a cruel way to console someone—removing all agency while creating an elaborate game of seek-and-find for the mourner to play for the rest of her days. Could *this* be the reason? Or wait, maybe *this* is the reason, the reason my dog died, the reason my house flooded, the reason my brother killed himself or my mother left. There are things that happen. There are reasons, often never revealed, why people do what they do. Two separate categories.

Mozart's Sonata No. 8 is open in front of me, in a book that I played obsessively from last summer, before leaving for school. Mom always preferred Mozart; Dad, Beethoven—specifically hits like "Moonlight Sonata" and "Für Elise." The book hasn't been touched since then, and it pains me now to think about one year ago, how different the notes sounded, how little I knew. My fingers feel clumsy and swollen. I pick up the phone and scroll through the caller ID to the last number, Joan's number, and press CALL, and it's ringing before I have figured out what I am doing or why. I imagine the sound of the ring on her end, a shrill sound in a sad house, Joan and her parents thinking, even for a fraction of a moment, maybe there's been some mistake, maybe she's alive and well, maybe this really has been just a horrific dream. Joan picks up on the fourth ring, just as a machine has also picked up, and for a few seconds, there is confusion, followed by a beep.

"Sorry, hi, Joan. It's Agnes." I can't tell whether our conversation is being recorded.

"Oh...hey. What's up?"

This is the second interesting thing that happens today—something inside of me decides, without the rest of me fully consenting to this decision, to let Joan in, as I had let her in months ago, when the only one of us with a dead sibling was me. The simple fact is that I owe her the truth. Or in some weird extrapolation of guilt, I am deluded enough to believe that telling her the truth will console her. As though this new life that will be brought forth out of my carelessness, out of the wreckage of my bottomless loneliness, can somehow make her feel better.

"I'm pregnant. That's the reason I'm not going back to school. I'm due in about a month."

"Oh my God. Oh my GOD, Agnes." Joan's mouth seems very close to the phone. I can't tell if she's angry or just surprised or, I don't know, offended. I can't tell what she is.

"Yeah, so, I'm sorry it's taken me this long to tell you. I honestly haven't known how to even say it. I've barely been able to, like, admit it even to myself."

"What are you, I mean, how are you going to...like, you'll just live with your dad, then? I mean, he'll help out?" There is a frenzy in Joan's voice, maybe even something like joy. "And oh my God, whose is it? *Tea Rose*? Agnes, is it Tea Rose's baby?"

"Yes, I think so, in terms of my dad, and yes, it's Tea Rose's baby. I mean, it's my baby," I say, surprised to feel, for the first time, a sting of possessiveness—as familiar as a paper cut and just as painful. It's the way, I realize, I used to feel about Tea Rose himself. "But, yeah, he's the father."

Is there anything less mysterious than a father? I wonder. Then my doorbell rings, and I hear a click on Joan's end—the answering machine clocking out.

"Someone's at the door," I say. "I have to go. I'm actually not even supposed to be out of bed but...anyway, I have to go." I suddenly feel like telling her everything but I'm flustered by the shadow of someone outside, as though the shadow is me, eavesdropping on me.

"Agnes. Tea Rose called me. Like, a few weeks ago he called. He left a message but I never called him back. Does he know?"

The doorbell rings again. "Just a minute!" I call out. To Joan: "No. NO. He doesn't know. Do you know why he called? I have to go. Please, please don't tell him, okay? If you call him back? There's no point. I'll call you later. Is that all right? Bye, Joan."

I hang up the phone and move toward the front door and I feel like I'm in a dream, like I won't get to the door in time, won't be able to open it no matter how hard I pull, like in telling Joan about the pregnancy I have unsealed some kind of reverse Pandora's box that is sucking me down deeper into itself, where the real horrors lie. And worse, I have yanked Joan down with me. Joan, the last touchstone of the substandard Eden I just kicked myself out of, the life I accidentally traded this life for.

Who will I ensnare next? I wonder. Surprise? What if it's Surprise on my doorstep right now? "Surprise!" she might say, in the horrible sitcom version of this moment. "I hear you have some news!"

But no. It's not. It seems impossible, after all, that Surprise and I ever even inhabited the same space, and yet we used to sleep two feet apart and occasionally share towels. How can so much change so quickly? It might take a thousand years for one inch of soil to form but it took one ejaculation to get me here.

At the door is nobody. It's the packages from Pearlmann's, which is the third interesting thing that has happened today, interesting because I had pretty much forgotten that I'd ordered them and pretty much forgotten what I'd ordered. Interesting because I have no idea what to do with any of them, starting with where to put them. I lug each box into the front hall and then push them into a corner of the living room.

After doing this, I sit down on the piano bench again, tired, a faint throbbing in my abdomen scaring me back upstairs and into bed. The smell of my body on the sheets, in the sheets, in my ratty leggings and T-shirt, is weirdly intoxicating—something between gross and good. I pull up the covers and stick my nose in my shirt and huff at myself like I used to do with my baby blanket, which I called "dodo" and which Simon took upon himself to rid me of. He said, "That thing is disgusting," yanked it from under my nose, and tossed it effortlessly up on top of the kitchen cabinets—the highest point in our house and in the world, by my seven-year-old standards. Then he laughed, shoved something in his mouth, and left, banging the back door behind him. I couldn't get my dodo and nobody got it for me. Years later, during one of her big kitchen clean-outs, my mother found it, coated in dust. She asked me if I wanted it, and when I said yes, she said no, that it was too filthy and it was time to get rid of it. I felt too much shame to put up a fight, but I cried as bitterly that night as I had three years before.

I wake up to a darkening room, surprised at having been asleep. I hear the sound of muffled movement in the hall and then a soft knock on my door.

"Come in."

"How do you feel?" my father asks. He is carrying a box.

"I'm okay, I think."

"There are a lot of boxes downstairs. I don't know if you saw."

"I meant to tell you that I ordered some stuff. Um, baby stuff, with your credit card." I sit up in bed.

"Yes," he says. "I got the statement in the mail already."

"Is it okay? I can return it to the store I think. I just...I don't...we don't have, like, anything."

"No, no, I'm glad you got what you need. It's time to start preparing. I'm actually...I'm beginning to clear out Simon's room." The knuckles on his hands holding the box are white.

"Do you need help?"

"No, no. I think you should rest. I've wanted to do this for a long time."

"What are you going to do with it all?"

He indicates the box he is holding. "I'm boxing it up, putting it in the attic. The dresser and bed and night table—I think those things can stay. I'll put different blankets on the bed. A crib can still fit. Babies get up a lot. You might like having a bed to rest in. What do you think?"

I don't feel like pretending it's not weird to put my baby in my suicided brother's room, to lie in the bed where he died.

"I think that's a good idea, Dad." The relief on his face is as real as we are. It is the realest thing in the room. I did not know he needed this so badly. Maybe he didn't know, either.

He disappears with the box, his footsteps light.

"Dad?" I call out. "Do you think there will be space for the glider?"

"What's a glider?"

Chapter 35

Dad drives me to my weekly appointments. He sits in the waiting room outside the waiting room, which is two chairs in the hallway near the elevator. We don't speak on the way to the hospital. I pee in a cup, get weighed, have my blood pressure taken, get dopplered. Dr. Lang tells me everything is fine. He tells me I must go to the hospital immediately if I have any bleeding or sudden pain or if I feel faint. I feel suspended between panic and total oblivion—each, it seems, the utmost reach of the other. During the sonogram, I find myself unable to look at the screen. I stare down at the goo on my belly and refrain, each time, from commenting on the irony of what it reminds me of.

I will be induced in three and a half weeks, five days before my due date—October 16. A Sunday. Dr. Lang offers me this date, scanning the calendar on his computer, as though I will be meeting him for coffee and not bleeding and shitting all over him.

"How does that work for you? Get you prepped around seven a.m.? I'm on call that day."

At odd intervals I find myself thinking, *Fuck you, Dr. Lang.* Not with any particular malice.

Maybe the Dr. Langs have made things easier. But it dawns on me: He needs me more than I need him. I am what he does, in order to live. He is not my father, housing me, cleaning out his other, dead child's room so that my child can have one. He is not this baby's father, with a baby's father's rights. He is a man with a job. I am a woman with a body.

In fact, I think with a weird growing pride and fascination, without my body—without my historical body—there would be no Dr. Lang, no Dr. Langs. If everything but a dirt ditch and everyone but me were erased from the earth, I would figure it out. We would figure it out. As the last people on earth, we'd become like the first people on earth, and we would get born.

Dear Mom,

You would not recognize Simon's room. Dad undertook its transformation with a fervor I've never seen in him before. I'm not sure if the terms "happy" and "sad" apply to Dad—but he seemed almost happy as he worked. Relieved, maybe. And I guess it was his lack of crying that compelled me to compensate, somehow in the universal sense of checks and balances, and at various points over those few days, as he came home from work and immediately checked on me and then began moving, packing, and most recently, painting—a soft, celestial white, the color of light reflecting off snow—to get up from my lumpy bed and walk across the room and shut the door and cry, hard but quietly.

This dear father of mine, this island that is becoming a peninsula, for me, for my sake, for the sake of this baby, this man who wants nothing more than the end of all suffering, an erasure of whatever failures inscribed him before now— nothing steadies him like duty; nothing signals love for him like utility. How could I ever find fault with him? How could you, Mom?

When I eventually do coax myself all the way inside the

room, I see hanging on a hook from the ceiling a mobile with tiny multicolored airplanes. It was Simon's, Dad told me apologetically, and later mine. "If you want, we can get rid of it." No, I told him. I love it.

I have been spending what feels like an inordinate amount of time imagining what the baby will look like, but not in a moony, tender sort of way. I'm scared for it to look like Tea Rose.

And believing in you has become a bit like believing in God.

In the name of the mother, and of the daughter, and of this wholly holey body,

Agnes

Chapter 36

Alicia calls to tell me that she has given birth to her baby girl, that she labored for nine hours until the doctor asked her if she wanted to have a cesarean section, and Mary said yes.

"I would have kept going," she tells me. "But they said my heart rate was dropping. My mom was really worried."

"How was it? The, um, surgery?" My mind is racing—that is what a cesarean section means, right? Surgery?

"Well, I didn't feel a thing. And then all the anesthesia wore off and I was just sick and sore. I'm okay now, though. Except for my boobs. Breastfeeding is super hard!"

My eye falls on a wrapped box poking out of my closet. Alicia's nightgown. I feel a wave of shame colliding with fierce kicks so low down and far back that I half wonder if the baby has mistakenly rolled into some different, uncharted cavity. For a moment I am distracted.

"Agnes?"

"Sorry—I'm here," I say. I can't think of what else to add. "I'm so happy for you," I offer feebly.

That's all Alicia needs to forge ahead. "Ellery is sooo cute, Agnes. I can't wait for you to meet her."

Again, low, deep punches. I sit up straighter in my bed, which seems to make it worse. It feels as though the baby is fully underneath me. I take a deep breath. Punch. Chop. Slice.

"Hey," I say, suddenly remembering Teeny and the shower, "when was she born?"

"Oh! September twenty-second. My friend Tessa got it right. She says she's never been wrong about these things. Crap," Alicia says as loud, frantic crying pierces through the line. "Dammit. She's up."

I hear Mary, close to the phone. "Let me take her, Alicia? Get in your chair and I'll hand her to you? I have a bottle ready just in case?"

"Agnes, I have to go. I'll call you in a little bit, okay?"

We hang up the phone. My room feels extra quiet. I wonder what my baby's cries will sound like. *Not like that,* I can't resist thinking, Ellery's screeching still ringing in my ears. Another kick, alarmingly low. What if this baby comes through the wrong hole?

I stand up slowly and walk, slowly, to the bathroom. I feel cold with terror. Suddenly I want Alicia back on the line. I want to ask her how she knew labor was starting. I want to ask how much it hurt, how much painkiller she was allowed to take. I want to ask if it is possible to call an ambulance and ask politely if they will put me under, remove the baby, and wake me when everything is clean and over. I hold the edge of the sink and clench my buttocks and try to take some deep breaths. *I'm changing my mind,* I think. *I'm changing my mind. I'm changing my mind. People are allowed to change their minds.*

I think about sitting on the toilet to try to relieve some of the intense pressure, but I'm afraid of what might come out. Cautiously, I walk to Simon's room. On the bed is a package of newborn diapers that were not there yesterday, along with a tube of diaper cream and a few packages of disposable wipes. I sit on the bed, the items sidling toward me from my weight, the diapers practically crawling onto my lap. I look around the clean, white, hushed room, which feels like a mirrored reflection of my mind. *I belong here,* I think. *I belong here.* For a moment I consider moving to the glider, seeing the view from there, but I can't bring myself to do it. I haven't sat in it yet, and it feels as right of a superstition as any at this point, to wait until the baby comes. Without thinking too much, I open the package of diapers. I stack them neatly in the empty drawer of the bedside table, along with the wipes and cream. I get a clean towel from the Pink Bathroom and lay it on the bed, as a place to change the baby.

My blood feels warm. I want to do more. When Dad gets home that evening, I am vacuuming my room, having already done the baby's room. I opened the windows in there and in my own room. I am wearing a tank top with no bra, my sweatshirt a pilly mound on the unmade bed, my bed that has not been made in weeks. I don't hear Dad come in, and I don't hear him tell me to turn off the vacuum, but I do hear the silence following the cord being yanked from the wall by his hand.

"Agnes! You're supposed to be in bed! And why are all the windows open? You're going to get a cold!"

I know I look crude in my thin top, my big breasts and belly barely concealed. I know I smell ripe and worried, exactly how I feel. But for a split second it feels good to pretend that my father is some other person, another man who loves me, and he has come home not because he had to but because he wanted to, and he has found me stooped and manic, not his college dropout daughter but the almost-mother of his almost-child. In a flash I grasp the edge of that fantasy, and just as quickly it succumbs to a present moment made even sadder and more humiliating for the contrast. In that narrowest of windows, I saw why people do on purpose what I have done by mistake.

· · ·

At my appointment the following week, Dr. Lang tells me I am 3 centimeters dilated and 40 percent effaced. He tells me this after sticking something inside of me with surprising force. I lift off the table in pain.

"Sorry about that," he says, handing me a tissue and washing his hands.

"What does that mean?" I ask, still on my back. I use the tissue—meant, I suppose, to catch the lubricant that will fall out of me when I stand up to get dressed—for my nose, now dripping. I am tired of the wetness of my body.

"It means," he says, drying his hands one finger at a time, "that you're coming along. We should be in good shape for your induction. You are still what I'd consider preeclamptic, but there's slightly less protein in your urine, and your blood pressure has come down a bit."

I prop myself up on my forearms and dangle my feet from the stirrups. It's difficult to be casual from this position. "I read somewhere that preeclampsia is caused by 'maternal-fetal conflict.' Does that mean my body is turning against the baby?" I read this in the *P* volume of Funk & Wagnalls encyclopedia that I'd asked Dad to bring upstairs the other day, along with *C*, where I'd read the five-page entry on childbirth. I fell asleep that night, having read widely in both volumes, wondering why people bother reading other books, why books besides encyclopedias even exist.

Dr. Lang looks at me like I'm a child, and I immediately feel like a child. "We don't really know what causes preeclampsia. There are a lot of theories but nothing definitive." He offers his delicate hand and I sit all the way up, keeping the paper cover close around my lower half. "So, assuming nothing unforeseen happens, we'll see you back here in a few days and get this party started."

"Um, okay. Sounds good."

"I'll let you get dressed. Take care, Agnes." He turns back just before leaving. "By the way, have you taken any classes?"

I must look confused because he quickly adds, "You know, childbirth classes? Breastfeeding? CPR?"

I shake my head. "I, um, well, I've mostly been in bed."

Dr. Lang laughs, a harsh *ha*. "Right, true. Before that, though? Did it occur to you to—"

I must look a certain way because Dr. Lang stops speaking, clears his throat. "You'll be fine. Are there any questions that I can answer?"

I hold the paper sheet tighter around me. "Yes." I look him in the eye. "Just one, really. What exactly is going to happen?"

Another *ha*. "Well, you probably remember some stuff from biology class, right?" I can tell he regrets his last-minute due diligence. "Every birth is different." He shrugs. "We will let you know everything that we're doing before we do it, and we'll do our best to keep you as comfortable as possible. The rest is up to you."

"Okay," I say, hoisting myself off the table, my lower half exposed for a brief second before Dr. Lang hastily exits, the door clunking shut behind him.

The next evening, I am distracted by how I smell. I take a shower, despite having taken one this morning. Standing under the hot water, I feel increased pressure in my abdomen, squeezes of pain that have come and gone over the past couple of weeks. It is as though an invisible belt is being tightened around me, slackening just as I feel I might pop. I have a vague idea that these are contractions, but aside from them, my body feels the same.

My belly button looks grotesque. How strange, I think, that it was once an opening, a portal into my mother. I soap and resoap my belly, fascinated by the shallow, creased circle that used to be a real dent. I look at my crisscrossing veins, extra blue in the pinkish light of the bathroom. What was that joke we used to love to say on the playground? "Your epidermis is showing! Your epidermis is showing!" Unbelievable that this same skin is now the baby's outer layer. That if I just dug inside a few inches, there it would be.

I stop soaping and squat down in the tub, the hot water on my back the only form of touch I can handle these days. What poetic irony, that each of us comes into the world attached to another and then immediately gets severed. All of us, walking around, cut off from our mothers, all with the same mark to prove it, the tunnel that connected us closed up and filled with skin.

As I stand back up, holding on to the tiled-in soap dish, I feel something softly come out of me. In the tub between my feet is a snot-colored mass the size of the small bar of soap I'd just been using. *What happened to the soap?* is my first thought. Bending down to get a closer look, I see that it is something that has something to do with my body, which has everything to do with the baby, and watching the water swirl around it, whitish and jellyfish like, I begin to fear that the worst is happening, right now, in my shower, that the baby's brain has somehow oozed out of me, and soon the rest of the baby will follow in haphazard pieces.

I push the thing toward the drain with my foot and, reviled by how it feels, gag after it. I get out of the shower, wrap myself in a towel, and walk unsteadily to my room. I lie on my bed, damp and cold and terrified. I wait for the next dreadful thing to happen. I wait and wait. I'm scared to move, so I stay still on my wet towel. My dad calls up the stairs to ask if I need anything. I force myself to say no, I'm fine. I hear him start the dishwasher and lock the doors. I hear him walk past my room and down the hall to his room. The house goes completely quiet, except for the screaming panic in my head.

I try to write a letter in my head, to calm down, but I keep switching back and forth between addressing Mom and addressing the baby. *Dear Mom, what is happening?* **DEAR BABY, WHAT IS HAPPENING?** *Dear Mom, tell me what I should do.* **DEAR BABY, ARE YOU STILL IN THERE?**

Eventually, I must fall asleep, because I wake up shivering with cold and in dire need of the toilet. I stand up carefully and hang my towel over a chair. I find my robe in the dark and put it on and walk across the hall to the bathroom. I pee. I brush my teeth. I feel better, calmer; I wonder if maybe I dreamed the whole thing in the shower. I fix my matted, damp hair into a loose braid and take a few relieved deep breaths, checking, as I breathe, for any strange sensations. There are none. Back in my room, I put on sweatpants and a T-shirt and, feeling not quite sleepy, decide to read. My bed is wet, so I stand beside it, holding an encyclopedia, unsure of what to do, before deciding to sleep in the baby's room. *The baby's room* is exactly how it occurs to me—not Simon's room.

Just as I reach the room, I feel an enormous pressure between my legs, and then a pop, and then wetness. I think, *Well, this is great. I've somehow, despite having just gone to the bathroom, peed my pants,* but the wetness seems to have nothing to do with my bladder, and there is suddenly more of it, and then still more. Fear overcomes me, the same fear from the shower, and I stand frozen, dripping God knows what on the hallway carpet. I recall a long-ago soap opera episode, watched in secret when I was home sick once from school, where a pregnant woman stood in a puddle of her own water before being rushed to the hospital. The memory soothes me somewhat. *This is supposed to happen,* I tell myself. I drop the encyclopedia and walk stiffly to my parents' room, hesitating outside the closed door as I've done so many times before. How many minutes of my life spent hovering outside their room, and what on earth does that mean? Finally, I make myself knock and open the door. As my eyes adapt to a new shade of darkness, I can make out my father's shape in the bed. He is sleeping on his back, his hands clasped over his middle, like an arranged corpse. My mother's side of the bed remains taut.

I hover over him. "Dad. Dad?" His eyes flutter open.

"I think I need to go to the hospital. I'm, um, all wet."

He flies out of bed. "Okay, okay. Are you all right?" He rubs his face as though trying to see me better.

"I feel fine I think. I don't know. I'm not really sure what's happening."

"Let me get dressed. Why don't you change your clothes? Can you do that? Maybe put a few things in a bag? I will meet you downstairs in five minutes." He rushes into their bathroom and closes the door.

The clock on his nightstand says 2:11 a.m. Back in my room, I strip off my clothes and pat myself dry with them before throwing them in the hamper. I put on underwear, a tank top, clean sweatpants, and a soft sweater. I slip into my Doc Martens but can't fathom bending down to tie the laces. I'm aware that I must look slightly deranged. Into a bag I put more underwear, socks, a hairbrush, another shirt. I see the wrapped box—Alicia's present—in my closet and impulsively tear into it and shove the nightgown in my bag. I look around my room, suddenly desperate for something else to bring along, a rabbit's foot or some other amulet, but finding nothing, I go downstairs. Dad is already there.

As we drive in the dark, Dad's knuckles on the steering wheel look almost fluorescent. At one red light, a wave of pain doubles me over—pain like the worst cramps I've ever had but more sinister. I hug my belly and try to breathe. I arch up out of my seat, trying to hoist myself out of the pain. At the next red light, I feel completely fine. Dad's face looks desperate but he keeps his eyes straight ahead. Another surge of pain hits as we arrive at the hospital, and again, I picture myself clawing out of my body, which feels not like a body but like a fanged and barbed monster, a torture machine. Dad parks the car and the agony lifts. Nobody told me that labor would be so schizophrenic. Then again, I sheepishly realize as we enter the hospital, I was pretty resolute about not asking.

It feels strange to walk into the emergency room. A few people are in the waiting room. Nobody looks to be in excruciating pain.

"My daughter is beginning to have labor," Dad blurts awkwardly to the woman behind the Plexiglas. She looks at me. "How far apart are your contractions, dear?"

I draw a blank. Am I supposed to know this? Why is math always trying to sneak into my life? "I'm not sure. I had two on my way over here. We live about fifteen minutes away." *She's the one not in labor,* I think. *Let her figure it out.*

"Okay. I'm going to send you two up to maternity. They'll get you settled there. Do you know where you're going?"

"Yes," Dad and I say at the same time. Which is funny considering that we have, generally speaking, no idea where we're going. On the seventh floor, I am given some paperwork to fill out. Midway through, I have another contraction, and somehow, knowing what to call it now—a contraction, something I'd previously believed only happens when you're lying down in a hospital bed—makes it slightly less scary, if no less painful.

A nurse leads Dad and me to a room. There is a hospital gown and an oddly shaped plastic bottle on the bed. She tells me to get undressed in the adjoining bathroom. "You might want to use the enema too."

For what feels like the twelfth time today, I get undressed. I use the toilet. I contemplate trying out the enema but feel queasy at the thought. When I come back into the room, Dad is sitting on a built-in bench near the window, staring at the ground.

I get into the bed. The nurse works on me silently, taking my blood pressure, hooking me up to a monitor. She tells me she needs to take some blood. I nod, not knowing why or what this means, amazed by how docile I am, by the docility that hospitals seem to manufacture. If she had told me she needed a part of my frontal lobe, I might also have nodded. I have another contraction as she is drawing out my blood, and the needle slips out, and she holds my arm roughly as I quake in pain and she jabs around, trying to refind the vein. It slips out again and she tries two, three more times, before getting it in.

"Sorry," she says, "that's going to be a big bruise."

I stare at her pale, impassive face, feeling almost impressed by her unconcern. I could be anyone, or no one, or everyone. I don't matter. She is performing her job on my body, which would seem, by her demeanor, to have nothing to do with my person. After taking what feels like a gallon of my blood, she tells me that the doctor will be in soon.

"Is it Dr. Lang?"

"No," she says. "Dr. Lang is off tonight. You'll be with Dr. Howard."

"Dad," I say when she leaves the room. "You okay?"

He comes over to the bed. He looks confused. "Yes, of course. Are you? How do you feel?"

"I'm fine right now. Until the next go-round."

The door opens and Dr. Howard strides in. She is Dr. Lang's opposite—a tall robust black woman with shiny magenta lips.

"Dr. Howard," she says, taking my hand. "You ready to have a baby?"

I start to reply and have a contraction instead. They seem to be happening faster. "You're okay. Try to breathe through it. That's good. You're okay." I realize that I am gripping Dr. Howard's hand. She pats my back firmly with her other hand. My dad stands near the bed awkwardly. *Of all his awkward days,* I think, trying not to writhe, wanting to spare him the distress of seeing me writhe, *this is his most awkward day.*

"I want to check your cervix. If you want an epidural, now would be the time to get one."

"Will it hurt?" I ask.

Dr. Howard smiles. "There will be some pain and pressure, yes. But it's nothing compared to squeezing out a baby without one. Given your preeclampsia, we do not want a drawn out and unnecessarily painful labor, so I'd recommend it. I think Dr. Lang would agree. Says here your induction was scheduled for midweek next week—you beat him to it!"

"I'll get one. An epidural."

"Good. I'm going to take a peek at the baby too." She turns to

Dad. "Hello," then, looking at me, "do you want your—friend?—here in the room?"

"I'm her father," my dad says at the same time that I say, "He's my dad." He looks like he wants to hurl himself into the sealed window, less to escape than to knock himself unconscious.

"I think probably, um, outside—right, Dad?"

Dad nods, turns to go, then fumbles back toward me. We both wince—me as another wave of pain begins and him as he kisses my head briefly before bolting out the door.

Dear Mom,

Here's what I remember:

Dr. Howard checking my cervix, which set off a contraction so powerful I temporarily went blind. A nurse—the same one as before—coming in to say there was a problem at the lab, and she needed to draw more blood before the anesthesiologist could give me an epidural. Me, shuddering in the aftermath of the contraction as the nurse sought out a vein yet again. The doctor telling me I was 9 centimeters dilated and the baby would be born sometime this morning, possibly before sunrise. Me, crying and asking for water. Not getting any water. Dr. Howard in the room, Dr. Howard leaving the room, two more nurses in the room, both of them women—girls—who looked barely older than me. I held and clawed the hands of one of them during a contraction that was so bad I felt I was actually ripping in half.

A handsome, sullen man coming in—the anesthesiologist—and telling me to sit up, hunch over, and stay completely still. Me, crying harder at his request as another contraction shredded through my ass and spine. One nurse holding me from the front, trying to keep me steady, as another one tried to brace me from the back, and the man repeating, "Hold still, hold still," as he jammed what felt like a screwdriver into my lower back. Me crying and shrieking, shrieking and crying, burying my face in the nurse, repeating "I can't, I can't, I fucking can't," like some kind of Little Engine That Couldn't. The nurse behind me murmuring, "She's 10 centimeters," and Dr. Howard's voice ringing out like a field hockey coach, "Agnes, it's time to start pushing," and me asking what does that mean, and what felt like every three seconds a new contraction pummeling me, so that the moments in between felt like cruelty more than relief.

Beeping from machines. One of the kind nurses wiping my face and telling me how great I was doing. I felt as though I were mutating into Pain Itself. Then she told me that when it came time to push, to do it as though I were emptying my bowels. This is what life is. A shitting.

I heard Dr. Howard's voice coming in and out. At one point the beeping was long and loud and her voice was almost entirely drowned out. And then it pealed—"time to push, honey, push for ten seconds, hard as you can"—and I focused on her beautiful shiny lips and shiny eyeglasses and took a deep breath and pushed like I was trying to disappear, like I was trying to rid myself of myself through myself. It hurt so badly that I wondered why anyone bothers with the epidural at all. It hurt in a medieval way—as in, how can we have skyscrapers and computers and this degree of pain? The nurse told me to hang in there, that the epidural would start working soon, and then that I had progressed quickly and the epidural had come too late.

I pushed and pushed, whenever they told me to push. I pushed for a long time. At some point the sky outside the window grayed and then pinkened, and I could notice it because the epidural did, in fact, start working, and the pain became more storied—I knew it was happening but it wasn't happening to me, or something like that. At another moment I felt the need to go to the bathroom and I think I probably did. I kept turning my head to look at the sky, getting bluer, and I heard Dr. Howard say, "This is it, last push. I can see the head," and I pushed with the dark force of everything I've ever wanted in my life, as though it wasn't just the baby I could make emerge but every single wish, hidden and unhidden—your return, Simon's return, Dad's happiness, my own happiness, immortality for all of us, a better life for each of us—fulfilled. When I opened my eyes, that sky was bluer than a sky should be, and the room was filled with an otherworldly yowling and the cheers of Dr. Howard and the nurses.

"A boy, and he's perfect," Dr. Howard said, putting him on me, his face a squashed mask of alarm, his eyes squeezing shut against the light, the commotion, the indignities of being forced into this bizarre, nonviscous world. "You have a son."

I started crying and couldn't stop. I cried so much I soaked the baby, who had found my breast and gone quiet and busy with it. I cried so that I could barely see him, but what I saw through my tears was a face I somehow knew from the depths of me, a déjà vu face, as if from a dream I'd forgotten until that moment. Is this what it means, I wondered, when something is your own, when something belongs only to you? His eyelashes, the matted clump of dark hair on his head, his very intense little expressions—all of it was just astonishing to me, overwhelming beyond anything I've ever felt. When the nurses asked if they could take him to be weighed and cleaned up, I said okay, because I had no fight left in me, and because, honestly, I was afraid. Afraid that somehow all of this feeling would crush him.

The hours since then have been a blur. He doesn't have a name yet. I'm scared to name him, to mess him up with a name. It seems he should just be able to be Mine, and His Own, and not, say, Jack. He is 8 pounds, 4 ounces, and 21 inches long. I am sitting in my bright hospital room, propped up on pillows with two ice packs underneath me, and he is here on the bed with me, swaddled and still between my legs. There is not one part of me that isn't sore, but somehow I don't feel it, or I feel it but I've been expanded enough to feel past it.

Dr. Lang came to see me a little while ago and seemed almost miffed that things had gone on without him. He was courteous and curtly congratulatory. Nothing is bothering me. Everyone keeps telling me to try and get some rest. I'm not tired.

I am apparently pretty torn up down below. What nobody probably tells you is that babies seem to come more out of your ass than your vagina. At least that's how it felt. Dr. Howard stitched me up, and the nurses have been plying me with stool softeners and pain medicine. I take all of it. I'm taking everything in. I feel incapable of saying no or feeling no. These wonderful fairies called lactation nurses have flitted in and out, holding my son to my breast, massaging my breasts, showing me the proper way to get him latched. They say my milk hasn't come in yet, but still he sucks happily, greedily, his eyes opening briefly before rolling shut again, as if in ecstasy. I'm stunned by this new ability, to soothe and sate someone so completely, with so little effort. How can mothers not feel superhuman?

Dad seems about ready to fall apart. He didn't want to hold the baby, which I think I understand. I don't know if I'd want to if I were him, if I were anyone but me. He looked at him for a long time, his eyes filled with what looked like love and anguish. Finally he said, "He looks like you," and squeezed my hand.

I did have Dr. Howard circumcise him. I don't like to think of the pain it caused him, but I also don't like to think about uncircumcised dicks. I had an experience with one once, and I didn't like it. I know that's entirely weird and subjective but the thought of some person far off in the future not enjoying any part of this boy bothered me more than allowing him to be cut. I'd just been cut, so it makes sense for us to heal together.

Dad stayed until just a little while ago, when I made him go home and get rest. He sat in a chair near my bed, leaning in to look at the baby, or pretending to, and when I'd try to nurse, he'd leap up to go stand by the windows, looking out.

A pediatrician is supposed to come look at the baby tomorrow morning, and provided everything looks as it should, we will be discharged. The two of us will go home to begin our new lives together—his new because he is literally hours old, and mine new because of him. I keep thinking about baptism. Probably because he feels like a baptism.

The absolute strangest part of all of this is that I'm not scared. I will never be alone again.

Finally,
Agnes

Chapter 37

I don't mind the wheelchair the hospital makes me take down to the ground floor while Dad goes to get the car. He'd come to my room first to hand me the car seat.

"Do you know how it works?"

"I'll figure it out," I said. "Thank you."

I adjusted the straps and gently propped my sleeping son inside. His eyes fluttered open, and for a few seconds, he stared hard at me, the room, his foot. His eyes darting and lingering, until he closed them again, as if worn out from the effort. It took a few attempts, but I managed to maneuver the straps and buckle him in securely, his tiny body encased in plastic like a baby turtle in a too-large shell. I put on his hospital cap and hospital socks and covered him with his hospital blanket. An orderly wheeled me downstairs and outside, and a nurse held the car seat. "He's precious," she said to me.

"I know," I told her. "Thanks."

She hugged me goodbye and I hugged her back, hard. Martha. She'd been administering to the both of us for the past forty-eight hours with immense care, and I felt a lump in my throat as we parted ways. How peculiar, I think as I latch my baby into the car seat base that Dad must have installed, then strap myself in beside him, how intimacy has nothing to do with time. How you can feel bonded to someone in a matter of moments, if that person allows it. How you can spend years with someone—I look at Dad's profile—and only ever remain adjacent. I remember how we were told in high school that there were certain SAT questions that you can effectively not answer and not be penalized for not answering, and I think, well, that is Dad's idea of love in a nutshell. He would rather not answer than answer wrong. His biggest fear seems to be losing points, and you can't lose points if you don't hazard a guess. Dad turns on the classical station. I recognize the Mozart sonata, one I learned to play during my final year taking lessons. I tap imaginary keys on my lap.

"I've heard that babies like classical music," Dad says.

I try not to smile, but I smile. I'm not going to ask him where he "heard" this from, because I know he didn't hear it anywhere. I know he is trying to be with me, on my side, a father. A grandfather. We pull into the garage. My father turns around to me in the dim light. "Welcome home," he says in a voice that can only be described as weird.

"Thanks!" I try to be sunny.

The house smells different. The dryer is whirring but the smell is not laundry. My son remains asleep as I nestle him against my shoulder and ascend the stairs to the kitchen. In my mind I am narrating to him each new scene: *This is a house. This is your new home. This is a washing machine. These are stairs. This is a door,* rhythmically, like some kind of lullaby. I feel uneasy, a fist of pain undulating down low, and I'm unable to separate my physical sensations from my emotional ones. Ahead of me in the kitchen, Dad is turning on lights, putting on the kettle.

"Can I make you some tea?"

"Um, sure, thanks." The smell persists. The pain deepens. I want to sit down in the glider, at last, with this baby. To feel what it feels like.

"I'm going to change his diaper. I'll be back in a minute," I say to my dad.

My dad gives me a long, inscrutable look. I step out of the

kitchen and shift the baby a little. *These are more stairs. This is more carpet. This is a handrail. This is wallpaper.* I move slowly, concentrating on my feet.

Midway up the stairs, I look up.

Standing at the top is my mother.

Chapter 38

She is wearing the yellow dress and the red shoes but not the red belt. The absence of it makes the dress look completely different, almost frumpy. Pinned to the dress, over her heart, is a gigantic button that says #1 GRANDMA. The strange smell rolls off of her, the way the smell of the sea rolls off the sea. The smell is strange because it is her smell, but it does not match the smell in my memory of her. I manage not to drop the baby or fall down, although in my mind, I'm doing both those things—falling, falling, my baby slipping from my grasp, along with my vision of us gliding serenely in the nursery, cocooned from all harm.

"Agnes. Look at you."

I can't look at me. I can't stop looking at her. I climb the rest of the way up the stairs and we stand facing each other in the narrow hallway, her back toward my bedroom and mine toward the Pink Bathroom. Something in her energy makes me draw the baby closer.

"You came back. Where have you been?" I manage to speak, to make words, but my voice sounds mangled.

My mother shakes her head. "Not important. We can discuss all of it later. May I—for now—hold my grandson?" She steps toward me hopefully. "I just washed my hands. It's important to wash your hands every time you touch an infant."

I don't know what to do. To refuse seems harsh, punitive—and yet. "Sure," I say finally, handing him to her. She cradles him, cooing softly, her eyes going slightly moist.

"What is his name?" she asks, without looking up.

"I don't know yet. I'm still waiting for it to come to me."

"He looks so much like Simon," she says, touching one finger to his chin. "Simon is a good name. I've always thought so. I still think so." She looks at me. "It's yours to use if you want it, you know."

"Thanks," I say, the knot in my stomach getting pulled tighter and tighter, fibers fraying. "I don't think I'll be naming him Simon, though."

I hold out my hands. "I was going to change him, see if he needs to eat again."

My mother looks at me, her face open but unreadable. "Would you like me to do it? Change him I mean?"

"That's okay. I kind of need the practice." I try to laugh, but the words just sound rueful.

My mother puts the baby back into my arms and the pulling in my stomach eases slightly.

"You've really changed," she says, and walks down the stairs.

Alone in the nursery, I close the door and sit in the glider with my son. I wipe my clammy hands across the back of his swaddle to try to dry them and then feel guilty and use my pants. I have a strong, solitary desire to not leave this room, to somehow figure out how I can make it habitable for the two of us. A small refrigerator could fit on the dresser. The baby twists his tiny head to and fro and begins to cry, a shy bleat that becomes a throaty wail faster than I can unbutton my shirt. My breasts ache terribly, and as I try to connect the baby's desperate mouth to my nipple, the pain becomes so acute that I cry out. A moment later there is a knock.

"Do you need help?" My mother's voice seems like it's coming from inside the room.

"No. We're fine. Thanks."

After a few minutes, I hear her footsteps descending the stairs. I switch the baby to my other breast. He is quiet now and seems to be working very hard for what must be mere milliliters. His brow is furrowed. I wish for floodgates to open and wash us both away, away from here.

I doze some with the baby. When I open my eyes, the room is dim. The sun has set. I'm thirsty and stiff from being in the same position, my top still unbuttoned. A moment before I feel his exquisitely painful latch, I hear little suckling noises—as though by making them he causes the breast to appear. His mouth goes slack after a minute or two. He does not open his eyes. I feel the pull of his world, the world of sleep and comfort, sleep only interrupted by discomfort, and I want to enter it alongside him.

The house is quiet. I get up slowly and turn on the bedside lamp. Carefully, I unswaddle my son—his arms boing upward as if on springs, those little gates in a pinball game—and grab a clean diaper. As I'm reaching for the wipes, a spray of pee hits me in the face, and as soon as I clean myself off, it happens again. I get another wipe and hold it at the ready. He sighs and stops wriggling, closes his eyes. Finally I get him changed; then I rewrap him and place him in his crib. I marvel at the swift return of his sleep, the profound simplicity of his needs.

Downstairs, the light over the stove is the only one on. A plate wrapped in foil sits next to the sink. Mom and Dad are in the den watching the news, the light from the TV making them look superimposed, two-dimensional. They sit next to one another on the couch, their hands close but not touching.

"Are you hungry?" Dad calls out. "There's a plate for you there. Chicken."

"I saw. Thanks."

I get a glass and fill it with ice, and then with water. I drain it in big freezing gulps and enjoy the ensuing cold headache. I fill up the glass again and drink it just as quickly. My thirst feels bottomless. I don't know how to be in this house, this house that refuses to not be impossible. I was just starting to figure it out, to at least glimpse a future in which I could glimpse a day when I might have a firmer sense of things, a life, a life furnished with appropriate and not insurmountable feelings, a life of safety and peace for my child, a life with at least one important thing figured out. I did not know how but I believed in a how. Now that belief feels hollow, stillborn.

My mother has returned, and I am disappearing.

I eat the food because I am hungry. I eat standing at the counter, since sitting down seems too much like forgiveness. It is my mom's cooking, and the taste of it fills me with a kind of fermented joy, a pleasure that's gone acidic from too much shelf time. I keep thinking, *Where was this food when I needed it the most?*

I put the plate in the dishwasher and go upstairs. I wash my face and brush my teeth and put on Alicia's nightgown. It stretches over my still-swollen belly and breasts and makes me feel indecent, doubly so for having stolen it from her. *Oh well,* I think. We can't always do the right thing, or we don't always want to. I put a robe on over it and go back downstairs. My mother, my father tells me, has gone to bed. He is watching the nature channel, a program about the African savanna. I have the odd sense that the African savanna is 75 percent of the nature channel's programming, that we have all, all of us in the entire universe, seen it before.

Sitting on the edge of the couch, I ask quietly, "So what's the deal?"

Dad glances at me. On the TV, a lion is taking down a zebra—that old scene. "With what? Your mother coming home? Isn't it great?"

"But where has she been? And why has she been gone so long? And what made her come back? And how much have you known about all of this?" There are questions upon questions. Now that I've started asking, I'm not sure I will be able to stop. I want to peel everything back to the very beginning, to the beginning that predates me, to the beginning before the beginning. I have just had a baby, and I feel I deserve certain answers, certain answers about origins.

"Mostly she has been at Ingrid's old place. She likes it there. She wants to keep up the place, and she's good at that sort of thing," Dad says matter-of-factly, as though what's at issue is my mother's prospects as a property manager.

"Why didn't you just tell me? Why the secret?"

Dad looks at me. He looks tired. On the screen, an elephant munches grass sullenly, his tail whipping the flies around, as opposed to away. "Agnes, it's complicated. I'm sure she'll tell you in time. She didn't want to bother you with it—she barely wanted to bother me with it. She just needed some time. Some time away from . . . everything."

"But do you have any idea what I've been through? The worry? The wondering? Not to mention, I really kind of needed her this year!" I am crying now, which I thought I was too angry to do.

Dad shuts the TV off. We sit in near-darkness. I wipe my nose with my sleeve.

"I'm sorry, Agnes. I know it must have been difficult for you. It was difficult for me, too, believe me. But we have to also think what's best for your mom. She's been through a lot."

"How has she been through more than we have?"

Dad is quiet.

"The important thing," he says, after a minute of what seems like careful deliberating, "is that we're all here together. I would think you'd be happier. Mom is so excited to help you with the baby. The baby is the whole reason she came back. Doesn't that mean something to you?"

It seems as though he really wants an answer. I try to decide. "I don't know," I say honestly. "I don't know anything. I feel like I've been . . . lied to, like you've been lying, this whole time. How often did you guys talk? Why didn't she ever want to talk to me?"

Dad rubs his eyes. "She called me once a week or so, at work.

She always asked about you first. She feels a lot of guilt, Agnes. But...she just...she needed to...get well first—before she could, you know, be here. Once you left for school, I think she allowed herself to fall apart in a way she couldn't before."

"But why is her falling apart more important than ours? We've all fallen apart! And she—and you—both of you, have made it even worse for me!"

Dad touches my hand, wet with tears. "Maybe one day you'll understand. Life isn't fair—you know that as well as anyone. Your mom took what she needed, Agnes. At some point, we all do."

I imagine leaving my baby. I imagine my baby killing himself. I cry harder.

"You've been through a lot"—that phrase again—"in the last forty-eight hours. Why don't you get some rest? Things will feel better in the morning."

I feel like I could collapse under the featherweight of Dad's sad attempts at consolation, the tired dictums, the futility of it all. I feel newly abandoned—abandoned by this unabandoning. I feel like a husk, and—catching a glimpse of Dad's face as I leave the room— like a daughter of husks.

I get into bed in the nursery. Simon's bed. I think about how two months ago, a month ago, I could not have conceived of it. Now it is a place to sleep where I can be near the baby. What must Simon think of any of this.

The baby stirs as I begin to doze off. In a flash I am beside him, lifting him from the crib. I sit in the glider and we glide. I nurse him on my left side and feel a thorny surge on my right. In a moment, my nightgown is soaked. After he falls asleep again, I lay him in his crib and tiptoe down to my room, where I peel off my nightgown. I find the stretchy bra I'd worn in the hospital and put it on, stuffing a maxi pad in each side. I didn't realize that when my milk came in, my milk would come out. I put on different pajamas and go back to Simon's bed.

The next time I wake up is not to a baby's cry. I feel a disturbance of air, movement somewhere in the room. I feel electrically awake. Propping myself up on my elbows, I can make out the outline of my mother in the glider, the bundle of my baby cradled in her arms.

I stand up. My breasts are heavy and the front of my bra feels waterlogged. "What are you doing?" I whisper. A tingling moves through me, as in the moments of waking up from a bad dream. Here, now, I feel I am waking into one.

"He was crying," my mother whispers back. "I thought you could use some sleep."

"He was not crying. I would have heard him."

"He did cry. Sort of a whimper, off and on for several minutes."

"He didn't whimper. He didn't cry. Why are you in here?"

"I'm telling you, he was starting to get upset. It's not good to let them work up to a big cry when they're this young. I want you to be able to rest whenever you need to. That's why I'm here."

I stand in front of them. My mother continues to glide, just barely grazing my foot. "Go back to bed," she says. "He's fine now."

"I need to feed him."

"He doesn't need to eat. He's asleep again. You should go back to sleep. He just needed to be held."

"I need to feed him, for me. My boobs kill."

My mother makes a sound in her nose, as though trying to decide if she believes me. I feel a cross between fury and fear. "Please give him to me."

Bending forward, my mother kisses the baby's face and whispers something to him I can't make out. She looks at me and shrugs. "Here. Take him."

I gather him from her and bring him to the bed, not wanting to sit in any spot made warm by her body. I place him on the bed and he wriggles his head like an earthworm.

My mother pauses at the door. "How about a hug?"

I put a pillow on either side of the baby, even though I know he can't move. I don't want to hug her. For over a year I have wanted nothing more than to hug her. From that place—that memory of wanting her, needing her—I move toward her and we embrace. She feels small, smaller than me, with my protruding flesh and leaking systems. I try to feel what I should be feeling but am more preoccupied with the sense that I am sullying her. "I know you're mad," she whispers near my ear. "Dad told me. I hope that one day you understand. I think you will."

Chapter 39

The next morning, I feel a fuzzy sense of wanting to start again somehow, to set things to rights. In the shower, where my breasts respond to the hot water by leaking milk down my body, I resolve to call Alicia, to ask how she's doing, to tell her about my son. Maybe I'll even tell her about the nightgown, and we can laugh about it. I'll try to be happier, less paralyzed, around Mom and Dad. I'm the one who got pregnant and had a baby, I tell myself. It's not as though there's a codified way for everyone to act. We're all in it together, figuring out our new lives in light of this new life.

When I go to check on the baby, I discover my mother in there, bent over his crib. When she straightens up, she is smiling. "I can't believe how much he looks like Simon. They have the same jaw and nose. The eyes are debatable. Have you given any more thought to his name?" All of my goodwill from the shower dissipates. "No. And I'm definitely not going to name him Simon."

"Simon is an excellent name for a boy."

I feel that there is nowhere in the house for me to be. I want to run but my sore body won't let me, and what would I do with the baby even if I could? I realize I do not have a stroller, the discovery hitting me like a rebuke—*what kind of ill-prepared inadequate mother doesn't have a stroller?* I feel stuck in my body, stuck in the house, stuck in a swarm of silence. I reach for the baby to feel calm. Late in the morning I dress him in the warmest clothes I bought for him, double swaddle him in two blankets, and secure a tiny cap on his head. My father is at work and my mother is in the attic. I put on sneakers and my coat and take my baby outside. Holding him close to me, I walk.

The air is crisp and feels like a balm—I wish for it to enter me at every hole. My son opens his eyes and for a moment, the clear blue sky is reflected in them. On doorsteps are pumpkins; strewn across bushes are fake cobwebs. It is the season of ghosts and candy— my favorite. I dressed as a gypsy for four Halloweens in a row and wore the same bohemian skirt and flowing top borrowed from my mother, pinned clumsily at the hems, each year. The most exciting part of the costume were the fingernails—Lee Press-on Nails, long and with the slightest curl, that I painted blood red.

I turn down a street I haven't been on in years and remember a childhood classmate whose mother was rumored to be a gypsy. The rumor, I think, was started by her daughter. She would invite us over to look at her mother's crystal ball, which was kept in a box on the living room mantel and looked, now that I think about it, a lot like a snow globe. I wasn't as impressed with the idea of telling fortunes as I was with the idea of living nowhere, of wandering.

I walk until I feel calm. I touch the baby's cheek and it is chilly. I press him closer to me and we make our way back home. When I open the front door, I am greeted by large boxes in the hallway and piles of clothes on the floor.

"I was getting so worried," my mother says, stepping over and around stuff as she comes toward us. "It's too cold for him to be outside. Let me warm him up."

I don't give her the baby. I try changing the subject. "What is all this stuff?"

"Baby stuff! Clothes and toys, stuffed animals, some books. Simon's mostly. I tried to find yours, too, but it must be somewhere else."

I don't ask where else it could be. There's nowhere else in this house it could be.

. . .

A few days later, there is a moment where this returned mother becomes my mother, returned. I am in my room, attempting to exercise, using two dumbbells I found in the garage. I have been occasionally seized by the fear that my body will never resemble its former shape. I don't really know how to exercise. I'm lifting one dumbbell to my shoulder and then back down, counting to ten, when I hear a low knock. I shove the dumbbells under my bed.

"Come in."

My mother comes in and shyly puts two objects on my desk. "I just remembered a couple of things that really helped me after I had your brother and you," she says. She holds up a maxi pad, unwrapped. "I soaked this in witch hazel and put it in the freezer for a bit. Put it in your underwear. I know it sounds strange but it really helps."

"Oh. Okay. I'll try it." The other fear I have occasionally been seized by is that my ass and vagina, which seem now curiously fused into one throbbing muddle, will never stop hurting.

"And this is . . . well, basically it's a corset. But it's elastic." She holds up a wide beige band with Velcro running down one side. "You wrap it around yourself and wear it under your clothes. It's supposed to sort of push everything back into place. Come here," she says. "I'll help you."

Maybe it's because I've wanted to hear those words—*I'll help you*—for so long, that I walk over to her and allow her to push my shirt up and my sweatpants down. She wraps me up tightly. "Is that too tight?" she asks.

It is too tight, but it feels right, the tightness. It feels like I feel, pleasantly suffocated, tenderly crushed, by something purported to restore me.

Days pass. I keep a cold witch hazel maxipad in my underwear and the relief is immense. When I throw one out, another appears in the freezer. It is a kindness I don't know how to repay and so I do not try. My mother moves like a shadow but her presence is like a glare that my eyes and my senses cannot adjust to. I alternate between hiding in the nursery and taking my son for furtive walks. His umbilicus heals, and shortly after, his penis. He opens his eyes for longer stretches. Flakes of skin cover his scalp and forehead, and I wipe them away with some baby oil on a cotton ball. In the evenings, I bathe him in the sink of the Pink Bathroom, trying to ignore my mother, whose breath and movements I can hear outside the door. Caring for him feels meditative and intuitive, an experience wholly divorced from my mind. My mother's hovering is constant. She offers commentary and advice whenever I'm within earshot.

"Keep his head covered."

"*That*—that cry—it is identical to Simon's."

"He should learn to take a bottle."

"I bought some pacifiers—sometimes he just wants to suck but not eat."

"Make sure to dry his bottom before putting on a fresh diaper."

"I think he's cold. You are underdressing him."

Before leaving the room, I brace myself. I imagine a cloak that I can put over myself and my son to make us invisible, impenetrable. When we walk, I bundle him up and zip him into my big winter coat. It's like having him inside me again, but I can see him, his nose that might one day be described as regal, his surprising eyelashes. He sleeps, every once in a while pursing his lips and sucking—as though figuring, *Why not? Maybe I'll get lucky*—every once in a while opening his eyes and tilting his head back, as if to look at my face.

Every day I plan to call Alicia, and every day I do not call. She leaves two messages, one on the machine and one with my mother, who tells her I am busy with the baby and cannot come to the phone. Curiously, I feel no guilt.

Nighttimes are my favorite. I wake up multiple times and feel more alert than exhausted. It is easy to pretend we are alone in the house. My milk flows easily now, predictably, and the two of us find one another with a kind of rapture. One night, around two in the morning, I place him back in his crib and tiptoe to the door to refill my water glass in the bathroom. When I open the door, my mother is standing there.

"I thought I heard something," she says.

My heart beats wildly. In the stark silence, we both can almost hear it. I feel that I cannot continue in this house. But there is nowhere else.

Dad exhibits increasingly odd behavior. He rents a power washer and power washes the driveway, something he has never done before. He buys canisters of air freshener for every room and uses them liberally upon entering or leaving. One night he comes home with two large pizzas and two bags filled with Chinese takeout.

"Something for everyone!" he says. It is as if he counts the injuries in this house as mouths to be fed.

One day I see them from the window where I sometimes stand holding the baby. They appear to be arguing, Mom's hands making erratic circles in the air while Dad leans squinting and motionless against the car. After a while, he steps toward her and forcefully grasps her shoulders. It stuns me a little, this break in character, unless the real break in character is how he acts around me—halting, unsure. I can't see his face. A moment later, they embrace, his arms around her like he's afraid of what will happen if he lets go.

Some nights from the nursery I hear them talking in their room. I become afraid, to hear something I shouldn't, and yet my whole body tenses to listen. One time I hear her say, "You never said it but you always blamed me," and then Dad's voice, cracking with rage, "You have no right, no right." Another night I overhear him ask her if she wants to move, to live in another house. The baby wakes with a sputtering whimper and I pick him up quickly and try to hear her answer. Maybe she says it too quietly, or maybe she's fallen asleep, I think, but then—a long, low sob.

Chapter 40

Joan calls one day while my mother is out shopping and my father is at work.

"Hi! Oh my God, hi. I'm so glad you answered. Did you have the baby?"

"Yes! A boy."

"Oh my goodness. Congratulations! How are you doing? What's his name?"

I laugh for the first time in a long time. What a relief, to laugh. "I don't know. I feel like I might not ever know. Poor thing has his one-month checkup next week."

"Tea Rose Junior?"

I feel the laughter blink out of my body. I had all but forgotten that my baby has a father, that every baby has a father. *For what?* I think, bitterness curling my edges like a flame on paper. I'm the only one here. I've always been the only one here. I'm the only one this child needs.

"How is school? Did you find a roommate?"

"School is fine. My classes are easy this semester. My parents agreed to pay the balance on the rent for the rest of the term. After that I'm on my own. I'll cross that bridge when I get there. Not having any roommates is pretty nice."

I am quiet. Everything Joan is saying seems like a transmission from another planet.

I remember spring break, playing house with Joan. The coziness of it. Something about how she defined the spaces she inhabited— even the front desk at the music library, when she was working, exuded a certain quality. The feeling of *I could rest here. I could have a quiet mind here.* An aura of tea steam and soft light and throw blankets, even when those things were absent. I think about how in my one year of college, everything that could have happened, did. College, I realize, is not school. It is a backdrop.

"What if I went back?" I ask, half to myself. Joan was in the middle of a sentence about the new director of the music library.

"What? Where? Here? *Here?*"

"My mother came home," I tell her.

"Oh my God. Really?"

"It's not, um, working out. I can't seem to . . . be here. And she is trying to turn this baby into my dead brother."

A heavy sigh comes from Joan. "I know how that is." Then, "I have a car, you know. It was my sister's. It's not mine to keep, the way nothing of hers can be. It's like I'm borrowing from her soul or something. I constantly feel like I'm offending them by being alive."

We sit in silence for a minute.

"Um, Agnes. The other reason I'm calling, besides the baby . . . " She trails off.

"Go ahead."

"Tea Rose is, um, asking about you. A lot. He comes by at least a couple times a week, wanting to hang out. We had lunch twice, and I went with him to a party where he got fantastically drunk and talked about you the whole time."

"Wait. What about the—"

"The girl? The love of his life? Yeah. She's not in the picture any-more. Something about how she tried to steal from him? Or his family? I don't know. It ended badly."

"Wow. So I'm, what, the rebound from the girl he broke up with me for?"

"I don't know. He seems pretty obsessed with you."

I have to laugh. "He'll probably be obsessed with you soon enough, if you give him the chance."

"I still think it's crazy that he has a kid and doesn't know it."

"For all intents and purposes, he doesn't have a kid. There's no reason for him to know."

Joan makes a sound like she is huffing her breath onto a cold windowpane. "I love ya, Agnes. But I don't know if I agree. I know I have no idea what you've been through, but doesn't every kid deserve to know where she comes from? Like, even if they don't end up having a relationship?"

From the other room, I hear the baby stir. "I have to get going," I say reluctantly. "Thank you for calling me." I don't really want to hang up. Talking to Joan feels like a place, a room with a view of weeping willows and sighing brooks.

"Okay. Wait. Write down my number. In case you ever need a rescue."

• • •

My mother has bought the baby a little bouncy seat. She insists on being the only one who knows how to put him in it.

"Give him to me," she says. "The straps are tricky."

I give in, because I am tired. Tired of fending her off. Tired of sneaking around. Tired of waking up multiple times a night, not to feed the baby, although I am waking up to do that, too, but to glance around the room and listen outside the door for her. Tired of seeing the containers of formula lined up near the toaster, the photocopied articles about feeding schedules and sleep training.

One evening, we are sitting in the den. My mother crouches near the baby in his bouncy seat. He stares fixedly at the plush bumblebee suspended above his head. My father is lazily playing solitaire on the coffee table. It is a placid scene that evokes nothing but dread inside of me. That knot again, pulling tighter.

"I'm thinking about going back to school," I say.

"Wonderful," my mother jumps in. "You could come back whenever you wanted, to see the baby—weekends, breaks. I think it's important to finish college."

My mouth opens and then closes. My father looks from my mother to me, lays down a card. "What, uh, were you thinking, Agnes? A local school? Like, community college? Or reenrolling in your old school . . . ?"

"Well, first," I say, trying to stay calm, "I just want to say that whatever we decide—whatever I decide—I'm not going anywhere or doing anything without *my* baby." I don't intend the emphasis, but there it is.

Mom's eyebrows seem to birth new eyebrows. "What do you have in mind, exactly?"

"I don't know, exactly. But I think I could try to enroll for next semester, go part-time, get a job. It wouldn't be easy but it wouldn't be impossible." I didn't really have a plan before I started talking, but what I'm saying feels right, and it gives me a flicker of hope, and until I feel its feeble warmth, I don't realize what a sad person I've turned into.

"Agnes, be sensible. Who are you thinking would pay for college? Let alone child care?" My mother sounds insulted.

"You helped me pay for college this whole past year! And I worked, and we had financial aid! I don't understand what's changed." Seeing my mother's face, I add, "I mean in terms of the financial stuff."

"What's changed," my mother says, her words gathering like a summer storm, "is that you got pregnant at nineteen and had a baby. You will not be able to manage without help. You're still a child yourself."

"Who says I won't have help? I could have help. I have . . . friends. I could hire someone. I will figure something out!"

"Friends? You think friends are going to help you raise your baby? What, on their way to the bar? If the father wasn't willing to stick around, don't be so sure your friends will."

The baby wriggles in his seat and begins to cry. My mother beats me to him and turns the seat to the "vibrate/music" setting. A music-box version of "Twinkle Twinkle Little Star" loudly fills the room, the interstices of our anger. My son cries harder. My mother unfastens the straps in what seems like an exaggerated way and bounces him in her arms. He quiets down. She gives me a look, a look meant to prove something to me. My father looks helplessly on, and I find myself pitying him. He doesn't deserve this. I feel as though he's eddying down the drain of this house, this house that has become like a living drain ever since Mom returned. For a while, we lived in the still, shallow water. Now we are being pulled under.

The difference between Dad and me is that I want to get out and dry off. He wants to get the going under over with, to start a new life down there beneath the one he used to know. Good or bad, he just wants to get where he's going and know it swiftly and entirely so that he can stop having to feel things. I wouldn't call my aspirations lofty but I still want to believe in an up, a reaching toward.

The baby begins to bleat quietly, and then louder, and I tell my mom that I need to feed him, and she pretends not to hear me, so I say, "MOM. PLEASE HAND ME MY SON."

She gives me a flinty look and kisses his head languidly before handing him to me, in the manner of a mother handing her child to someone she does not one hundred percent trust. I take him upstairs and find a revenge-tinged satisfaction in nursing the hell out of him. He finishes on one side and then the other, and when I burp him, he vomits all over me. I clean him up, change his outfit, wrap him up snugly, and lay him in his crib. His eyes flutter and he gives me a

Kristen Iskandrian

look—not quite a smile, almost a smirk, a charming, flirty look, the look, I realize, of his father.

Without changing my shirt, I find the portable phone and carry it outside. A stiff breeze hits my vomit-soaked chest and I shiver, with cold and excitement. I dial Joan's number.

Dear Mom (Hi Dad),

I know you're probably still mad. I hope that in time you won't be mad. I'm not writing to change your mind about being mad, but I did just want you to know that we're fine, in case you're worried. I can live with your anger more than I can live with your worry.

I know it wasn't a good scene, our goodbye. I know you want to blame Joan, too, but she's really not at fault. I told her to come. I know it seems irresponsible and juvenile. But I can't be at home, in your home, at least not right now. One day I will come back, and it will be because I want to be there. Maybe Thanksgiving. Maybe Christmas. I can't keep you from coming here but if you do I hope you come knowing you will not change my mind, knowing that my son and I will not be driving home with you.

I have to figure out what home means now, because the home I left became alien to me, and I lost all footing. Joan feels like home to me. And she really loves the baby already. She helped me find a pediatrician. She is probably the most caring person I have ever known. The baby's father is here, but so far I have not seen him. It's a situation I'm treading lightly around.

The registrar granted me an official leave for fall semester, no penalties to my existing credits. It'll take me longer to graduate but that's okay with me. I will start taking classes in January, just two. Joan is trying to get me a job in the music library and if that doesn't work out I may be able to work in the dining hall

274

again and if that doesn't work out I'll find something else. She is going to babysit when I have to be away. I trust her as much as I trust myself. Sometimes it's easier to trust her than myself.

I took out all the money from my savings account because I'm going to need it until I pin down a job. I have already used some of it to set us up here. The baby and I are sharing a room and it's very comfortable. We have a bed and a crib. Also a small rocker that I found on the curb. We scrubbed it down and Joan made a slipcover for it in less than two days. I know I'll need more stuff eventually but we're okay for now. He sleeps well and feeds well and has started to smile. My love for him is exhilarating. I keep waiting for it to be hard, like everyone says it will be. I know it will, one day, be hard. Maybe once it gets hard it will only get harder, and I'll never know this ease and joy again, and I will disappoint him and he will disappoint me in irrevocable, unthinkable ways. I know things change. But until they do, I am enjoying each day for what it is bringing me: peace.

I hope you stay, Mom. I hope you and Dad can be happy there, or maybe somewhere else, but together. I will always be your daughter and my son will always be your grandson. I didn't leave to rebel. I didn't leave because I was angry. I have to be a mother to this boy and I couldn't do that under your watch.

I am grateful for everything you've done and tried to do for me.

Dad: whenever I was in your office as a kid, I used to read that "Footprints" plaque that someone—Nancy, I think, which seems crazy to me now—gave you. I loved the punchline of God carrying that man on the beach. And then as I got older it started to make me furious—the schmaltziness, the idea of this beachy God announcing his good deeds, glibly solving the mystery of why some of us make it and some of us don't, why some of us stay on the sand while others hurtle themselves

275

Kristen Iskandrian

headlong into the sea. The only thing that stupid plaque gets right is that it is impossible to know sometimes if you're being carried. God never shows up in my dreams to tell me if I have. But that I'm here, with this baby, is proof that someone or something did. You did, Dad. You carried me through this most impossible year, even when I had no idea you were doing so.

In my closet, behind the stuffed animals, is a box of letters. It's for you, Mom. The letters are in order. I still want so badly for you to know me. And I want so badly to know you too. Let us try from a distance. I think we're better from a distance.

Yours,

Agnes

PS: His name is Daniel.

Acknowledgments

Many people loved this book into being. Heartfelt thanks to my agent, Emma Patterson, for her always-astute advice and guidance, from which has sprung a real friendship. To my whip-smart editor, Libby Burton, who saw the book inside the manuscript and made it hum; and to Sean Desmond, Paul Samuelson, and the rest of the team at Twelve for taking such good care of it. A debt of gratitude to Jennifer Pitotti MD, for her obstetrical fact-checking in key passages of the novel.

To the women: Jenn Blair, who rooted for Agnes from the very beginning. Porochista Khakpour and Laura van den Berg, for their gifts of early enthusiasm. Melissa Broder and Lorian Long, my virtual coven. Sabrina Orah Mark, whose work has changed me, whose friendship has sustained me. Jennie Marable, my longtime co-conspirator, for accusing me of being a writer long before I felt like one.

To the places: The weird and wonderful town of Athens, Georgia, where I learned and unlearned so much. The Wingate Hotel on Route 280 in Birmingham, Alabama, and my room overlooking the Dumpster, where I spent several scattered weekends away from my regular life in order to finish this book.

And to my family—my first, toughest, truest teachers: Greta and Ami Iskandrian, Basil and Kimberly Iskandrian, Susie and Brendhan Buckingham. I love you. Thank you for loving me. Mom, thank you for showing me always to seek. Dad, thank you for showing me always to strive. For the immense support of my Connell family, too—how lucky I feel to have gained you.

To my daughters, Beatrice and Simone, for reinventing my world. And to Brian—for everything, everything.

Mission Statement

Twelve strives to publish singular books by authors who have unique perspectives and compelling authority. Books that explain our culture; that illuminate, inspire, provoke, and entertain. Our mission is to provide a consummate publishing experience for our authors, one truly devoted to thoughtful partnership and cutting-edge promotional sophistication that reaches as many readers as possible. For readers, we aim to spark that rare reading experience—one that opens doors, transports, and possibly changes their outlook on our ever-changing world.

12 Things to Remember about TWELVE

1. Every Twelve book will enliven the national conversation.
2. Each book will be singular in voice, authority, or subject matter.
3. Each book will be carefully edited, designed, and produced.
4. Each book's publication life will begin with a monthlong launch; for that month it will be the imprint's devoted focus.
5. The Twelve team will work closely with its authors to devise a publication strategy that will reach as many readers as possible.
6. Each book will have a national publicity campaign devoted to reaching as many media outlets—and readers—as possible.
7. Each book will have a unique digital strategy.
8. Twelve is dedicated to finding innovative ways to market and promote its authors and their books.
9. Twelve offers true partnership with its authors—the kind of partnership that gives a book its best chance at success.
10. Each book will get the fullest attention and distribution of the sales force of the Hachette Book Group.
11. Each book will be promoted well past its on-sale date to maximize the life of its ideas.
12. Each book will matter.

About the Author

Kristen Iskandrian's work has been published in *Tin House*, *Zyzzyva*, *Crazyhorse*, *EPOCH*, and *Denver Quarterly*, among other places. Her story "The Inheritors" was included in the *O. Henry Prize Stories 2014* as a juror favorite. She has a BA from the College of the Holy Cross and an MA and PhD in literature and creative writing from University of Georgia. Born in Philadelphia, Kristen currently lives in Birmingham, Alabama, with her husband and two daughters.